Dryftwood Outlaws on the Bayou

James Brennan

Copyright © 2022 James Brennan

All rights reserved.

ISBN: 9798433956858

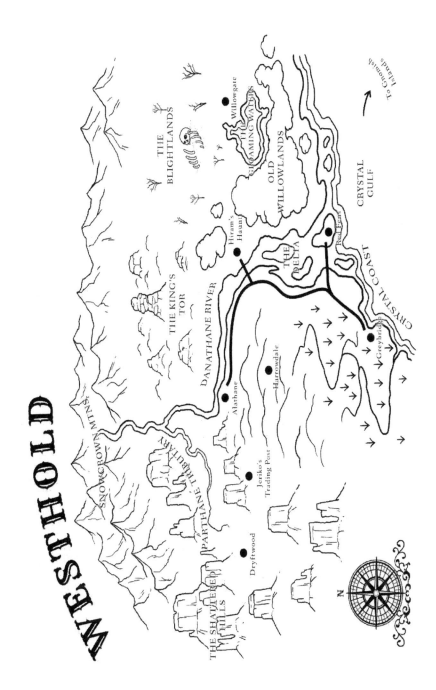

CONTENTS

Chapter 1	Pg 1
Chapter 2	Pg 4
Chapter 3	Pg 9
Chapter 4	Pg 13
Chapter 5	Pg 18
Chapter 6	Pg 23
Chapter 7	Pg 27
Chapter 8	Pg 32
Chapter 9	Pg 38
Chapter 10	Pg 46
Chapter 11	Pg 52
Chapter 12	Pg 58
Chapter 13	Pg 64
Chapter 14	Pg 69
Chapter 15	Pg 73
Chapter 16	Pg 77
Chapter 17	Pg 82
Chapter 18	Pg 88
Chapter 19	Pg 92
Chapter 20	Pg 96
Chapter 21	Pg 100

Dryftwood Outlaws on the Bayou

Chapter 22	Pg 105
Chapter 23	Pg 109
Chapter 24	Pg 113
Chapter 25	Pg 118
Chapter 26	Pg 124
Chapter 27	Pg 128
Chapter 28	Pg 133
Chapter 29	Pg 138
Chapter 30	Pg 143
Chapter 31	Pg 147
Chapter 32	Pg 151
Chapter 33	Pg 157
Chapter 34	Pg 160
Chapter 35	Pg 165
Chapter 36	Pg 168

CHAPTER 1

The outlaw spit out a crimson blob of chewing weed as a horde of swamp flies buzzed around his hatless head. The tall, lanky Plains Human stood boot-deep in a fetid pool, trying to gauge the distance between his spot and the dense copse of blackwood trees standing in the middle of the swamp. The outlaw hoped to find Ophelia Delphine, a witch of supposedly tremendous power, in that very grove of trees. He had tramped all over the Delta searching for her, in every backwoods bayou and overgrown bog, and he was running out of swamps to wade through and swarms of insects to swat.

The outlaw scratched the burgeoning stubble on his chin as sweat poured down his forehead from the sticky, humid air. Water flowed into his rough brown riding boots, and he sunk deeper in the mud with every step. On his back, a well-used longsword filled a weathered scabbard. On his waist, a battered belt buckle with the emblem of the Alathanian Marshals—a sword pointing downwards along the spine of an open book—glinted dully in the fading sunlight. Underneath his soaked, buckskin riding tunic, he bore the scars of countless battles.

A dry-mouth winder slithered past him in the brackish water at his boots, unperturbed by the intruder in its land. Weeping willows stretched down to the muck, throwing up a veil of vegetation for the outlaw to cut through and navigate past. All around him, the sounds of the Delta filled the air—chittering swamp flies, croaking bullfrogs, the occasional snapping of some rotten log in the distance. The Delta was an area of incredible fecundity; legend had it that the mythological monsters that used to roam Westhold were birthed in the humid stewpot the Swamp Elves now called home. For the outlaw, though, it was the more mundane critters—bugs, errant winders—that he had to contend with now. The outlaw wasn't from around these parts, and he still wasn't used to the raw nature of the Delta. He had a singular purpose, however, and he was going to follow the trail no matter where it led. He took a swig of Sweetfire from his wineskin, swished it around in his mouth before swallowing, and moved towards the copse of blackwood trees with each step making a loud sucking sound in the mud.

"By the Good Light," the outlaw cursed as a swamp fly bit him on the back of his neck. He went to crush the pest with an open palm, but the insect was long gone by the time his hand hit skin. The constant buzzing grated on his nerves and only made moving through the swamp more agonizing. "These flies will be the death of me before anything else."

When the outlaw stood about fifteen feet away from the strip of semi-dry land that housed the stand of blackwoods, his ears perked up, stopping him dead in his tracks. An old instinct honed from years on the run had sharpened his senses to a fine point. He stood stock-still as he strained to listen to his surroundings. There wasn't a particular sound that drew his interest but rather an absence of sound. Moments earlier, the swamp had been full of life, but now, it seemed as if everything had simply ceased to exist. The outlaw took in a slow breath and reached for the handle of his longsword.

The creature's long, leathery snout snapped out of the water with the speed of a lightning bolt; that same second, the outlaw brought his boiling blade out of the worn scabbard. The creature, a powerful, hefty reptile with sharp, jagged ridges along its back, bore down on the Plains Human, sending him sprawling into the water before he could bring his weapon to bear. Brackish water, filled with fly eggs, tiny fish, and choking weeds, flooded over his black hair and into his nostrils, leaving the outlaw sputtering. He flailed wildly in the water, trying to gain purchase in the muck. The creature snaked towards the prone outlaw, opening its jaw to reveal a mouthful of razor-sharp teeth flecked with chunks of meat.

As the outlaw waved his sword through the pool, it sent bright rays of light through the weeping boughs of the willow trees, and the heat from the metal turned the water to steam. He swung the molten blade in a wide, defensive arc to ward off the approaching beast as he tried to stand. Avoiding the clumsy first strike, the creature brought around its thick, scaly tail and slammed it into the outlaw's thigh, sending him ass-over-teakettle back into the muck. White-hot flashes of pain thundered through his leg, virtually paralyzing the outlaw.

He pulled his face free of the clinging mud to see the creature circle around and snap at him again. The outlaw ducked back into the water to avoid the powerful jaws and waited as the beast's momentum propelled it past him. As the back half of the reptile slithered overhead, the outlaw stood up in one fluid motion, bringing his hissing blade up through the water and neatly lopping off the beast's scaly tail.

The creature thrashed and screeched in mad pain as its heavy tail sunk to the depths of the swamp. It turned around and tried to snap its jagged maw onto the intruder's outstretched arm, but the outlaw managed to step back just in time and save his limb. Now, the hulking reptile was right in front of him, its jagged teeth inches away from his torso. The outlaw, covered in swamp gunk, grasped the worn leather handle of his blade with both hands, rotated the tip of the sword downwards, and brought great vengeance on the beast's scaly, reptilian head. The molten edge slid effortlessly through the creature's tough exterior, into the soft insides, and to the decaying swamp bottom. The reptile whipsawed madly against the magical blade, but the more it tried to free itself, the more the sword seared through flesh, bone, and scale until, finally, it shuddered and died.

The outlaw pulled the sword from his foe, its edge slowly dimming. The beast, now free from its pin, bobbed lifelessly at the water's surface. The creature's corpse rolled over onto its back and floated gently to the side as the flies hungrily eyed their feast. Around the outlaw, life came back to the swamp—the bugs buzzed, the winders slithered, and the bullfrogs sung their arias. The outlaw looked up at the purpling sky and then over to the copse of blackwood trees standing quietly above the waterline.

Jeremiah Blade sheathed his cooling longsword and made his way to dry land.

CHAPTER 2

"You killed my pet!" the wizened old Island Gnome screamed at the top of his lungs. "Intruder! Why did you kill my pet?"

"Your pet tried to bite me in half," Jeremiah Blade retorted as best he could in the syrupy Swamp Elf language—he was still getting used to the intricate phonetics—while standing on the bank sopping wet and trying to get a dry pinch of chewing weed out of a pouch on his belt. "It was my only option, really."

"That's what he's there for!" the Island Gnome shouted, stamping his feet in the moist loam of his tiny island. "I put him there specifically to keep interlopers like yourself out of my garden!"

Jeremiah looked around for something that resembled a garden in the dank swamp, but the closest thing he found was a few mysterious tubers poking their way up from the wet ground. He almost hocked out a crimson blob of chewing weed backwash, but he thought better of it in case he accidentally spit in the Island Gnome's garden.

"Look, mister," Jeremiah answered, hoping the Island Gnome would identify himself. "I didn't mean…"

"I ain't no mister!" the ancient Island Gnome bellowed. "Do you do this often? Trespass on people's properties, kill their pets, and start lobbing insults around? You've got some nerve, young man."

Jeremiah narrowed his eyes and found, to his mild embarrassment, that it was indeed an old woman. A particularly hairy and baritone-voiced old woman, but an old woman nonetheless. Jeremiah sighed and pinched the bridge of his nose with two fingers.

"I'm sorry, miss…" Jeremiah tried again.

"Hilda, young man," the crone answered, wagging a crooked finger as a curious look spread across her ancient features. "Yes, that's it. Hilda Von Wanderway."

Jeremiah was surprised to hear the Von Wanderway name, one of the Five Families of the Gnomish Islands, tossed around on this forgotten bayou. The Von Wanderways had ruled over the Gnomish Islands for centuries with the other four major families—the Bastimars, Klinkhammers, Rumblebumbles, and Von Verblins—and, by all accounts, had brought great prosperity to the island nation. He found it unlikely that this weathered Island Gnome could be related to royalty. Then again, in his current state, few would guess he was Alathanian nobility.

"Miss Hilda Von Wanderway," Jeremiah pressed, adopting a semblance of high-society decorum that felt tremendously out of place. "I didn't mean to intrude and kill your pet. I'm looking for the one called Ophelia Delphine. The Hoodoux Queen. Does she happen to be here?"

Hilda Von Wanderway turned her bent, crooked body sideways as she assessed her visitor. Her stringy, white hair swished from side-to-side, and she held up her bony fingers as if she were calculating some obtuse math problem.

"I thought she was dead," Hilda Von Wanderway offered. "Done got eaten by some ornery swamp critter. Real shame, that."

Jeremiah's heart sank. He had been looking for Ophelia Delphine for years, from the Red Fens to every backwater in the Delta. He couldn't tell if the wizened Island Gnome was telling the truth, or even knew the truth, but he couldn't help but feel disappointed at yet another dead end.

"Is that a marshal's belt buckle?" Hilda Von Wanderway, her cloudy white eyes suddenly alight with interest, asked pointedly. "I thought them marshals were done for."

That wasn't exactly true, but explaining what really happened to the Alathanian Marshals would be a tall task for the circumstances. After Jeremiah discovered the Arkstone—the source of the Blight that destroyed the Savannah Halfling civilization of Willowgate decades ago—in the Shattered Hills, the Alathanian Marshals, under the command of Chief Marshal Godwin Malmont, rode hundreds of miles to take control of the powerful ore. The Mesa Dwarves, the folks native to the Shattered Hills, had other plans and cast an ancient ritual to hide the dangerous ore away, hopefully, forever. The marshals ultimately failed in their task to commandeer the Arkstone, thanks in no small part to Jeremiah Blade, and Chief Marshal Malmont paid for the outing with his life. It would be an even taller task to explain that Jeremiah was the one who had cut Malmont's thread, why he did it, and now he was the most wanted man in all of Westhold because of his actions.

The following years proved to be tumultuous for the Alathanian Marshals. Word got out that it was the Arkstone—not general Duskstone use—that had caused the Blight. For decades, the Alathanians had tightly controlled magic use based on the simple premise that Duskstones caused the Blight and no one could be trusted to wield them responsibly. Now that the Arkstone was known as the cause of the Blight, the Alathanian Marshals lost their raison d'être, and Duskstone use exploded once again across Westhold. Without the risk of causing another Blight, people turned their backs on the marshals and towards the arcane to supplement their lives. Additionally, the discovery and subsequent disappearance of the Arkstone set off a massive hunt around Westhold for the powerful ore by everyone from the remaining marshals to outlaws looking to use its power for their own nefarious purposes. However, years had passed since the events in the Shattered Hills, and, as far as Jeremiah Blade knew, the apocalyptic ore remained hidden.

Whether the Arkstone remained tucked away or not, Jeremiah Blade was still the most wanted man in Westhold. Betraying your order and killing its leader, who also happened to be one of the most famous people in all of the Five Civilizations, would do that to a person. That's why the Island Gnome crone noticing the Alathanian Marshal belt buckle came as a surprise—he had originally moved to the Delta because he thought its backwaters would be the last place anyone would recognize the trappings of an Alathanian Marshal.

"I won it in a game hall in the Red Fens," Jeremiah lied smoothly, referring to the Swamp Elf capital. The outlaw mimicked throwing a pair of dice for emphasis. "Some old Alathanian thought it would fetch him a pretty copper. Enough to get him back in the Sweetfire, at least. He said it was an antique. Whatever it is, I took a shine to it and thought he'd fancy a wager."

"Did you win that pretty sword off of him too?" Hilda shot back, eyeing him suspiciously. "It's an awfully nice piece of steel to be gambled away so easily."

"Ah, you know," Jeremiah flinched at the inquisitive Island Gnome's curiously intuitive insights. "With the marshals out to pasture and their treaties torn up and whatnot, it's never been easier to pick up a magic weapon or two."

"Ain't that the truth," Hilda squealed. "Now that we don't have to worry 'bout some up-jumped Alathanian spouting off about this and that treaty, I might pick me up one, too."

Jeremiah flinched again; it had only been a few years ago that he was an up-jumped marshal spouting off about this and that treaty. He had ridden into the Shattered Hills with all the piss and vinegar of youth and barely left with his life. He had been so young and determined to make a name for himself. Jeremiah had wanted the bards to sing his name, not the bounty hunters to bay for his blood. It was a long and winding road from the day the Arkstone disappeared, but it had led him here, to this swamp, staring down a crooked, ancient Island Gnome.

The image of Lucille 'Iron Eyes' Ledoux dying on the Arkstone cavern floor blazed to life in his memory. She had stood by him through everything.

She had been as good and true and honest a person as he had ever known, though he was too young to see it at the time. She had told him that his blind faith would bring nothing but death and destruction, and Jeremiah grimaced at how true her words rang. Lucille's blood stained the red earth of the Shattered Hills like so many before her. Before she died, she gave him the name that Jeremiah clung to like a sailor on a piece of driftwood—Ophelia.

Since that day, Jeremiah Blade had searched the Delta high and low for someone named Ophelia. He had never been to the Swamp Elf nation before, and it was a steep learning curve. Between their intricate language, insistence on having the 'Good Times', and the endless miles of bayous and swamps, Jeremiah quickly learned that the rules he grew up with in Alathane no longer applied. He had picked up drinking, gambling, chewing, cavorting, cursing, fighting, swindling, lying, blaspheming, and sleeping late—all things that were vices in every corner of Westhold except for the Delta, where they were held in high esteem. It had been a long few years.

Despite the Swamp Elf reputation for being polite, it was difficult to get a straight answer from damn near anyone on the whereabouts of an 'Ophelia'. Eventually, Jeremiah learned that her full name was Ophelia Delphine, and she was the meanest, nastiest, cruelest, and evilest of all the Hoodoux Witches in the Delta. He also learned that she was the 'queen' of the Hoodoux Witches, though he never quite nailed down if that title was given to her by some sort of witches' council or she just claimed it for herself. Either way, Jeremiah learned from a fishmonger near the docks in the Red Fens that this Ophelia Delphine lived down where the black trees grow, which sent him scrambling and sloshing through every bayou in the Delta searching for some damn black-barked trees.

"Ma'am," Jeremiah pressed, summoning up all the politeness he could muster with his fraying patience. "I don't want to disturb you further, or kill any more of your pets, but if you have any information on the whereabouts of Ophelia Delphine, I would greatly appreciate it. If you had anything at all, then I'll get out of your hair right quick and in a hurry."

"I'm telling you," Hilda Von Wanderway insisted as she pulled a fat swamp bug from her hair. She eyeballed it hungrily and then popped it into her mouth. Bits of carapace and gossamer wings clung to her crooked teeth. "The Queen of the Hoodoux Witches is dead. Nobody has seen her in ages. Least of all Hilda Von Wanderway."

Jeremiah felt a slight buzz in one of the pouches that hung off his belt. The outlaw flashed a big smile and turned off to one side to surreptitiously check his aging Raeller Counter. Despite having been rode hard and put up wet after many years of use, the device still worked, and a dazzling display of sickly green lights danced across the interface. Jeremiah coolly turned back to see Hilda Von Wanderway's eyes narrowing dangerously.

"It's funny that you mention that," Jeremiah persisted as tendrils of green mist started seeping from the Island Gnome's gnarled hands. "Damn near everyone in the Fens told me the Hoodoux Queen lived down where the black trees grow. I've searched every crooked waterway for this damn witch and, looking around, I must say that these are some mighty fine blackwood trees, Ophelia Delphine."

CHAPTER 3

In an instant, a bolt of sickly green arcane light burst forth from the Island Gnome's hand and screeched towards Jeremiah Blade. His Alathanian Marshal belt buckle flashed its protective blue shield, sending the eldritch energy ricocheting off into the surrounding blackwood trees. Jeremiah pulled his sword from its scabbard, and, for the second time that day, its edge burst with a primal heat.

Before Jeremiah's dark brown eyes, Hilda Von Wanderway started to transform. Her bones broke and elongated, causing her to grow two feet in mere seconds, and her skin darkened to a deep mahogany color with numerous black tattoos inked across her body. Her hair turned from stringy, snow-white to thick, dark braids that swirled around her head like the stars in orbit. Underneath each emerald green eye were three identical lines of Duskstone tattoos that ran across her cheeks. These tattoos, much like the artwork that adorned the Mesa Dwarf Sandscribes in the Shattered Hills, glistened with an otherworldly, iridescent light. Terrible waves of arcane energy rolled off her thin frame as she came into her true form. In the space of time that it took to flash a yellowed smile, Hilda Von Wanderway had transformed into a fearsome, cackling Swamp Elf Hoodoux Witch.

Before Jeremiah could react, the ground underneath his boots turned into a thick morass of mud and dead foliage. He instantly sank up to the top of his rough brown riding boots as if the decaying mess was actively trying to eat him alive. Jeremiah fought and struggled but only managed to sink deeper into the mud. The fully transmogrified Hoodoux Witch shook with mad laughter.

Jeremiah, thinking quickly, dipped his sword into the grasping muck and flicked it upwards, sending a spray of superheated mud flying towards the witch. She held her forearm up to protect herself, and the flecks of molten swamp popped and sizzled on her exposed flesh. The Hoodoux Witch hissed and reeled, breaking her concentration long enough to allow Jeremiah to pull himself free of the mire, though he left both riding boots behind.

Jeremiah stumbled into the stand of blackwood trees, the moss hanging from their limbs rough as a Mesa Dwarf's beard. The Hoodoux Witch rattled out a variety of incantations and, before Jeremiah realized what was happening, the hanging moss had insidiously wrapped around his throat. Jeremiah tried to protest and explain his situation, but the moss snapped upwards and would have jerked the outlaw right out of his boots if he had still been wearing them.

Jeremiah writhed under the tightening foliage, but, in an instant, he could see above the tree line as the magically-infused moss lifted him through the scraping blackwood branches. A full moon and a carpet of silvery stars hung above Jeremiah and the muggy swamp, painting the Delta in a pale, ghostly light. Below him, the Hoodoux Witch tittered like a crazy person as she commanded the violent flora. The ancient Swamp Elf had brought the very bog around them to life to thwart the intruding Jeremiah Blade.

Jeremiah could see darkness creeping into the edge of his vision. In an act of desperation, Jeremiah whipped his molten sword through the strangling moss just as it launched him over the tops of the trees. Once gravity reclaimed the pinwheeling outlaw, he plummeted through the snapping branches and into a thick briar patch between the blackwood trunks with a thunderous crash. Next to the stunned Jeremiah Blade, his molten blade pierced the loamy earth like a fallen star.

Fortunately for Jeremiah, the ground beneath the briar patch was soft and wet, saving him from any broken bones. The tiny daggers on the brush, however, cut him in a hundred different places, from his bootless feet to his hatless head. Stars streamed across his vision, and the incessant buzz of swamp insects mingled with the ringing in his ears. Jeremiah tried to stand, but every movement dug the thorns deeper into his skin, sending tiny rivulets of blood streaming down his exposed flesh like trails of chewing weed spit.

Jeremiah did not have to wait long before another bolt of misty green energy blew up his briar patch. The marshal belt buckle's cerulean shell shielded him from the brunt of the attack, but he still felt the searing, sickly heat from the magic as it raised him from the bush and launched him into an imposing blackwood tree. His body gave way to the hard trunk, his bones and joints popping loudly through the thick, humid air.

The witch's shrieks of laughter pealed through the blackwood trees, coming from every direction at once. Jeremiah cursed under his breath at the formidable witch's powers, though such resistance was not completely unexpected. He had heard tales about the Hoodoux Witches and their prowess with the arcane; virtually everyone in the Red Fens had told him that they were far more powerful than any greybeard Mesa Dwarf Sandscribe or daft Island Gnome Klinkhammer. Now, tangled in a mass of decaying vegetation and assaulted by waves of terrible magic, Jeremiah could truly appreciate the terrific power this cabal of powerful Duskstone users wielded. His deeply ingrained naivety still believed he could reason with the wild Swamp Elf, but he quickly tossed that idea when a poisonous fog started to seep over his prone figure.

Jeremiah was once again saved by his old marshal belt buckle as the noxious yellow gas stretched for his lungs; the cerulean light completely enveloped Jeremiah, protecting the outlaw from the arcane vapor. He saw the fog peel away the bark from the surrounding trees, sizzling and popping the thick wood. The laughter suddenly stopped, replaced by a wave of whirring insects. In that brief moment, Jeremiah was impressed by her mastery over Duskstones and the sheer range of spells the Hoodoux Witch had at her disposal. He took the respite and picked up his smoldering longsword, steam from the moist earth drifting lazily off its edge. Outside of the stand of trees, Jeremiah could see the eerie green light start to glow again.

The bootless outlaw quickly made a beeline through the swirling, sunflower-colored mist and to a narrow blackwood tree. He brought his sword down in a long, sweeping arc through the trunk of the tree moments before the Swamp Elf launched the gathered vortex of green mist from her outstretched hand. The blackwood tree pitched to one side, soared to earth, intercepted the screaming bolt of energy, and exploded in a shower of splinters.

Jeremiah Blade then planted his molten sword in the earth and blasted through the blizzard of blackwood bark to tackle the mad witch before she could let loose another spell. His momentum carried the two into a line of mesh cages holding a host of delta fowl and swamp critters. The night air filled with the raucous cries of squawking, tumbling bog varmints and water birds. Feathers and fur flew everywhere as the witch and the outlaw rolled around in the muck, trying to gain the upper hand.

Eventually, Jeremiah grabbed the Swamp Elf by both wrists and bent them up and backwards in a painful jumble—an old lesson from his days at the Academy in Alathane. He then threw his weight on top of the witch as she tried to violently wiggle out from his grip. Jeremiah didn't weigh very much—he never had—but he certainly outweighed the waif of a witch, and he used that to his advantage by shoving her head in the mud.

"I'm not here to hurt you!" Jeremiah shouted over the din of disturbed fowl. "I need Ophelia Delphine's help! I'm looking for someone!"

The Swamp Elf lifted her head from the mud, straining her neck to catch Jeremiah in her periphery.

"There is no Ophelia Delphine 'round these parts," the witch spat back, writhing in Jeremiah's grasp. "You found the wrong grove of blackwood trees!"

"You are the only one who can help me find her, witch," Jeremiah grunted as he pressed the spirited hag down into the ruins of the poultry coop. "I'm searching for someone called Lucille Ledoux."

The Hoodoux Witch stopped struggling and raised an incredulous eyebrow at the name. All the magic filling the blackwood grove ceased as she arched painfully to get a good look at Jeremiah Blade. The lines of Duskstone tattoos under her eyes dimmed from a bright iridescent to a faded black against her mahogany skin. The Hoodoux Witch flashed a smile full of yellow teeth.

"Well, why didn't you say so, cher?"

CHAPTER 4

Ophelia Delphine placed a steaming, savory bowl of yambeau in front of Jeremiah Blade, and the delicious fragrance of the famous bayou stew filled the tiny cottage that the Hoodoux Witch called home. If it had been years earlier, back when Jeremiah was still accustomed to the finer tastes of Alathanian banquets, he would have recoiled at the unidentifiable hunks of meat floating in the rich broth. Jeremiah thought of the swamp critters that had been locked up in the now-ruined cages in front of Ophelia Delphine's little hovel and briefly wondered if he had seen any empty spots. But, the first taste of the yambeau, poured over rice with the right amount of added swamp spice, reminded him why the culinary reputation of the Delta was known throughout Westhold.

"What did you say your name was again, cher?" Ophelia Delphine asked her unexpected house guest. "Jeffery something? Ol' Ophelia's hearing ain't what it used to be, you understand."

"Jackson," Jeremiah lied, a trait he perfected during his time in the Delta, his cover name sliding effortlessly off his tongue. "Rose is my family name."

In the years since the events in the Shattered Hills, Jeremiah had been hunted by an uncomfortable number of bounty hunters and glory seekers looking for the man who slew Chief Marshal Godwin Malmont. Despite the fact that he was pretty sure this was Ophelia Delphine, he wanted to make certain his cover was still firmly in place. One could never be too safe with the hounds constantly nipping at one's boots.

"You've got some fire, Jackson Rose," Ophelia mentioned suspiciously as she poured herself a bowl of yambeau and sat down to enjoy the feast. She had a certain way to her—she was rail-thin, giggled at unknown jests, and, even though her body was bent under the weight of many seasons, every crooked move and random twitch she made exuded strength. "Not many men walk into the home of the Hoodoux Queen Ophelia Delphine and live to tell about it, cher."

That line sent Ophelia into an uncontrollable snicker, a sinuous sound that filled every corner of the cabin. Jeremiah grimaced; his aching back and crushed trachea could attest to the truth of her words. He was still filthy from their fight, covered with the lifeblood of the swamp, and, looking around the cabin at the potions filled with critter carcasses, dried lizard skins hanging from the walls, and exotic delta plants growing in clay pots, he figured she probably didn't have many visitors.

"I've been looking for you for years," Jeremiah explained in between spoonfuls of yambeau, pausing occasionally to let the spicy heat dissipate from his mouth. "I was riding companions with Lucille Ledoux, also known as Iron Eyes Ledoux. She was a good friend of mine."

"And how is my dear cousin doing, cher?" Ophelia asked as a brilliant green winder slithered across the table and curled around the witch's left wrist, up her arm, and then encircled her thin neck like a piece of jewelry. "Still rolling around in the dust of the Shattered Hills? I never knew why she went out that way. I mean, we got everything you need here in the Delta. Ain't that right, Woodroux? She was always a hard-headed one, though. It's been a while since I saw her hide."

Jeremiah sat there quietly for a long moment, mindlessly stirring his bowl of yambeau, with memories flooding through his mind. In a cramped cavern, flecks of dissolving Arkstone swirling around them, he could see her slate-grey eyes, the light fading behind them, looking up at him. Ophelia stopped eating, cocked her head to one side, and peered at the outlaw with her endless emerald pools as if she could gaze directly into Jeremiah's past.

"I'm sorry, but she's dead," Jeremiah replied, his voice barely above a whisper. Even after all these years, it was still painful for him to vocalize. "She died a few years ago in the Shattered Hills."

Ophelia Delphine continued to slurp her bowl of yambeau, her eyes never leaving Jeremiah Blade. She didn't seem particularly distraught, or even distracted, by the news.

"Well, good for ol' Lucille," Ophelia replied calmly as she fed a piece of meat to the winder slithering around her neck. "You know, I was talking to her ma a while back, and we got to wondering when that girl was ever going to do something with her life. Her ma was always asking me, 'Why is she always stomping around the Shattered Hills?' We never could understand it. But, good on my cousin."

"I said she was dead," Jeremiah exclaimed incredulously. "I didn't say she became the Marchioness of the Red Fens. She's gone. Gone for good."

"No one is ever gone for good, cher," Ophelia explained, waving off Jeremiah's concern with a bony hand. "The spirits, they're always with us. Well, that is until everyone forgets about you and your memory is lost to this world and the next. Then you're really gone. But ol' Lucille seems to have made an impression on you, young Jackson Rose, so I'd say she's doing pretty good."

Jeremiah stared at Ophelia, unsure of how to proceed. Her nonchalance took him completely by surprise. It wasn't every day that, upon hearing the death of a family member, you congratulated them for dying and being worth remembering. Hoodoux Witches were famous, or infamous, for their connection with the dead, but some around Westhold thought it was just hocus-pocus. Ophelia didn't seem to be putting on an act, however. Maybe she did spend a lifetime talking with spirits; at the very least, Jeremiah figured, chatting with dearly departed souls would probably give a person a little perspective on life and death.

"I'm here because she is dead," Jeremiah said, unsure of how to impress upon her the seriousness of the situation. "Lucille told me to seek you out before she died. She didn't say much more than that, but I can only imagine she meant that you could contact her somehow. And, if you can reach out to her, I can tell her all the things I didn't get a chance to say before she passed."

Ophelia Delphine took another long, unhurried sip of yambeau, this time bringing the bowl directly to her lips. She looked down thoughtfully into the bowl after she finished and picked out a hunk of unidentifiable meat with her crooked fingers and popped it into her mouth.

"I don't believe you understand how this works, cher," Ophelia explained. "The spirits, they talk to me. Not the other way 'round. I can't just knock on their door and ask them how the azaleas are coming along."

"There has to be a way to contact her," Jeremiah implored, desperately looking for a way forward. "Why else would she tell me about you?"

"That's a good question," Ophelia answered as she fed her last piece of meat to the emerald winder like it was a pet dog. The swamp critter then slithered back down to the floor and disappeared under the table. "She's my cousin? I'm touched she thought of ol' Ophelia before she moseyed on over to the other side. Maybe, she didn't want me to be surprised if she showed up in my fevered visions one day. Maybe, she thought of that time when I pushed her into a mud pit and left her there for an afternoon. I bet she is still pissed about that. The possibilities are endless, cher."

"You are supposedly the most powerful Hoodoux Witch in all the Delta," Jeremiah pressed as the pet winder wrapped its way around his bootless feet in search of food. The suddenly-tense outlaw tried to shake off the persistent winder but to no avail. "You're the Hoodoux Queen! You apparently talk to these damn spirits all the time. She's your cousin and you don't want to even try?"

"This ain't some fairy tale, cher," Ophelia said, her accent as thick as the yambeau. "Where you find the old Hoodoux Witch and she grants you three wishes. I'm a busy lady. You know, it ain't easy being the Hoodoux Queen. I may have given myself that title, sure, but there are still queenly things for me to do. Plus, I got plenty of cousins."

Jeremiah looked down at the emerald winder peering up at him, its tongue flicking with the expectation that the outlaw would feed it. He tried to shoo away the pesky pet, but it only side-slithered out of the way of his swatting hand.

"Fair enough," Jeremiah sighed as he tried to stop the winder from wrapping around his thigh, though the critter was stronger than its narrow frame suggested. "How about we make a trade then?"

Ophelia's devious smile flashed, and she leaned forward, bending her body at a dramatically sharp angle. Something akin to curiosity flashed on her peculiar features. Despite Ophelia rambling on about her being so old, Jeremiah couldn't pinpoint her actual age—each time she slipped through the shadows, she seamlessly shifted into an entirely different person. Ophelia drummed her long fingernails—clack-clack, clack-clack—on the table.

"Now, cher, you trying to charm ol' Ophelia now, aren't you?" Ophelia cooed as she placed her chin daintily on an open palm. "Ophelia knows when she's being courted by some handsome young blade. What do you got for me?"

Jeremiah hesitated; he still wasn't sure if this was a good idea, but it was something he had planned as a contingency. He looked down at the book-and-blade emblem on his Alathanian Marshal belt buckle, the powerful artifact that had saved him countless times. It was a link to his youth, and he could still remember vividly his pride when he received it on his graduation day. Jeremiah didn't want to give up the belt buckle, but he knew he needed to tempt Ophelia Delphine with something. Plus, every time he used it, the unique Duskstone profile made him easy to track for anyone with a Raeller Counter—a device that had been increasingly easy to get a hold of after the events in the Shattered Hills. Having the belt buckle was too dangerous and, if it could help him get to Lucille, then all the better.

Jeremiah slowly unhooked the buckle and held up the tarnished metal against the low, gold, arcane lights in Ophelia's hovel. He turned it over in his mind and his hand; Jeremiah thought about everything the belt buckle meant and what it represented. He didn't want to give it away but, looking at the leering Hoodoux Witch across the table, he figured he may not have a choice.

"I don't know how much access you have to Duskstone artifacts all the way out here," Jeremiah started, his voice low and conspiratorial. "But, if there is, in fact, a way to talk to Lucille, then I have something that is awfully hard to come by nowadays that you may be interested in acquiring."

Ophelia's eyes narrowed on the belt buckle, its book-and-blade emblem glinting dully in the arcane light. She extended a bony hand, palm upwards, across the table.

"Let ol' Ophelia have a gander at that, cher," Ophelia instructed, her interest piqued. "I'd hate for you to sell me a false bill of goods here."

It took Jeremiah a good long moment to release the belt buckle. Despite the fact he had taken pains to hide his identity, the marshal belt buckle was one of the last links to his past, and it was difficult for him to let go. Eventually, Jeremiah slid the artifact across the table to Ophelia, who snapped it up gleefully.

Ophelia Delphine held it up to the light, turning it over delicately, examining every facet. She ran her hand over the book-and-blade emblem and eyeballed the cerulean Duskstone implanted in the back. Ophelia started mumbling to herself in a language Jeremiah had never heard before and calculated some unknown equation on her crooked fingers.

As Ophelia examined the belt buckle, Jeremiah tried to shoo away the persistent winder that was snaking its way into his bowl of yambeau. He had spent all day trudging through the muck and had no intention of sharing his dinner with the annoying animal. The emerald green swamp critter hissed at the outlaw and flicked his tongue menacingly but made no move to bite Jeremiah.

"Get out of there," Jeremiah hissed back at the winder, desperately trying to save the last of his stew. "Why do you have to eat mine? There is a whole big pot of it over there. Stop it. Hey!"

"Shh!" Ophelia shushed as she stood up suddenly, her countenance severe. She leaned towards the flimsy wooden door, her sharp ears tuned for the slightest disturbance. All around them, there was silence—even the pot of yambeau seemed to have stopped bubbling. Ophelia slid the belt buckle back across the table to Jeremiah. "Put that back on, cher. I get the feeling you're 'bout to need it."

"What is it?" Jeremiah asked, confusion playing across his youthful features. He grabbed the belt buckle and slipped it back onto his belt. He stood, tightened his belt, and looked across the dingy room to where his longsword lay. "You need…"

Ophelia raised her withered hand to quiet the outlaw. The only sound that filled the hovel was the incessant slithering of the winder's flicking tongue.

"Did you come alone, cher?" Ophelia Delphine asked in a low, sinister voice.

CHAPTER 5

"Jeremiah Blade!" the Savannah Halfling called out across the swamp. "You're a hard man to find! But, not hard enough, it looks like."

Jeremiah Blade, Ophelia Delphine, and her winder marched out of the witch's hut to see a Savannah Halfling, dressed in a black, wide-brimmed ranching hat with a silver band around the crown and an odd, old-fashioned, black-and-silver vest, standing waist-deep in water with six heavily-armed Plains Humans standing behind her. The ragtag group surrounding the Savannah Halfling had the bearings of mercenaries, probably dug up at some dockyard tavern in the Red Fens. Around her and her crew, the heavy, dark night crowded in to watch the showdown among the blackwood trees while the summer insects filled the air with their incessant buzzing.

"By the spirits, why do I got so many visitors tonight?" Ophelia cursed under her breath as she eyed the new intruders upon her property. "This is more excitement than I've had in a long time. Who is Jeremiah Blade?"

"There is no Jeremiah Blade here," Jeremiah Blade called out to the Savannah Halfling as his sword started to warm on his back. On his waist, his old Raeller Counter buzzed quietly, indicating the presence of a powerful Duskstone source nearby. Whoever this woman was, she had come prepared. "You must have the wrong copse of blackwood trees, ma'am."

The Savannah Halfling's hands were underneath the water and she made no moves despite the swarming insect clouds. She had a thick wad of chewing weed in her lower lip and spit out a bright red blob of saliva that floated on top of the water like cooking oil. Behind her, the Plains Humans bristled with a variety of swords, polearms, and crossbows, anticipation flashing in their eyes.

"That's interesting," the Savannah Halfling answered in a strangely antiquated accent, matching her outfit. It was as if she had been plucked from the old Willowgate Halfling court at the peak of its glory. "It's not every day that a profile of an Alathanian Marshal belt buckle shows up on my Raeller Counter. Add that to another powerful ore profile associated with your person, and that leads me to believe we have one of Westhold's most dangerous criminals on our hands. Did you think you could run away forever, marshal? Or should I say, ex-marshal?"

Jeremiah set his teeth. He knew it was risky using the belt buckle, and now it had come back to bite him. He didn't have much of a choice, though; Ophelia would have cooked him alive if he hadn't worn it. Soft laughter echoed over the swamp.

"So, you are the one who found the Arkstone," the Savannah Halfling chuckled, a sneer painted on her pale, delicate face. "The one who found the most powerful Duskstone of all. Looking at you now, I can see why things spiraled out of control."

Jeremiah didn't rise to the bait, though it did surprise him that she was more focused on the Arkstone than the death of Chief Marshal Malmont. Usually, when the hounds came baying at his door, they were only focused on the killing, not the events that led up to it. There was no bounty on his head for finding the Arkstone.

"My name is Hallincross, and I aim to take you back to my people, Jeremiah Blade," the Savannah Halfling continued over the riotous chorus of insects. "I'd like to bring you back kicking. I've got some questions for your sorry hide. But, if you force me, I'll bring your corpse in all the same. There are ways to make a dead man talk."

"What's she talking about, cher," Ophelia whispered to Jeremiah, though she, of all people, knew how a dead man could talk. "Did you bring trouble to ol' Ophelia?"

"Not on purpose," Jeremiah answered, his voice low and honest. "I guess it's a good time to mention that I have a bounty on my head the size of the Snowcrown Mountains. I don't mean to get you involved, Ophelia. I'll be able to handle these bloodhounds on my own."

"Nonsense, cher," Ophelia shot back. "If you're on good terms with Lucille, that's good enough for me. Plus, they're stomping all around my garden."

"I'll give you ten seconds," Hallincross shouted across the swamp. "Either you tell me everything you know about the Arkstone, or I'll flog it out of you, Jeremiah Blade. You can either come the easy way or the hard way. Your choice."

Before ten seconds could pass, one of the Plains Humans standing behind Hallincross snapped down into the swamp water and started to thrash violently. The rest of Hallincross' posse froze in place, their eyes growing wide with fear. Hallincross, however, just rolled her eyes and waded through the brackish water towards dry land, her visage hateful.

Jeremiah saw Ophelia mumbling under her breath, the Duskstone tattoos on her face glowing, and green vapor dripping from her upturned palms. The water churned and bubbled, catching two more bounty hunters in the growing maelstrom. These men looked like hardened mercenaries, but stories of the strange and bewildering magic Hoodoux Witches wielded were well-known throughout Westhold, and Hallincross' posse was breaking like scared cattle. Jeremiah could sympathize with them—he had just recently been on the business end of Ophelia's terrible arcane might.

Jeremiah Blade unsheathed his now-burning sword as Hallincross and the remaining bounty hunters fought their way through the roaring water. The warm orange glow of the heated metal threw long, sharp shadows across the blackwood trees.

As Hallincross plowed through the swamp, a lavender Duskstone ore in the shape of a lidless eye flared to life on her throat. Her eyes shifted from midnight black to the same color as the Duskstone, and she brought out of the water an energy blade of swirling lavender and silver magic. Suddenly, Hallincross leaped up from the water in one explosive blast, soaring high and closing the twenty-foot distance between them with ease, leaving only a fading silver mirage behind. The move caught Jeremiah flat-footed; he barely had time to bring his sword up as Hallincross careened towards him with the energy blade, now running up to the elbow of her right arm, flashing with a ghostly light.

Arcane power rippled across the swamp as the two blades met. Jeremiah had become accustomed to overpowering foes with his magic sword forged in the heart of a dust storm, but Hallincross' force blade proved an equal to his molten edge. Jeremiah had spent the past few years fending off bounty hunters and fortune seekers, and they were usually ill-prepared and under-equipped to deal with the magic he had at his disposal. Hallincross moved with a fierceness and swiftness that told Jeremiah that she was no regular bounty hunter. She jumped, flipped, and dashed with impressive agility as she pressed the attack on Jeremiah. She wasted no extra movement in her attacks, and it took everything Jeremiah had to keep her at bay. Her movements harkened back to an older time; a memory flashed in Jeremiah's mind of scrolls in the Academy detailing ancient Savannah Halfling warriors utilizing such acrobatic displays against their foes. The two weapons clashed and receded and clashed again as magic surged across the swamp. Jeremiah was hard-pressed to keep up with the flurry of blows and had a difficult time finding a weakness to exploit in Hallincross' defense.

The three remaining Plains Human mercenaries managed to make their way to shore and launched themselves with wild abandon at Ophelia Delphine. The emerald green winder around her arm hissed, slithered down to the loamy soil, and bravely charged the oncoming mercenaries. With green mist dripping from her hands, Ophelia drew a complex pattern in the air that hung suspended for a moment before dissolving above the serpent.

Immediately, the winder grew to monstrous proportions, expanding well beyond thirty feet tip-to-tail, and it bore down on the mercenaries, its razor-sharp fangs glistening in the moonlight.

One of the mercenaries lunged at the beast with his polearm, but the winder corkscrewed on the ground, avoided the jab, and snapped forward like an emerald lightning bolt, catching the bounty hunter directly over his head with its hungry jaws. The Plains Human thrashed and shrieked as the scales quickly wrapped around his body. The other two mercenaries started to hack away at the exposed, overgrown winder, but two sickly green bolts of arcane energy ripped through the night, their armor, and their chests. The two mercenaries looked down at the gaping holes in their bodies, eyes wide in disbelief, before crumpling to the muddy embankment and into the foul water.

Jeremiah had no time to worry about the bounty hunters as the relentless Hallincross pressed the attack. The lavender and silver blade cut through the thick swamp air and swarms of buzzing insects, searching for any gap in the outlaw's defense. The Duskstone on her throat pulsated with every swing of the energy blade. Jeremiah had to utilize every skill he had learned from his time at the Alathanian Marshal Academy and his life on the run to deflect the attacks. Hallincross commanded considerable arcane power, the likes of which Jeremiah had not seen in many years.

Jeremiah Blade stepped to the side a half-second too late, and the lavender energy blade, dripping with stars of silver light, cut towards him with alarming speed. His belt buckle immediately flashed, and the protective cerulean shield grew between the antagonists. The force of the blow was enough to stagger Jeremiah, and he scrambled to gain purchase on the slippery ground. Another swipe of the energy blade came towards his belly, but the blue light held once more, sending more silver sparks fluttering through the moonlight. The force knocked Jeremiah to the wet earth, and his sword left his hand and skittered into the brackish water, sending a column of steam towards the stars. Hallincross leaped sky-high to bring her lavender and silver blade down once more to finish the outlaw Jeremiah Blade.

As the energy blade touched the cerulean shield one final time, a massive concussive force radiated outwards from the point of impact. Though he was protected from the brunt of the blast, Jeremiah was pushed further down into the sucking mud while Hallincross was sent flying backwards into the grove of blackwood trees. Jeremiah took this reprieve, quickly pulling himself from the muck, and scrambled towards the bank to retrieve his molten edge, tendrils of steam still clinging to the weapon. As soon as he found his footing, he charged towards Hallincross as she tried to extract herself from a forest of splintered blackwood trees. He brought down his molten blade just as she raised her right arm to defend herself. Jeremiah aimed for the elbow, where the magic turned to flesh, and, as the edge sliced through tendon and bone, the energy blade died, and Hallincross reeled in pain and confusion. The severed limb fell into the mud and laid steaming at the elbow. Jeremiah then brought his bootless foot into Hallincross' temple, sending her wide-brimmed hat flying, and a spray of stringy, black hair exploded out from underneath the old-fashioned cap. Hallincross crashed into the muck, dazed, disorientated, and in searing pain. Jeremiah then reached down, wrapped his bleeding fingers around the Duskstone implanted in her throat, and ripped out the ore in one swift motion, leaving behind a gaping, bloody wound.

The lines of lavender energy faded from Hallincross' body and she writhed in pain on the wet vegetation. Jeremiah could feel the arcane energy from the lavender Duskstone pulse through his body—his belt buckle even flared momentarily to combat the blistering waves of magic. But he held tight until the energy faded and eventually subsided back into the stone. Jeremiah looked down at the darkened ore and wondered how this bounty hunter came upon such a powerful Duskstone. Without thinking, he crushed the ore in his hand, leaving shards of dark lavender glass scattered on his palm. It was an instinctual decision, one that was meant to deny Hallincross of her power, but Jeremiah immediately regretted his haste. Before he could further ruminate on his actions, a thick accent interrupted his thoughts.

"Hot damn, cher," Ophelia exclaimed to the muggy night. "Who'd you kill to get this spitfire after you?"

CHAPTER 6

"You're a bit more famous than you let on, cher," Ophelia remarked casually as she cast a spell to reconstitute one of the swamp fowl coops. "I didn't know ol' Lucille ran with outlaws the likes of 'Jackson Rose'."

Jeremiah grimaced as he struggled to jam the squirming Hallincross into the impromptu jail. Off to the side, the enlarged winder continued to wolf down one of the bounty hunters, his boots protruding from the animal's maw. Jeremiah tried not to look.

"He is not just any outlaw," Hallincross spat from behind the bars of the mesh cage, her strange accent becoming more pronounced the more agitated she became. "He found the most powerful Duskstone known to Westhold—the Arkstone. He knows more about that epoch-defining ore than anyone living today. This outlaw has knowledge that could change the very face of our world. The fact that he killed Godwin Malmont is just salt to get the tongues of idiot bounty hunters and fortune seekers wagging."

Ophelia turned and eyed up Jeremiah Blade, her countenance impressed. With a wave of her hand, the bars of the cage twisted around Hallincross, limiting her movement.

"Not bad, cher," Ophelia said as Hallincross struggled against her prison. "You certainly weren't anything to look at when you first strode up here, but you're growing on me. It's not every day that ol' Ophelia gets to see a world-famous outlaw on her front porch. You should have opened with that. What's this Arkstone she's rambling on about?"

Jeremiah shifted uncomfortably on his bare feet as he weighed Hallincross' words in his mind. She only seemed concerned about the Arkstone—Chief Marshal Malmont was an afterthought to her. Every bounty hunter he came across only cared about him killing one of the most prominent leaders in all of Westhold, so why wasn't she?

"It was the Arkstone that caused the Blight," Jeremiah answered. He looked over to Hallincross, crushed between the wood and metal of the coop, and saw her face bright with fury. "Everyone thought the Blight that ruined the Willowgate Empire was caused by excessive Duskstone use. In a way, it was, but not just any ordinary kind of arcane source. It was the Arkstone, an ore of obscene power, which brought the Savannah Halflings to their knees. Lucille and I found it in the Shattered Hills, and she paid the iron price for it."

"Where is it now?" Hallincross spat at Jeremiah, the narrow wires digging into her flesh. "I don't believe that horseshit story about the Mesas banishing it to some forgotten corner of Westhold. You know where it is, Jeremiah Blade, and you will tell me."

"That would be a neat trick," Jeremiah responded as he dug in his chewing weed pouch for a slick pinch of the pungent leaf. He handed it over to Ophelia, who took it gratefully and stuffed some into her lower lip. "I don't care if you believe it or not. The Mesa Dwarves banished it so something like the Blight could never happen again. Sorry to disappoint you, but I have no idea where it is, and Westhold is the better for it. A Savannah Halfling, of all people, should know that."

"Then you are a fool to throw away such power," Hallincross hissed. "A power like the Arkstone is meant to be used, not discarded like an old toy. We could resurrect our entire civilization with a Duskstone of that magnitude."

Jeremiah stared incredulously at their captive. The realization dawned on him that she was raving mad. He took a menacing step towards the cage, his temper flaring dangerously.

"You know that the Arkstone destroyed Willowgate, right?" Jeremiah whispered, his voice as cold and hard as fresh steel. "The Blight turned people's flesh into maggot-ridden burlap, drained the very life from the soil, and twisted the minds and spirits of those who survived. Surely, you've heard the tales, and your desire is to use that very same destructive force to resurrect your fallen empire? Are you out of your mind?"

"With or without your knowledge," Hallincross retorted, her voice as cold and hard as Jeremiah's. "Willowgate will return…"

Before Hallincross could continue, the wood and wire of the cage snapped down further into her pale flesh, her face and body turning a bright red from the pressure. Ophelia waved a bony hand in the air, manipulating the coop's natural material and constricting the Savannah Halfling's ability to talk.

"Alright, cher, that's enough of that," Ophelia told the still-squirming Hallincross. She turned to Jeremiah with a curiously bemused look on her ancient features. "Why did you kill the old marshal?"

"He killed Lucille," Jeremiah responded mournfully, the wound still fresh despite the years. "He shot her down, and I reaped vengeance upon him in a mad frenzy."

"You best tell the truth...bastard," Hallincross sneered from her tightened confines. "Everyone in Westhold...knows you struck him down...in cold blood...to keep the knowledge of the Arkstone to yourself..."

Jeremiah heard a soft mumble from Ophelia, and Hallincross instantly fell asleep. With a wave of the witch's crooked hand, the cage loosened and blood rushed back through Hallincross' body. Ophelia picked up her winder familiar, now shrunk back to its normal size, and moseyed to her cabin.

"Well, it don't matter much now why you killed him, cher," Ophelia thought out loud. "He's with the spirits now, just like old Lucille. He might be a little sore if he saw you, I'd reckon."

"This is why I came here," Jeremiah insisted as he followed Ophelia back to her cabin. "Lucille died by Malmont's hands but indirectly by mine. I led her to the gates of oblivion, and she crossed. I didn't."

"Look, cher," Ophelia explained as she stepped back into the savory atmosphere of her swamp hut. "People die all the time. People are dying right this second. Dear cousin Lucille was sweet and all, but it's not like she did anything special. They get used to being dead, for the most part."

Jeremiah stood at the doorway of Ophelia's hovel, his mouth agape. He could feel his temperature rising dangerously—why wasn't she taking this seriously?

"Maybe this is commonplace for you, witch," Jeremiah snapped, more harshly than he intended. "But I have her death on my conscience and I am honoring her memory by coming here. She sent me to you for a reason, and I fully intend to find out why she did!"

"By the spirits," Ophelia spat as she stirred the pot of yambeau. Her winder familiar wrapped around her shoulder and hissed at the temperamental outlaw. "I can see why you and Lucille got on. Yall are both as hardheaded as old mules. Look, cher, you really ain't going to like where we have to go if you want to see her."

"I'll climb any mountain," Jeremiah pressed, an eagerness creeping into his voice. "Wade through any bayou, swim any ocean, to get to her."

Ophelia chuckled quietly as she scooped the remaining yambeau over a bowl of rice and then swatted the winder after it snatched a piece of meat from her bowl. She headed back to the table, sat down as if the events of the past hour never happened, and tucked into the steaming bowl of stew.

"Alright, cher," Ophelia sighed as it became apparent that she wasn't going to get rid of her nagging guest. "If you really want to see Lucille, there is only one place in Westhold that we will be able to do that. The Priory of Memory."

Jeremiah had never heard of the Priory of Memory. In fact, he didn't know any of the details of how Hoodoux Witches communicated with the dead; he always assumed they did so through some special type of Duskstone. He never thought it might be a physical location.

"I'm willing to take the chance," Jeremiah explained as he sat back down at the table. "Wherever it is, we can make it. I have to talk to Lucille one last time."

"If we go there, cher," Ophelia warned, her voice suddenly serious. "You have to be willing to cross to the other side. And, once we do, your pretty sword and fancy belt buckle ain't going to be enough to save you. The Priory of Memory lies at the heart of this world, where the veil is thin and narrow. If you get lost, you'll be on the other side for all eternity. Not a spirit, but forever cast adrift in a world not your own."

Jeremiah wasn't sure if Ophelia was trying to scare him, but regardless, ever since the Shattered Hills, his dreams had been haunted by the memory of Lucille Ledoux and he had to find a way to rest his troubled mind. He had thought about what he would say to her a thousand times. When she appeared to him in his dreams, Jeremiah tried to explain to her his feelings, but he could never formulate the right words. Lucille would always slip away before he could speak. Even if he had the slimmest of chances of reaching her, he had to try; he had to say one last goodbye and finally be able to sleep at night knowing she was okay.

"I'm willing to take any risk, Ophelia," Jeremiah said quietly as his spine straightened. "I'll go anywhere in Westhold to find Lucille, no matter the cost."

"Well, I guess it don't cost that much, come to think of it," Ophelia explained as she cleaned up her bowl of yambeau. Her heavy locks swirled outwards as she turned towards her room. "The Priory of Memory is in the Red Fens."

CHAPTER 7

Jeremiah couldn't help himself. He tried to explain to the incredulous Ophelia that, despite the fact that Hallincross had just tried to eviscerate him the night prior, he couldn't kill her in cold blood. They would just have to bring her to the Red Fens and leave her in the care of the local constabulary. Jeremiah wouldn't be doing that, of course—he was wanted by the local constabulary as well—but he felt that Ophelia would be able to explain how Hallincross had trespassed upon her property, and she would be jailed forthwith. Ophelia was none too happy about the development, but after some lively back and forth, Jeremiah convinced her to drag Hallincross through the swamp and to the Red Fens. It wasn't the best or most thought-out plan, but old habits died hard, Jeremiah told himself.

Jeremiah tugged on the rope that held Hallincross captive as they trudged through the bayou. She had to raise her chin to keep from drowning and, tied up as she was, all it took was one misstep and she'd be submerged. Jeremiah didn't want to kill her outright, but he also didn't want to make her life easy— she did try to kill him, after all. Plus, with all her ranting and raving, he needed a way to keep her relatively quiet before she riled up some swamp critter to come eat them alive.

"We got a long way to go before we get to the Fens, cher," Ophelia complained loudly as they waded through the brackish water. "And we ain't getting there any quicker with this one 'round our necks. Let's just cut her loose, and the swamp will take care of the rest."

"I know we are in the Delta," Jeremiah explained as he swatted away a swarm of persistent insects. "And the rules are a bit different out here, but all we have to do is deliver her to the Marchioness' guards and we will be done with her."

"It won't matter much longer, witch," Hallincross spat as she tried not to drown. The cloudy water lapped right underneath her pale chin. "It doesn't matter whether I live or die. I will return either way. We will all return. We will rise and claim what is ours. We will not be kept under the boot of tyranny any longer."

Jeremiah didn't have any idea what she was going on about, and she hadn't shut up about how "the forgotten will return" since they started their journey, but Ophelia stared intensely at Hallincross. She started to count to herself as if she was solving some unknown and unimaginable equation. The sound of Ophelia's crooked fingers tapping on a dead tree stump—clack-clack, clack-clack—echoed through the muggy swamp.

"You gave us the perfect opportunity, Jeremiah Blade," Hallincross continued, her voice feverish and eager. The more she spoke, the more Jeremiah was convinced she was out of her mind. "We would have the Alathanian Marshals breathing down our necks if it wasn't for you. You did Westhold a great service by getting rid of those bastards."

"The marshals still exist," Jeremiah shot back, uncertain and angry. His words were technically true, but Jeremiah couldn't deny the organization had been de-fanged as a result of the Arkstone revelation, despite the Alathanian efforts to contain the knowledge and keep it secret. They were a ship without a sail now, and Duskstone use ran rampant across Westhold because of it. "Marshal Sundown commands them."

It was no small miracle that Marshal Sundown was even still alive. After suffering grievous injuries during the Battle for the Arkstone, she was captured by the Mesa Dwarves for the second time in her long life and locked away under the Shattered Hills. With Chief Marshal Godwin Malmont dead, and Sundown captured, the Alathanian Marshals floundered and saw mass desertion among their ranks—many of whom became bounty hunters searching for Jeremiah Blade. By the time Sundown escaped captivity—also for the second time in her long life—the Alathanian Marshals were essentially no more.

"Sundown!" Hallincross' mad laughter filled the humid swamp air. "That Half-Elf and her clutch of failed marshals aren't going to stop us! We will reclaim our glory. We will return to this world!"

Jeremiah jerked the rope angrily, sending Hallincross splashing face-first into the bayou. He let her thrash around for a long moment before pulling her to the surface. Hallincross coughed and sputtered as life-giving air rushed through her body. Jeremiah gave her no time to rest and drugged her through the dark water, forcing her to half-stumble, half-swim to keep up.

Jeremiah Blade felt enough guilt for what happened without his prisoner gloating over his past failures. Despite the fact that the Mesa Dwarves successfully managed to hide the immensely powerful Arkstone away from the world, Westhold reeled from its discovery. A small stone cast on the red earth had caused a tsunami across the face of Westhold—a small stone cast by Jeremiah's own hand.

"If it makes you feel any better, cher," Ophelia opined to her new companions. "The Hoodoux Witches have thrived for centuries whether Alathanian Marshals existed or not. Maybe, it's because we don't venture very far out the Delta, or them marshals were scared of us. I can't say. It's probably the latter, I reckon."

Ophelia's chortle curled around the weeping willows and skipped along the bayou. It would have been a terrifying sound if Jeremiah had been trekking through the bogs all by his lonesome, but now, it just annoyed him. He watched wide-eyed as the ancient Swamp Elf splashed around barefoot in the mud and decaying vegetation, mumbling and laughing to herself all the while. They had been hiking through the swamp for less than a day, but the road to the Red Fens kept getting longer.

Suddenly, the rope jerked taut and stopped Jeremiah dead in his tracks just as he was about to vault over a rotten log. He looked back to see Hallincross slip her one good arm out of her bounds and shimmy her whole body out of the tight coils. She bit and scratched furiously, trying to make her great escape. Jeremiah, awkwardly straddling the rotten tree, lost his balance and fell face-first through a film of insect eggs covering the surface of the bayou. He immediately snapped up, sputtering and soaked, and fumbled for the loose end of the rope that had fallen from his hand.

Now free of Jeremiah's grasp, Hallincross waded through the throat-deep water to a higher patch of wet ground, desperately looking for something she could use as a weapon. The Savannah Halfling in the old-fashioned dress broke off a substantial limb from a decaying stump of wood with her single arm.

Jeremiah, uttering a creative string of curses, high-stepped through the muck after her. As soon as he reached the high ground, he tripped over a hidden root and fell to his hands and knees. Hallincross, sensing an opportunity, cracked Jeremiah across the jaw with her new cudgel, sending him sprawling into the morass. Jeremiah, more stunned than injured, turned over and peered through the swirling stars and into the dense canopy of willow branches and clinging moss.

"We will return!" Hallincross shouted in her antiquated accent as she descended on the prone outlaw, her tree branch flying. "We will reclaim what is ours!"

Jeremiah threw his hands up to defend himself from Hallincross' onslaught. Shards of broken, decaying wood splintered around him as she beat down until there was nothing left of her makeshift club. Jeremiah, rapidly losing his patience, rolled backwards in the mud, bringing his soggy boots over his hatless head and down on top of Hallincross' skull. She crashed into a jumble of swamp grass, giving Jeremiah enough time to scramble to his boots. As he turned to face his foe, Hallincross leaped at Jeremiah, her single arm clawing furiously.

Before she could land, however, her flight was arrested mid-air by a snaking root growing through the decomposing plant life. The root wrapped around Hallincross' leg and jerked her upside down, leaving her dangling above the bayou. Several other roots and vines likewise crept towards Hallincross, wrapping around her body and locking her away in a natural prison.

"As amusing as this is, cher," Ophelia Delphine called out across the bayou. "We ain't never going to get to the Red Fens at this rate."

The roots and vines tightened, enough to restrict Hallincross' movement but not enough to choke the life from her, just as Ophelia commanded the wood and metal of the critter cages the previous day. Jeremiah looked over to Ophelia, who was sitting cross-legged on the very same log Jeremiah had tumbled over at the start of the whole episode. She casually twirled her hand through the muggy air, bending the flora around the prisoner in increasingly clever patterns.

"It's two weeks to the Fens in the best of circumstances," Ophelia continued as she weaved her witchy magic. "With this one threatening to murder you at every opportunity, I'd give us a solid month and a half. I don't think you want to keep my cousin waiting, cher."

Jeremiah gnawed at his lower lip. He knew Ophelia was right, but he had no idea what they would do with Hallincross if they didn't bring her to justice. They couldn't just kill her.

"We could just kill her, cher," Ophelia whistled cheerfully as she tightened the strangling roots for emphasis. "The spirits would be mighty obliged, and I'm sure the Marchioness will appreciate having one less mouth to feed in her dungeon. Or we could just leave her like this. I'm sure something in this swamp will take the opportunity for free food."

Jeremiah twisted and turned as he decided what to do about Hallincross. He had taken a life before—killing Godwin Malmont was what got him into this mess in the first place—but he avoided it as much as possible in the intervening years. Occasionally, a bounty hunter would give him no choice, but killing did not come naturally to him, even in the brutal circumstances he found himself in as an outlaw. Violence was a tool that came with a heavy responsibility.

"This is just like a Plains Human," Hallincross spoke up through the bars of her natural prison. "Magnanimously deciding the fate of some poor castaway Savannah Halfling. You make me sick. Decades ago, the Willowgate Empire led the world, made history-altering decisions, and handed out charity to lesser civilizations in Westhold. It was a glorious and prosperous time. Can you imagine how advanced we would be if the Blight never occurred? The Savannah Halflings are the natural leaders of this world and deserve the respect that comes with that responsibility!"

"Willowgate has been a wasteland for decades," Jeremiah shot back, conjuring up his history studies from his days at the Academy and blending it with the revelations unearthed in the Shattered Hills. "The Savannah Halflings found the Arkstone, abused it, and paid the iron price for it. Even if they were great stewards of Westhold, that capability has clearly not been passed down to later generations."

The words were cold, cutting, and painfully unvarnished, but they rang true—the Savannah Halflings barely congregated in groups of more than a few dozen, much less magnificent, epoch-defining empires. Nonetheless, Hallincross raged against her bonds, threatening to break free from her magical prison and strangle Jeremiah with one arm.

"We will return, Jeremiah Blade," Hallincross threatened menacingly through clenched teeth. "And, on that day, Westhold will tremble."

The words clung to the hanging moss and rotten wood. Jeremiah had a hard time believing the vagabonds the Savannah Halflings had become could shape the events of Westhold, but Hallincross said the words with such conviction. It was no doubt that the Savannah Halflings had suffered a cataclysm unlike any other in the history of Westhold and been cast adrift and forgotten by the other civilizations, but what the struggling Hallincross was saying was beyond reason. The Savannah Halflings were a broken people, scattered upon the winds.

"We're burning daylight, cher," Ophelia Delphine called as she examined a particularly large bullfrog on the log next to her. "Do you really want to hear her ramble on like this for the next few weeks?"

Hallincross' deep black eyes bore a hole into Jeremiah. There was a hatred in those dark orbs, but also a confidence; whether that confidence was born of delusion or some unknown, hidden power, he did not know. Around them, the insects chirped and whirred as the day grew long in the west.

"Leave her," Jeremiah said with a cold finality. It amounted to a death sentence, though Jeremiah did not swing the blade. "If she survives, it will be her own doing."

CHAPTER 8

"I've been thinking," Ophelia complained as her winder flicked its tongue in support. "We really should have fed the Halfling lady to Woodroux. At best, some old swamp critter is going to come eat her for breakfast. At worst, she's going to find a way out and come kill you in your sleep."

"We couldn't kill her outright," Jeremiah retorted as they finally made their way through the outskirts of the Red Fens after weeks on the road. "At least this way, she has a chance to survive. Fairer that way. If she doesn't make it, then it's on her."

"Do you make a habit of leaving one-armed foes stranded in the middle of nowhere?" Ophelia asked as she gazed upon the magical green, gold, and purple lights that lined the streets leading towards the Swamp Elf capital. "Now, you got to worry about her chasing you down for whatever it is you know about that rock you found in the Shattered Hills."

Ophelia did have a certain logic to her argument—if Hallincross survived the wilds of the Delta, she would most certainly start hunting Jeremiah again—but Alathanian decorum was a hard habit to shake.

"Hey, friend," a Swamp Elf juggler looking to bilk Jeremiah for a few coins shouted in the native Swamp Elf language. "Have you ever seen someone juggle cutlasses before? Well, now's your chance! Not one, not two, not three, but four! Four swords! Amazing!"

Jeremiah waved off the enthusiastic jester and tried to step around him. They were just making their way into the city proper, and, despite the late hour, the Red Fens pulsed with an energy unlike any other city in Westhold. Lively bayou music mingled with the wafting smell of savory spices, while brilliant Duskstone lights shone above the streets and on the buildings. Game halls, brothels, and taverns stayed open all hours of the day while street vendors wound their way through the crowds selling all manners of snacks and drinks. If Jeremiah had still been a marshal, there would be no way he would accept such rampant lawlessness, but that was a lifetime ago, and the Swamp Elf enthusiasm for life and the 'Good Times' was hard to condemn.

"Ooo, cher, look!" Ophelia squealed in delight as the fool started tossing the rusty swords into the air with a goofy grin plastered on his narrow features. Despite her advanced age, Jeremiah had learned over the past few weeks of traveling with her that she had a childlike wonder for the little delights in the world. "I ain't seen anybody toss four swords in the air at the same time!"

Jeremiah shook his head. This was the same Hoodoux Queen who, weeks prior, transformed her pet winder into a gigantic version of itself to eat a man alive, called upon nature itself to do her bidding, and supposedly talked to the dead, and she was giggling like a crazy person at some obnoxious, garishly-dressed street performer. Ophelia Delphine was a strange being—certainly not unpleasant company, but certainly strange. From his time traveling with Ophelia, Jeremiah became accustomed to her odd habits. Eating insects, refusing to wear boots, and mumbling to herself about 'the spirits' had unnerved Jeremiah in the beginning, but, knowing that he would never find the Priory of Memory without her, he kept his opinions to himself. Jeremiah dug in his belt pouch for a few coppers and tossed them into the jaunty hat the performer used as a money bucket. The fool snickered as he finished with a dramatic flourish that sent Ophelia into another tizzy.

The pair continued down the road into the Red Fens, surrounded by the light and fury of a city that circulated day and night. As they walked, Jeremiah and Ophelia primarily spied Swamp Elves, naturally, but also a large number of Island Gnomes, thanks to the Red Fens' status as the major port of call for the merchant ships of the Gnomish Islands. The Swamp Elf capital was as cosmopolitan a city as was possible in Westhold, though; not just Swamp Elves and Island Gnomes, but members of all the Five Civilizations—Plains Humans, Savannah Halflings, and Mesa Dwarves included—populated its Duskstone-infused streets and architecture. The Red Fens was a bastion of commerce, culture, and vitality open to everyone.

All of this was precisely why Jeremiah had called these streets home since leaving the Shattered Hills—it wasn't the first time Jeremiah Blade had walked under these arcane lights. Since recovering from the injuries he received during the Battle for the Arkstone, he had left the red earth behind and made his home, as it was, in the Red Fens, figuring that his best way to avoid the bounty hunters that dogged his existence was to hide in plain sight. For the most part, it worked, as long as he made sure his Duskstone use was at a minimum and he kept to himself—it was a big city and easy to disappear among the crowds. In all of his time in the Red Fens, however, he had no idea that his way back to Lucille was among the shades of green, gold, and purple the entire time.

"Where exactly is this place?" Jeremiah ventured as he followed the swaying, barefoot Ophelia through the colorful streets. "I've been in the Fens for years now, but I've never heard of the Priory of Memory."

Ophelia stopped abruptly under a purple streetlight and gazed up at a loose wooden sign that read "The Stumbling Pelican" swinging over the entryway of a ratty tavern. From inside, Jeremiah could hear an old squeezebox and the sounds of revelry whining through the windows. Ophelia stood there with her eyes closed, a soft smile across her face, while her pet winder mimicked her mannerisms. Suddenly, the old Hoodoux Witch seemed much younger—her wrinkles smoothed out, her muscles toned, and her thick black hair less speckled with grey. She had turned years younger before his eyes.

"Is this the Priory of Memory?" Jeremiah asked after he started to worry that Ophelia wasn't breathing. "This doesn't really look like a priory to me."

"Does the sign say 'Priory of Memory', cher?" Ophelia responded without opening her eyes, swaying in time with the music. "It's been a lifetime since ol' Ophelia has been 'round these parts. I do miss the music here so much. All there is to listen to on the bayou is the insects singing. I'm pretty sure this is where he said he would be. I got to see if he is still playing that squeezebox of his. He always played so pretty."

"Who is he?" Jeremiah asked. "A friend of yours?"

When Ophelia failed to answer, Jeremiah cleared his throat, grabbed a pinch of chewing weed, jammed it into his lower lip, and watched her and her familiar writhe to the music.

"Let's go in," Jeremiah stated as his patience started to wane. "I'll buy us some drinks."

Jeremiah moved past Ophelia and entered The Stumbling Pelican. As he opened the aging wooden door, he could see a haze of men and women milling about, downing ales and fluorescent drinks, as an old skin-and-bones Island Gnome stood on stage with a squeezebox almost as large as he was. The coffee-colored Island Gnome with long, luxurious silver locks of shoulder-length hair crooned across the bar, and an amulet on his throat shone with a fierce tangerine light that pulsed in time with his song. The bright orange glow stood out against the heavy Duskstone lights casting wild shadows on the rotting walls and antique furniture of The Stumbling Pelican.

As the Island Gnome bard finished his song, the crowd erupted into applause and whoops of encouragement. Before Jeremiah could clap, Ophelia appeared next to him, whistling enthusiastically. The handsome Island Gnome bowed low before the crowd, his full head of silver hair sweeping low. As he whipped his hair out of his face, the bard swiped a tankard of ale off a low stool that shared the stage with him, took a drink, and scanned the crowd, his grey eyes finally alighting on Ophelia Delphine. The Island Gnome jerked back with a curious look on his weathered features—it was somewhere between despair, relief, and nostalgia—but he recovered quickly and made a sweeping gesture towards the crowd.

"If it's alright by yall, I'm going to take a small break," the bard called out to the gathered host in the Swamp Elf language. "These bones aren't as young as they used to be. I imagine some of yall out there can sympathize."

The patrons of The Stumbling Pelican were disappointed but grumpily acceded that the old bard probably did need a rest. He came off the stage with his squeezebox slung over his shoulder, shook a few hands with the patrons, and made a beeline to the open arms of Ophelia Delphine.

"Lukas Sing-Low, it's awfully nice to see you, cher," Ophelia declared as they finished their hug. "You look like you're doing alright. Maybe a few more silver hairs on your head, but none the worse for wear."

"You're too kind, Ophelia," Lukas Sing-Low responded in a much softer voice than his booming, onstage baritone. He spoke with an ease and fluidity in the Swamp Elf language, but the faintest hints of an Island accent still shone through the syrupy tones. "You haven't aged at all. It must be that fresh bayou water keeping you young. Or are you casting some Hoodoux to keep the wrinkles away?"

Ophelia Delphine fluttered her long eyelashes like a tavern maid, flashed a sly smile to the old bard, and flipped a lock of dark hair over her shoulder.

"You know the air is much cleaner in the Delta than it is here, Lukas," Ophelia cooed as the barman brought over three tankards of warm ale and passed them around. The three clinked their mugs and took long draughts before Ophelia continued with a chuckle. "But, you know, ol' Ophelia ain't opposed to a little bit of the Hoodoux every now and then. You know, I do like to call myself the Queen, cher."

Lukas Sing-Low laughed into his ale before turning his attention to his new drinking companion.

"Who's the young blade here?" Lukas Sing-Low asked, sizing up the newcomer. "You got yourself a boyfriend?"

Ophelia looked over to Jeremiah with a wide, toothy grin plastered on her mahogany features. Jeremiah quickly realized the situation—in front of a tavern full of people, she could easily oust him as Westhold's most wanted outlaw.

"Jackson Rose," Ophelia answered as she turned back to Lukas Sing-Low, giving Jeremiah a chance to breathe. "Not my boyfriend. He's a bit too young for ol' Ophelia. He's a friend of my cousin Lucille, and he's looking for a little bit of help finding her."

"How's Lucille doing?" Lukas asked as he took another tankard of ale from a grateful patron to add to his growing collection. The three moved over towards an empty space at the bar to get some air from the crowd of drunkards. "I haven't seen her in a lifetime if my memory serves me true."

"She's dead," Ophelia responded as casually as if she were telling him the weather. "Apparently, Rose over here was with her when she passed to the other side. I'm sure she's doing fine, though."

Lukas Sing-Low cast a quick glance up towards Jeremiah, his bushy eyebrow arching quizzically. Jeremiah nodded in response, and Lukas shrugged and took a long draught of his ale.

Unusual present circumstances notwithstanding, Jeremiah had already heard of Lukas Sing-Low and even saw him in person at one of the innumerable food festivals the Red Fens hosted throughout the year. He doubted Lukas would recognize him—he had just been part of the faceless multitude cheering for the Island Gnome. Lukas Sing-Low was one of the most famous bards in the Delta and had lived in the Red Fens for decades. He had made the Red Fens his home, and the people of the city embraced him wholeheartedly. In a land where music was an integral part of life, as critical as breathing, a bard of Lukas' caliber was a valuable commodity. Some said he was past his prime, but judging by his latest serenade and his formidable skill on the squeezebox, Lukas Sing-Low still had some fire in him.

"Well, I'm sorry to hear that," Lukas responded after he finished his ale. "I remember her being real nice. I'm sure she's doing right fine."

"That's why we are here, cher," Ophelia replied while letting her pet winder slither on the bar towards an unattended mug, much to the dismay of the bartender. "Young Rose over here wants to go see her."

Lukas Sing-Low's face turned pale, and he immediately dove into his drink.

"Oh, no, Ophelia," Lukas said, suddenly sounding and looking old. "I've been rode hard and put up wet. I don't think I'll be able to make it even if I tried. It's been a long time, and I intend to keep it that way."

"You know we will need you, cher," Ophelia charged ahead, undeterred. "You are the key. Plus, it ain't just Rose that has something to see over there. Over the past few weeks, I've been listening, and the spirits have been whispering about some strange going-ons over there."

This was news to Jeremiah. He had spent those past few weeks with Ophelia, and she had made no mention about the spirits talking to her in any capacity. Jeremiah wondered about her ramblings and mumblings as they trekked through the swamps, but he figured it was just part of the show. Maybe she had been talking with the spirits. She certainly hadn't let on that anything was wrong, though.

Jeremiah looked between the two and saw the anxiety obvious in Lukas' eyes. Ophelia, as always, seemed unconcerned. Lukas motioned to the bartender—who was busy trying to move the mug away from Ophelia's winder—for another ale.

"No offense to you, Ophelia, your cousin, or the young blade here," Lukas explained after another gulp. "But why would I want to risk these old bones to find someone I barely even know?"

"I'm telling you, cher," Ophelia responded as her familiar slithered into the mug in the bartender's hands, causing him to freeze in fear. "It ain't just about Lucille. The spirits are talking to me. There are faint whispers about the veil. Plus, I remember risking these old bones to look for someone I didn't know."

Lukas Sing-Low held Ophelia's gaze for a long, uncertain moment before downing the rest of his ale and shifting his squeezebox so that it rested on his narrow belly. He gave the instrument a tentative squeeze, and it sighed melodiously. Lukas gave a curt nod to Jeremiah and flashed a thin smile towards Ophelia Delphine.

"I wish you had come by for anything but this, Ophelia," Lukas declared before climbing onto the bar and scanning the crowd. "They always say it's an ill omen when a Hoodoux Witch strolls through your door. It's just too painful to go back."

With that, the famed bard launched into a raucous tune that rolled over The Stumbling Pelican like thunder.

CHAPTER 9

The upbeat, riotous song about a famous bayou dish faded away as Lukas Sing-Low swung his squeezebox over his shoulder so he could take an unimpeded drink from his mug. Jeremiah clapped enthusiastically with the rest of The Stumbling Pelican while Ophelia leaned forward and glared at the Mesa Dwarf card dealer, her face a twisted mask of contempt.

"If you deal me another pickaxe, cher," Ophelia warned the dealer as she cocked her head to one side and strummed her long fingernails on the gaming table—clack-clack, clack-clack. "I'm going to let Woodroux eat you alive. And everyone is going to ask, 'What happened to that longbeard card dealer over at the Pelican?' Oh, he made the Hoodoux Queen mad and ended up in her swamp critter's belly. Real shame."

The card dealer looked around at the other players at the table, hesitation flashing in his eyes, then to the winder curling around Ophelia's stack of coins. When Jeremiah caught the dealer's questioning eye, the outlaw shrugged in response, trying to impress upon the Mesa Dwarf that he was on his own. The dealer flipped over the top card and let out a sigh of relief when a shovel appeared as the card suit.

"I'm impressed that you have such famous friends, Ophelia," Jeremiah said after Ophelia stopped her victory dance and pulled the sizable pile of gold coins towards her. "But, what does he have to do with finding Lucille?"

"Lukas is a lot more than some famous barfly troubadour, cher," Ophelia responded as she smugly stacked her gold coins high. "Lukas is an ol' friend of Ophelia's, and we've been on many a grand adventure. He is the key, cher, and without the key, you ain't never going to see my dear cousin."

Lukas Sing-Low, as if on cue, broke out into another lively song on his squeezebox, causing a large swath of The Stumbling Pelican's patrons to rumble to their feet and start dancing. Even those too old or too drunk to dance clapped cheerily along. The only ones who didn't join in the merriment were the ones bleeding money on the card tables. Duskstone lights blinked in time with Lukas' music, heightening the mystic, otherworldly atmosphere in the tavern. Jeremiah couldn't help but tap his boot along with the music.

"What do you mean he is the 'key'?" Jeremiah asked as the dealer dealt out another round of hands. "If this place is as dangerous as you say, then wouldn't adding more folks mean we have a greater risk of losing someone? Whatever we are about to do, I don't necessarily want Lukas Sing-Low's blood on my hands."

"Oh ho!" Ophelia laughed as she looked at her cards. "So, it's alright if ol' Ophelia's blood is on your hands? That's awfully sweet of you, cher."

"That's not what I mean," Jeremiah stammered, though Ophelia didn't actually seem to be too offended. "It's just, the last time someone followed me to a dangerous place, they ended up dead. I guess that's why I'm here now. I don't want anyone coming along who isn't entirely necessary. You know, for their protection."

"There's about to be a lot of dead people where we are going, cher," Ophelia responded as her opponents at the table raised curious eyebrows at the conversation. "I like Lukas and all, but what's one more in the grand scheme of it all? It ain't going to bother ol' Ophelia none. This is the way of things, cher."

Jeremiah paused to rub his eyes as the card game continued hesitantly around the table. He was still having a hard time adjusting to Ophelia's curious outlook on life and death. After an extended moment, Jeremiah decided to take a different tack.

"How does a bard have experience with this?" Jeremiah asked as Ophelia's familiar slithered across the deck of playing cards, and the dealer looked on in abject fear. The winder flicked his forked tongue expectantly at the mortified Mesa Dwarf. "What adventures did you go on before? How does a bard know anything about the dead? I'm sure his experience is quite varied, but still, what spirits are talking to him?"

"Oh, well, you know, cher," Ophelia explained as she continued to eyeball her hand of cards. "Ol' Ophelia was young once. If it hadn't been for Lukas, I may not have ever made it to the other side. He came to me, much like you, looking for someone lost to him. Back then, I hadn't appointed myself as the Hoodoux Queen yet, so I didn't know anything about going over to the other side. But he had found a way. A key, if you will. Such was his determination to find a way back to the one he lost. Also like you, cher. Many of my kind turned him down. Said he was a damn fool that would doom us all. But young Ophelia took pity on Lukas and accompanied him past the veil. We damn near never came back. I like the spirits, cher, but ol' Ophelia doesn't want to spend more time with them than necessary."

"That sounds ominous," Jeremiah replied as he kept a wary eye out across the tavern. "Did you find who he was looking for?"

"Nope," Ophelia answered quickly as she gave a suspicious, evil eye around the table. The dealer and the other players shifted uncomfortably as Ophelia took her sweet time in deciding whether to raise or not. "The other side is a big place, and the one we were looking for was awfully small. We wandered for an eternity, but we were forced to retreat. We were losing ourselves, and young Ophelia wasn't as tough then as she is now."

The other players at the card table stared at Ophelia as she rambled on about spirits and the other side so casually. The Red Fens was a strange place, filled with all manner of strange folks, but it wasn't every day that you found yourself losing your week's wages to a Hoodoux Witch that spoke with the dead.

Jeremiah plucked a glass of Sweetfire from a passing barmaid, ran his free hand through his black hair, and gazed out over the bar. Lukas Sing-Low was jigging on top of the bar, leading the patrons of The Stumbling Pelican in a particularly ribald sing-a-long. The Island Gnome had terrific stage presence, at once commanding and sympathetic. Jeremiah could tell Lukas Sing-Low had been doing this for a lifetime. It was hard to believe that the lively and gregarious bard could have delved into as dangerous a place as Ophelia was describing, much less serve as the "key" for it, but the Hoodoux Witch had a habit of talking in vagaries, enjoying it as Jeremiah's face screwed in confusion.

As he scanned the room with his back turned to the game, lost in thought, Jeremiah heard another person slip into one of the empty chairs around the card table. He thought nothing of it until he heard the rough voice of the newcomer dance across the felt.

"You go ahead and deal me in, hoss," the male voice directed the card dealer. "I just burned into town, and I'm looking to fleece these fine folks of their hard-earned coins."

"You're a tall drink of water, cher," Ophelia retorted to the newcomer. "That pretty grin of yours ain't going to help you take ol' Ophelia's gold, though."

Jeremiah froze as Ophelia fenced with her new opponent, an icy spindle of fear spreading across his chest. The outlaw didn't dare turn around; he just kept tapping his foot and observing the crowded tavern, even though he strained his ears to pick up every cast-off syllable from the table.

"What are you in town for, stranger?" the dealer asked as the cards spun onto the felt. "You look like you just came in off the trail."

"I'm looking for a relative of mine," the new voice answered quickly. His voice was slightly slurred like he had a big chaw of chewing weed in his lower lip. "He owes me some money. He's kind of a bastard, but that's family for you."

"You from Alathane, cher?" Ophelia piped up cheerfully. "You look a little ragged 'round the edges to have come from the streets of gold."

"By the Good Light, no," the stranger exclaimed, sounding offended. "I avoid that place like the Blight. I'm from Dryftwood, though I've been long gone from there for many moons. I just came to the Fens to find this bastard cousin of mine."

"There ain't no way for you to make money in Dryftwood?" Ophelia inquired innocently, trying to throw the newcomer off his game. "I have a cousin who lives in Dryftwood. I hear it's an alright place to make some gold if you don't mind getting a bit dirty."

"Oh, yes ma'am," the stranger answered as the players called and raised the pot in turns. "If you know what you're doing out there, you can make a fair gold piece or two. But, my old cousin recently came into a significant chunk of money. Enough to make them short-stack Gnomish bastards blush."

A creeping sense of dread snaked its way up Jeremiah's spine. His mind raced back to the Shattered Hills. He thought about the dust storms, the hangings, the heat, the Arkstone. It couldn't be, he thought. Jeremiah ran a calloused hand along the hilt of an old hunting knife at his belt, preparing himself for the worst.

"Your cousin lives around here?" one of the other players at the table asked. "Or you just drifting through town before you dive deeper into the Delta or set sail for the Gnomish Islands?"

"Yeah, the old boy lives around these parts," the stranger answered, a hint of sarcasm in his rough voice. "But he spent a fair amount of time in Dryftwood. That's where he learned he had all this money coming to him. He set out for the Delta in the hopes of gambling it away before any of his kin could hit him up for a loan. Originally, dear coz is from Alathane. I doubt he's seen those marble walls in a while, though."

Jeremiah, still gazing towards Lukas Sing-Low, flicked his knife an inch out of its sheath in preparation for the coming storm. Of all the places in Westhold, he had no idea how he ended up at the same table as this ghost. Jeremiah cursed under his breath for letting his guard down twice in one month. It must have been his damn belt buckle, though he wasn't sure this newcomer knew how to work a Raeller Counter. Jeremiah's body tensed with every new word that tumbled out of the stranger's mouth.

"Hot damn, dealer," the voice cheered through the chorus of groans from his opponents. "You're alright to this old drifter! I knew today was going to be my lucky day. I had a good feeling about this table. Of all the game tables in the Fens, I'm a lucky bastard to choose this one, yessir. It's not every day that I get to sit across from a former Alathanian Marshal."

Jeremiah spun around faster than a bolt of lightning, threw his chair across the dance floor, unsheathed his hunting knife in one fluid motion, and caused everyone at the table, save the newcomer, to jump back in shock. The long and lean stranger sat there calmly, his narrow arms akimbo as he studied his hand. A dark ranching hat covered his face but, when he lifted his angular chin towards Jeremiah, a wide grin broke across the rough stubble of his jaw. Though Jeremiah had a good idea of who he was about to find, he still reflexively gasped when he saw the pale blues eyes of Breaker Calhoun staring back at him.

CHAPTER 10

"Well, what a coincidence," Breaker Calhoun chortled from his seat at the table. "Who would have guessed I'd find my old friend in such a big city. Jeremiah Blade! How are you, son?"

"What are you doing here, Calhoun?" Jeremiah growled. "I thought your blood stained the red earth of the Shattered Hills."

It was a testament to The Stumbling Pelican that an outlaw waving around a hunting knife barely drew attention from anyone not sitting around the gaming table. The music played, and the patrons danced unimpeded despite the theatrics.

"You didn't try hard enough to kill me, Marshal Blade," Breaker Calhoun explained loudly, his grin never leaving his face. "Next time, you and your girlfriend ought to make sure you finish the job. But, I guess yall learned that lesson pretty quick since we no longer have the esteemed Chief Marshal with us."

"If you are here for the money, you better reconsider, Calhoun," Jeremiah threatened menacingly. "I'll make sure I finish the job this time."

"By the Good Light, I'm quaking in my boots," Breaker Calhoun mimed dramatically, shaking his hands in mock terror. "You're a dangerous man, Jeremiah Blade. Killing someone of Godwin Malmont's caliber was no easy feat, especially for some up-jumped blade trying to make his way in the world. I always wondered why you did it, slaying that old stick-up-the-ass, but when I heard he killed that girlfriend of yours, I figured you must have been pretty hot. I tried looking for you to give my condolences, but you up and vanished like some narrow-boned ghost. I never thought I'd see you again, but you messed up right nicely when you flashed that pretty Alathanian belt buckle a few weeks ago. We wouldn't be having this little reunion if you hadn't. Got me right on your trail. Seeing my old friend, Jeremiah Blade, might just make me shed a tear or two."

Jeremiah felt his Raeller Counter buzz on his belt and heard Ophelia whispering under her breath as Her winder curled into a tight coil and hissed across the table. Though Lukas Sing-Low was singing a loud, raucous song from the bar, Breaker Calhoun's ranting was starting to draw attention from the nearby gaming tables. The patrons of The Stumbling Pelican were creeping ever closer to Jeremiah as the realization that the most-wanted criminal in all of Westhold stood among them. Breaker Calhoun, for his part, flipped one of the cards in his hand upside down, examined it closely, and let out a long, low whistle.

"Who is this, cher?" Ophelia whispered, her voice low, hard, and menacing. "He's got a smart mouth on him."

"His name is Breaker Calhoun," Jeremiah explained without tearing his baleful gaze away from the lanky, whistling human. "I know him from Dryftwood. He's a lawman, of all things. This rat imprisoned me and your cousin. Damn near killed us and left us to die."

"Well, what did yall expect?" Calhoun grinned as he laid his cards face down on the felt. "At the time, innocent me didn't think I was dealing with a lying, cheating, swearing, murdering son of a bitch, but I had an intuition! I'm guessing I would have done Westhold a mighty big favor if I had killed you that day. Let me ask you, Jeremiah Blade, how much is that bounty on your head now? Five thousand? Ten? Fifty thousand, wasn't it? You hear that? Fifty thousand gold pieces!"

With Calhoun loudly lobbing around such substantial sums, more patrons leaned into the conversation, even over the rowdy notes of Lukas Sing-Low's squeezebox. Out of the corner of his eye, Jeremiah saw a burly Mesa Dwarf pull out a bone-handled knife from his waistband. The hairs on the back of Jeremiah's neck started to rise as the whispers multiplied around him.

"I don't know what you are talking about, Calhoun," Jeremiah warned venomously as the drunks crept in for a closer look. "I recommend you stand up and walk out of here or else I'll drop your carcass in some forgotten bayou."

"That ain't very nice, Jeremiah Blade," Breaker Calhoun laughed casually as he dropped his hands underneath the table. "But it does sound exactly like something the murderer of Godwin Malmont would say!"

In an instant, The Stumbling Pelican exploded in a swirl of chaos. Rough hollering filled the tavern as Jeremiah whipsawed the hunting knife through the air towards his grinning antagonist, but Breaker Calhoun, anticipating a bit of violence, flipped the card table up in front of him, and the blade buried itself firmly in the green felt. Coins and cards cascaded to the floor while the erstwhile deputy sheriff of Dryftwood kicked the table, now on its edge, towards Jeremiah Blade. The outlaw tripped backwards under the weight of the card table and, as he fell to the floor, he saw Ophelia's emerald winder corkscrewing wildly past him in the air. Before Jeremiah could hit the ground, a puff of air cushioned his fall and gave him just enough time to catch the table and stop it from smashing him in the face. A wisp of green smoke curled around him and he fell the final inch to the Sweetfire-soaked floor of The Stumbling Pelican with a heavy thud.

A considerable weight dropped on the other side of the table and snatched the breath from Jeremiah's lungs. As he tried to press the table off of him, a long-forgotten hatchet blade split the wood directly above his forehead. The serrated blade glinted off shards of green, gold, and purple light from the swirling Duskstone lamps of The Stumbling Pelican. Jeremiah struggled under the weight of the table as the hatchet ripped out of the wood for another strike.

Before the weapon fell again, the table soared up and across the barroom like it was swept away by a crashing tide. Jeremiah saw Ophelia Delphine mumbling to herself, her clawed hand dripping green swamp mist, as Breaker Calhoun pinwheeled through the fields of drunks, degenerates, gamblers, and other fine, upstanding citizens of the Red Fens. Ophelia, the three parallel lines of arcane tattoos under her eyes glittering with an iridescent light, smiled at Jeremiah Blade.

"You got an awful lot of friends, cher," Ophelia declared flatly as The Stumbling Pelican descended into a riot, carried along by an upbeat tune from Lukas Sing-Low, who was not one to miss an opportunity for conducting a good bar fight. The old bard punctuated each act of violence he witnessed with a hearty squeeze on his instrument, gleefully adding to the devolving melee. "I didn't know you were going to have so many admirers come looking for you. You're more famous than ol' Ophelia. I won't lie, I might be a little jealous."

Jeremiah didn't have any time to answer as a portly Plains Human, taking advantage of the world's most wanted outlaw lying prone in front of him, jumped on top of him with a boot knife drawn. Jeremiah jerked his head to the side just in time, and the blade jammed deep into the wooden floor planks next to his ear. He whipped his head up and head-butted his attacker, breaking the opportunist's bulbous nose, and sending a spray of blood shimmering through the magical light. The outlaw followed up with a solid left hand that knocked out two rotten teeth from his attacker's mouth and sent the Plains Human sprawling into the ruins of the gaming table. Jeremiah scrambled to his boots, hoping to catch Breaker Calhoun while he was still extracting himself from the demolished furniture, but the late hour and the long trek through the Delta had dulled his edge and he stumbled over himself as he picked his way through the broken tables and chairs.

All those within earshot of Jeremiah's conversation with Breaker Calhoun converged on the lurching outlaw to bring in the biggest haul of gold The Stumbling Pelican had ever seen. Suddenly, everyone in the bar was a bounty hunter—it was only natural with so magnificent a prize laid out in front of them, ready for taking. This was the chance of a lifetime for the lost souls that populated the stained facade of The Stumbling Pelican.

Jeremiah reached behind him for his warming longsword to greet the swelling crowd, but before he could pull the blade from its scabbard, a Sweetfire bottle came crashing down on the crown of his hatless head. Flashing stars mingled with shards of shattered glass spiraling away from his skull. Jeremiah swooned, clomping his boot down heavily to maintain his balance as the throng of opportunists came down on him like an avalanche.

Before he realized it, Jeremiah's world was nothing but tooth, nail, and blood. Clenched fists and broken bottles rained down on the outlaw as he desperately tried to defend himself. Jeremiah booted some fat, pasty Swamp Elf in his rotund gut, then drove a knee into his nose, sending the drunkard sprawling into a barmaid who was still valiantly serving drinks through the storm. A cloudburst of alcohol plumed outwards, covering the brawlers with a fine layer of ale and Sweetfire. A Mesa Dwarf with a single eye lunged towards Jeremiah with a broken Sweetfire bottle but slipped on the alcoholic deluge and crashed face first onto the floor. Jeremiah lined up and booted the Mesa Dwarf in his good eye just as a meaty, dark-skinned Plains Human woman in a tight corset and a gangly, pale Savannah Halfling tackled him and brought him down to the floor sticky with spilled alcohol. Blood, glass, and clumps of hair flew skyward as Jeremiah fought for his life and freedom. At one point, someone broke a heavy bar stool over Jeremiah's back, but his longsword took the brunt of the force and saved him from never being able to walk again. Jeremiah was quickly becoming overwhelmed as more fortune-seekers jumped onto the dog pile, knives and broken bottles slashing indiscriminately.

Ophelia, who had been, up until this point, scrounging around the brawl looking for her familiar, finally emerged from underneath a heavy gaming table with her emerald green winder twisting on the floor next to her bare feet. Seeing Jeremiah crushed under a tangle of boots, limbs, and sticky liquor, Ophelia started chanting in a tenor that matched the fevered pitch of Lukas Sing-Low's bar battle song. Ophelia's Duskstone tattoos glowed brightly, and a sudden rush of freezing air blew up the dog pile and sent surprised patrons, Jeremiah included, cartwheeling through the stuffy tavern air. All around The Stumbling Pelican, bodies crashed into furniture, walls, and other warm bodies enjoying the show. Tables, chairs, mugs, and glasses all shattered under the weight of flying, opportunistic drunks. Jeremiah fell flat on a gaming table and into several stacks of playing cards which fell to the floor like cherry blossom petals in the wind.

Jeremiah was free of the tangle but saw no respite as a sharpened hatchet blade embedded itself in the green felt next to his head. Above him, the leering, stubbled, upside-down visage of Breaker Calhoun loomed over him. The former sheriff's deputy raised his second hatchet with no intent to miss the next strike.

Jeremiah rolled backwards and brought the point of his boot over his head and directly on the bridge of Breaker Calhoun's sharp nose. Calhoun reeled as a sheet of bright blood cascaded down the front of his rawhide vest. As Calhoun staggered back, Jeremiah shuffled off the table and pressed his advantage, splashing a full glass of Sweetfire in his old foe's face, searing the freshly broken skin, and smashing the glass right on Calhoun's ear. Jeremiah turned to grab a chair to finish off the former sheriff's deputy, but Breaker Calhoun feinted to one side, dropped down, hooked the backside of his hatchet behind Jeremiah's knee, and pulled his leg out from under him. Jeremiah once again found himself on the floor of The Stumbling Pelican looking up at the stained rafters. It had been an eternity since the last time Jeremiah saw Breaker Calhoun fight, but it was clear he had not lost his step in the intervening years. Jeremiah, dazed, looked to one side to see Ophelia's familiar, its eyes wide and curious, staring back at him.

"Anytime you want to eat somebody," Jeremiah whispered curtly to the winder. "That'd be great."

The familiar did not have time to respond as Breaker Calhoun leaped towards the prostrate Jeremiah, his hatchets raised high.

He never made it. Just before the blades came down, Breaker Calhoun's body froze in mid-air. Suspended above the chaos, his body broke, twisted, and started to shrink. Breaker Calhoun's long and lean body minimized until he was no more than a few inches high and he fell among a forest of broken table legs. Jeremiah could hardly believe his eyes as he watched Calhoun fight his way out of a piece of gaming felt. Jeremiah looked to Ophelia, her Duskstone tattoos glowing brightly, and saw a sly smile creep across her mahogany features.

Jeremiah, thinking quick, grabbed an errant Sweetfire glass and snapped it over the tiny form of Breaker Calhoun; he then slid a playing card under the upside-down glass, trapping his foe inside like a spider. All Breaker Calhoun could do was hop around the empty glass angrily and beat against the edges to no avail. Across the battlefield of The Stumbling Pelican, Lukas Sing-Low, keeping a watchful eye on the brawl, slowed the tune on his squeezebox, and the room slowed and sputtered in concert. Ophelia Delphine turned her attention to the rallying crowd of drunkards and lashed out with icy winds to keep off the punters and opportunists trying to reach Jeremiah Blade and claim the sweet bounty.

"We best make ourselves scarce, cher," Ophelia warned as she saw a flock of burly bouncers moving on their position. "Or else we're all going to end up in the Marchioness' dungeon. Take a deep breath and don't get lost now, you hear?"

With that, thick, billowing clouds of smoke filled The Stumbling Pelican. Lukas' song stopped suddenly as the sprawling green cloud spread to every corner of the bar. All around them, the vapor filled noses, mouths, and lungs, causing every soul it touched to wretch and stagger. Everyone who was still conscious scrambled for whatever exit they could find.

    Jeremiah took a sharp breath before the cloud washed over him, but the fumes stung his eyes and reduced his visibility to zero. Crashing his way towards what he thought was the exit and holding the tiny, angry Breaker Calhoun in the Sweetfire glass, Jeremiah felt a surprisingly strong hand grab him by his ear and drag him through the ruined interior of The Stumbling Pelican and into the muggy night redolent with the savory smell of fried seafood.

CHAPTER 11

Noxious smoke rolled outwards from the windows and doors of The Stumbling Pelican, scattering street food vendors and revelers in every direction like sailors fleeing a sinking ship. It was a testament to the Red Fens that this scene only heightened the festive spirit as enterprising patrons passed around pilfered Sweetfire bottles from the tavern to enjoy the show.

Jeremiah's eyes burned from the fumes, but he could tell from the increased humidity, stones beneath his boots, and salty tint to the air that he had successfully escaped from The Stumbling Pelican. The powerful grip continued to drag him along as Jeremiah kept his own tight grasp on the glass that contained the tiny Breaker Calhoun. The former sheriff's deputy tumbled wildly, crashing into the sides of the glass slippery with leftover Sweetfire.

"Ophelia!" shouted a voice over the growing scrum. "This way!"

The powerful grip obliged, and Jeremiah felt himself drug through the street towards the sound of the voice. All around them, people cursed, hollered, and clamored, not willing to give up the hunt for the outlaw Jeremiah Blade.

"Your friend sure kicked up a hornet's nest, cher," Ophelia's voice declared as she weaved her way through the drunks and the street vendors. "You got damn near all of Westhold after you. I'm impressed."

Jeremiah mumbled a reply but was mainly focused on putting one boot in front of the other. His vision was slowly returning to him, but he couldn't rub his eyes because both hands held Breaker Calhoun firmly in the cup. Jeremiah didn't want to lose Calhoun and have him crushed under-boot until he could find out more about how his old foe found him. Jeremiah blinked hard, trying to wash out the stinging fog, and stumbled after the surprisingly hale Ophelia Delphine.

Ophelia muttered something unintelligible, and Jeremiah heard a person

Dryftwood Outlaws on the Bayou

scream and take flight. A chorus of curses erupted as the unlucky soul crashed into a street vendor's cart, sending fried seafood skywards. Ophelia and Jeremiah rushed by, wasting no time for an opportunistic snack as the street descended into bedlam around them. By the time Jeremiah's vision was fully restored, they stood in front of a bemused Lukas Sing-Low sitting on a low stool next to an undisturbed street vendor's cart.

"Jackson Rose, huh?" Lukas drawled out, the slightest hint of sarcasm in his voice, as he munched on a skewer of fried dragon shrimp. "I did not know that Jackson Rose was the most wanted man in all of Westhold. It's never a dull moment with you, Ophelia. I'll give you that."

Jeremiah took a gander around the tumultuous street—drunks and gamblers sprung to life with knives and broken bottles in their hands, street peddlers guarded their wares against the marauding mob, and, more disconcertingly, several people were informing the rakish Vermillion Guard, the all-female Red Fens city patrol, that none other than Jeremiah Blade, slayer of Godwin Malmont, was tramping around their watch. Jeremiah took one look at the guards' famous Duskstone pikes and decided he wanted no part of that.

"Can I have one of those?" Ophelia cheekily asked Lukas despite the deteriorating situation. Lukas slid a handful of savory dragon shrimp off the skewer and handed them to Ophelia. Her emerald familiar, loosely curled around her neck, snatched a dragon shrimp from the witch and devoured it with great abandon. The three chomped away as the murderous horde searched for the outlaw Jeremiah Blade. "I'm mighty obliged, Lukas. Woodroux is, too."

"What happened to making ourselves scarce?" Jeremiah questioned as neither Ophelia nor Lukas seemed to be in any hurry now that street food was involved. Three of the Vermillion Guards, with their jaunty, feathered hats, were starting to head Jeremiah's way. "We best get to moving if I want to sleep anywhere other than the Marchioness' dungeon."

"I guess you're right, cher," Ophelia mumbled as she wolfed down the last of the shrimp. "Lukas, you got any idea where we can run to?"

Before Lukas could answer, a burly Swamp Elf tackled Jeremiah Blade into the street vendor's stall, sending shrimp and searing oil skywards. The cooking oil fell on the Swamp Elf's back and burned through his thick tunic, causing him to shriek in pain. Miraculously, Jeremiah managed to hold on to the glass containing Breaker Calhoun as he kicked and elbowed his way out of the shredded food cart. Lukas Sing-Low, thinking fast, grabbed a handful of wooden skewers in a tight bundle and jammed them into the fleshy cheeks of Jeremiah's assailant. The Swamp Elf howled in more pain as the sticks dangled from his jowls, giving Jeremiah just enough time to squirm out from the ruined stall.

The Vermillion Guards, their graceful, curving pikes lowered, were now almost upon them. As Lukas helped Jeremiah to his boots, Ophelia's Duskstone tattoos glowed brightly and her hands dripped with the viscous green light of the Delta. Suddenly, a narrow line of cobblestones rose a few inches from the ground right in front of the charging guards; the lead guard couldn't catch herself in time, tripped over the sudden hurdle, and went flying face first into the street. The other two Vermillion Guards tumbled over their comrade and lay in a jumbled heap as their feathered hats drifted daintily towards the ground.

"Time to mosey, young man," Lukas warned as the sharks circled around them. He spied a narrow alley and let out a sharp whistle. "Ophelia, that way!"

The three immediately set off through the streets of the Red Fens with a whole host of pursuers on their tail. Duskstone lights whirred by as they pounded through the alley. Looming gargoyles perched on building corners greeted them as they turned down a wider lane with elegant, decaying homes. These homes had a dignified character, like relics of a nobler time long forgotten. Jeremiah had never seen this part of the Fens and reminded himself to come back when there wasn't a murderous mob on his tail. He was broken from his temporary wonder when a large rock flew in front of his face and smashed into the creaking front porch of a nearby house.

"Heads up, cher!" Ophelia shouted from a few paces in front of Jeremiah. "You can gawk later!"

Three Mesa Dwarves blocked their path, heavy stones in their palms. Lukas spun around, grabbed Ophelia and Jeremiah by their arms, and drug them into a cloud of late-night revelers who had no idea who now stood in their midst. All at once, the Mesa Dwarves launched a rocky fusillade at the mob that contained the fleeing outlaw. The stones fell upon the revelers, cracking a heavily-inebriated Plains Human in the jaw and sending a crimson spray of blood throughout the crowd.

The drunken camaraderie immediately turned to affronted anger and confusion as the partiers cast about for the stone throwers. As soon as the revelers saw the three Mesa Dwarves lining up for another volley, they drunkenly charged their assailants, and a sprawling brawl erupted in the street.

Jeremiah, Ophelia, and Lukas took advantage of the distraction and sprinted down another alley sandwiched between two old, stately homes. After hurdling over piles of trash and an unconscious Savannah Halfling clutching a Sweetfire bottle, the three companions tumbled out into a smaller street lined with old magnolia trees. The heavy, fragrant smell of the blooming white flowers drifted through the humidity. The night soaked through their clothes, leaving a sheen of sweat across their bodies. The outlaw, witch, and bard paused momentarily to catch their breath.

"If we can make it to Stormview," Lukas said between gulps of air, referring to the most populated and popular district in the Red Fens. "Then we can hide out at my place. I don't think the Vermillion Guard will be looking for outlaws at my little abode. I usually don't have their pretty spears knocking down my door."

"You got enough room in there for the Hoodoux Queen, cher?" Ophelia inquired as she scanned the quiet street for pursuers. "You know ol' Ophelia likes to live in luxury. It's been so long since I've been to the Fens, so I expect a bit of pampering."

"Well, we aim to please at Château Sing-Low," Lukas chuckled. "There ain't finer accommodations in all of the Fens."

Jeremiah gazed around the leafy avenue, straining his eyes against the Duskstone lights. By all appearances, it looked like they had shaken the hounds. The three casually started down the avenue, with the broad, green magnolia leaves swaying softly above their heads.

As they walked, Jeremiah looked down at Breaker Calhoun, still locked away in the Sweetfire glass like a trapped insect. He could see the dazed look in his old foe's pale blue eyes, and Calhoun's face was starting to swell from the constant tumbling. Jeremiah paused momentarily to give his tiny antagonist some fresh air. Breaker Calhoun noticed the giant Jeremiah leering over him and lashed out with a long list of faint epithets directed towards the Blade family.

"I don't know why you don't squash him like a bug," Ophelia pondered aloud as they hurried their way through narrow alleys and broad lanes under the watchful eyes of gargoyles balanced on wrought-iron balcony railings. "If yall are such foes from your time in the Shattered Hills, now would be a good time to throw him to some hungry rodent crawling the streets for food."

Jeremiah had wondered that as well—Breaker Calhoun had never been his favorite person. Their relationship was tense from the moment they met. The former sheriff's deputy had stymied him at every turn in Dryftwood, and even tried to kill him on multiple occasions, including tonight. Regardless, Jeremiah felt a bizarre sense of kinship with Calhoun. After all, Breaker Calhoun was one of the few people who knew Jeremiah Blade before he became the most infamous man in all of Westhold. Jeremiah couldn't just end him without ceremony. Ignoring Ophelia, he kept a tight lid on the glass, only stopping to make sure Breaker Calhoun had enough air to breathe.

The three scouted their way across the Red Fens, wary of any followers, and eventually found themselves in a magnificent garden filled with all manner of flowers, magnolia trees, and marble monuments to long-forgotten battles and heroes. It was a haunted scene, with purple Duskstone lights mingling with the pale starlight to cast strange, shifting shadows around them.

The companions rounded a statue of 'Midnight' Rabideaux, the legendary warrior duchess who founded the Red Fens in a great and bloody battle that gave the city its name, and promptly ran into five heavily-armed Vermillion Guards. The two groups looked at each other in shock under the watchful gaze of Midnight Rabideaux.

Sensing his chance for freedom, Breaker Calhoun banged on the walls of his tiny, glass prison and yelled at the top of his diminutive lungs, trying to get the attention of the guards. Jeremiah quietly, but violently, shook the glass to get his prisoner to shut his mouth.

"Yall happen to see Westhold's most wanted outlaw 'round these parts, cher?" the lead guard, having recovered from her initial surprise, drawled out in a thick Red Fens dialect. The towering Swamp Elf lady looked at the three companions in turn until her eyes finally landed on Jeremiah Blade and the cup in his hands. "Lanky, young Plains Human, carrying a Sweetfire glass with a tiny man inside. He was accompanied by an Island Gnome and a barefoot Swamp Elf lady."

The gathered host looked down at Ophelia's bare foot tapping lightly on the stone pathway. Ophelia stopped moving her foot and shuffled off the path into the flower bed surrounding the statue of Midnight Rabideaux, mumbling something about having no idea what the guard might be talking about.

"By the Good Light," Jeremiah cursed at Breaker Calhoun. He was so close to finding Lucille—he spent years finding the Hoodoux Queen Ophelia Delphine and, when he finally did, his past caught up with him in the most unexpected form. Jeremiah wondered what the food would be like in the Marchioness' dungeon. "I'm going to feed you to that damn winder before this is all said and done."

"Gentlewomen, please, this must be some kind of misunderstanding," Lukas intoned while waving his hands in hypnotic patterns in a vain attempt to distract suddenly suspicious guards. "Surely, this must be some grave misunderstanding. You must be looking for some other barefoot witch and spindly-ass outlaw with a shrunken prisoner. Really, the Red Fens is full of all kinds of strange folks like this."

The Vermillion Guards lowered their pikes, but, as the lead guard started to declare that they were under arrest, Ophelia's Duskstone tattoos glowed, and the flower bushes burst from the inside, sending a blizzard of shredded flower petals swirling between the two groups.

"Run!" Lukas hollered, but his two companions needed no prompting as they slid past the swinging, grasping pikes and charged through the park.

The three companions sprinted over low, iron-wrought fences and moss-covered benches, hoping to put as much space between them and the guards as possible. Jeremiah risked a glance behind them and saw the flurry of flying foliage continue to swarm the Vermillion Guards like a cloud of angry hornets. The guards, as formidable as they were, were unable to handle the full, confounding might of the Hoodoux Queen Ophelia Delphine.

The park was huge, and the Duskstone lights few and far between, and the three eventually slipped off into the shadows, hurrying towards Lukas' quarters across the city. As soon as the shouts of Red Fens guards disappeared and the warm shadows embraced them, they slowed and vanished into the muggy night under the pale, marble visages of Swamp Elf heroes long dead.

CHAPTER 12

"I'm impressed that you kept playing," Jeremiah directed at Lukas Sing-Low as he nursed his injuries on the second story of the bard's cottage. Outside of Lukas' quarters, they could hear revelers dancing and singing in the street below, and the smell of spicy Swamp Elf cuisine drifted through the cozy living room. "That was really violent there for a moment."

"Well, it's like the Swamp Elves always say," Lukas Sing-Low replied modestly as he dug around his cabinets for a bottle of Sweetfire and some glasses. "There is always time for the Good Times."

"That's right, cher," Ophelia piped up as she lounged on Lukas' plush couch and swayed her bare feet side-to-side. "Nothing stops the Good Times. I've seen Lukas play through plagues, famines, riots, storms, prison breaks, and all sorts of cataclysms that have fallen upon this fair city. He even played for five days straight when the Island Gnomes' Grand Duke came to town, only stopping to refill his Sweetfire glass after one of the barmaids fell out in exhaustion. But he wasn't off that squeezebox for more than thirty seconds. It was quite a sight."

Lukas Sing-Low shrugged, almost embarrassed, as he poured the amber liquor into cups and distributed them to Ophelia and Jeremiah. The clinking of glasses filled Lukas' home, and a reverent hush fell after the toast.

Ophelia placed the glass on the lonely table next to her familiar and watched as the emerald winder dove into the Sweetfire with great vigor.

"That can't be good for it," Jeremiah declared incredulously as the winder slurped down the liquor. "Your friend there, I mean."

"He, cher," Ophelia waved off the unwanted advice. "Woodroux is a he. Plus, that winder is a mighty drinker. I've tried to tell him to stay out of the Sweetfire, but does he listen to ol' Ophelia? He's worse than some spoiled Swamp Elf noble who doesn't have anything better to do than drink and gamble away his mama's fortune. Gives me grey hairs. Never had a familiar who enjoyed the drink so much."

Woodroux, after finishing off Ophelia's glass of Sweetfire, purposefully ignored the discussion about his errant, youthful ways. His attention turned to the other Sweetfire glass on the table, the one that held a very angry and very tiny Breaker Calhoun. The familiar curled around the stolen glass from The Stumbling Pelican and bared his hungry fangs.

"How long is he going to be that little, Ophelia?" Lukas Sing-Low asked. "Not that he doesn't deserve it, mind."

"Still got a few more hours," Ophelia explained as Woodroux circled the glass menacingly. "We might have to dump him in the sewer before he pops out of it, though. He looks awfully mad."

On cue, Breaker Calhoun tapped lightly against the glass with one of his miniature hatchets. The three companions could hear a faint Dryftwood drawl from behind the walls of his prison.

"Alright, we have plenty of time," Jeremiah concluded as he picked up the playing card that served as the roof to Calhoun's prison. "How did you find me, Calhoun?"

"I ain't answering your damn questions, Blade!" Breaker Calhoun shouted, his tiny, distant voice amplified by the echo in the glass. "Damn you and that swamp thing witch! If it hadn't been for her, I'd be hauling your carcass to the Marchioness for all the gold in the Fens. You just can't help having some girlfriend defend you at all times, is that it, Blade?"

Ophelia Delphine leaned over the table and shook the Sweetfire glass violently, spinning Breaker Calhoun around in dizzying circles. Ophelia then slammed the glass on the table to stop his momentum, smashing Breaker Calhoun against the bottom of the cup. A smug, content look snuck across her mahogany features.

"Let's try this again, Calhoun," Jeremiah bellowed down into the glass. "How did you find me?"

"I already told you, hoss," Calhoun shouted, though his size made it seem like a whisper. "You used that fancy belt buckle of yours. You might as well have thrown a damn parade. Folks already suspected you were hiding in the Delta, and you just wrote it on the wind for them. Don't you know those Raeller Counters you marshals used to keep such a tight hold on are a dozen a copper nowadays? Without the marshals kicking down your door to bust you for lighting your campfire with a Duskstone, everyone and their grandmother has one."

Jeremiah cursed under his breath, but he knew he didn't have much choice. Ophelia had a command of the arcane unlike anything he had ever seen, so he wouldn't have gotten very far without the protective blue shield. Now, however, he was reaping the consequences. Jeremiah knew by the appearance of Hallincross and Breaker Calhoun that the sharks were circling. He needed to get out of the Fens as quickly and quietly as he could.

"Why did you leave Dryftwood?" Jeremiah asked harshly, and the tiny Breaker Calhoun held his hands up to his ears at the sonic tidal wave. "What are you doing chasing outlaws in the Delta? I thought Moss made you the Sheriff of Dryftwood and fulfilled your little dreams. Now, all of a sudden, you're a bounty hunter?"

"Oh, you know, a little holiday never hurt nobody," Breaker Calhoun retorted sarcastically. "You and your marshals damn near tore up the entire Shattered Hills, Jeremiah Blade. Turned everything upside down. You want to know what happened? Moss barely survived, the old bastard is hard to kill, but, as he recouped from his injuries, a group of rough-riding outlaws filled the power vacuum and completely upended Dryftwood. Took it for themselves. That meant poor ol' Breaker Calhoun was no longer the Sheriff of Dryftwood. You dashed my little dream, son. I had to find a new line of work as Moss struggled against the newcomers."

"You left a one-eyed fat man to fend for himself against the usurpers?" Jeremiah asked, cocking his head to one side. "That sounds just like you, Calhoun."

"Alright, smartass," Calhoun fired back vociferously. "What do you think I'm doing here? A war chest ain't no good if you got nothing to fill it with. That's when we cooked up hunting you down, since we're friends and all, and we fully plan to turn your scrawny ass in for a kingdom's worth of gold. We ought to be able to buy some pretty Duskstones with your bounty. That'll set the fear in those up-jumping, city-stealing bandits. My plan only went squeehawed because I didn't expect you would be friends with some bayou-trash witch."

Ophelia gave the cup another hard shake, sending the tiny Breaker Calhoun rattling around the glass again. Jeremiah couldn't help but chuckle at seeing his old antagonist spun around like a cup of dice.

"Ophelia is not one to make angry," Lukas Sing-Low recommended as Ophelia slammed the glass down again, bringing the dizzy Calhoun to an abrupt stop. "She blinded me once for beating her in a card game. She only restored my sight when I apologized, gave her money back, and said I'd never do it again."

Ophelia let out a hearty laugh at the memory while Jeremiah poured another long drink into his Sweetfire glass. As he saw the amber liquid tumble into its glass cage, an idea popped into his mind. The alcohol swirled, and Jeremiah started to formulate a way to shake off the hounds that pursued him. Losing the bounty hunters, fortune seekers, and Vermillion Guard on their mad dash through the Red Fens was a stroke of good fortune, but he knew his luck would run out soon enough with everyone from the Marchioness on down knowing that the outlaw Jeremiah Blade was in town. Every possible exit out of the Fens would be watched, either by the Vermillion Guards or some young blade looking to make a fortune. Ophelia had said that the Priory of Memory was in the Red Fens, but the Swamp Elf capital was a big place, with a lot of dark corners hiding hungry daggers. Jeremiah took a swig and swirled the idea around—at least this way, he'd get some use out of the skinny bastard.

"You and I go way back, Calhoun," Jeremiah started, his tone softer than before. "We got a lot of history. There is no need for us to fight like this."

Ophelia and Lukas looked up at each other, surprised at the sudden tenderness in Jeremiah's voice. Breaker Calhoun saw what was coming, however, and was having none of it.

"No, there ain't no way," Breaker Calhoun replied once he regained his balance and the world stopped spinning. "I ain't falling for whatever horseshit you're 'bout to say. I came to capture you and collect that sweet reward on your head. I might currently be heading backwards on that, but, regardless, nothing you say is going to make me take my eyes off the prize. I just got to figure out how to get back to fighting size and then you're in an awful amount of trouble. You can drown me in Sweetfire before I turn around and help you, hoss."

A slight smirk—the same one he had seen from Breaker Calhoun dozens of times before—crept across Jeremiah's youthful face. He certainly didn't want to disappoint his old friend.

"That's a shame," Jeremiah said mournfully as he poured the Sweetfire into the glass holding the tiny Breaker Calhoun. The amber liquor fell on top of the sheriff's deputy-turned-bounty hunter, cascading off of his wide-brimmed hat. "I did enjoy our working relationship. Doesn't look like you're getting back to Dryftwood. You always struck me as the most reasonable of the lawmen in Dryftwood. Moss will probably be fightin' mad when he finds out you lost yourself in the drink. Especially since getting his town back rests on your narrow shoulders."

The Sweetfire crashed on top of Breaker Calhoun's head and crept up towards his waist as the glass filled. The normal, smirking features were replaced with a look of shock. He started to scramble on the sides of the glass for a way out but only succeeded in sliding down deeper into the growing pool of liquor.

"Alright!" Breaker Calhoun called out desperately as the alcohol sloshed under his chin. "You obviously got a lot more fire in you than the last time I saw you. What are you proposing?"

"You are going to tell the world that you caught Jeremiah Blade," Jeremiah answered, leering over the lip of the cup, his voice now hard and unforgiving. "You are going to tell everyone you know, and everyone you don't know, that you were the winner of the race tonight. You've captured me, housed me in the Marchioness' royal prison, and plan to ship me off to Alathane forthwith. You'll tell everyone who will listen that you already collected a portion of the reward and plan on spending the money gambling, drinking, and cavorting around the Fens like the city has never seen."

Jeremiah paused to take another swig from the Sweetfire bottle and let the seeds of the plan take root. He wasn't entirely sure it was going to work, but he figured their high-speed chase through the city would be on the lips of every man, woman, and child in the Red Fens before the sun broke over the horizon and he had to get some breathing room to be able to leave the cover of Lukas' quarters. All Jeremiah needed was some time for them to find the Priory of Memory.

"This will send every bounty hunter in the Delta towards the Marchioness' jail," Jeremiah continued as he clinked the Sweetfire bottle against the table. "That should buy us enough time to go where we need to go, don't you think, Ophelia?"

Ophelia Delphine took a seat, cocked her head to one side, and mumbled to herself, turning the plan upside down and inside out. Lukas Sing-Low nodded slowly, figuring any plan was better than waiting for someone to bust down his door, wreck his house, and take the young outlaw by force.

"What makes you think I'll help you?" Breaker Calhoun shot back as he stood on the tip-toes of his boots to avoid drowning in Sweetfire. "As soon as I get out of here, I'm going to gut you faster than you can blink, son."

"I don't think you will there, hoss," Jeremiah replied coolly. "I'll make you a deal, Calhoun. If you do this for me, then once I am done here, I'll see to it that Moss gets his town back."

Ophelia and Lukas did not appreciate the gravity of that statement, but Breaker Calhoun did, and Jeremiah figured the former sheriff's deputy wasn't in a place where he could negotiate. He was trying to give his old foe a way out of his current predicament, and, hopefully, Jeremiah would find a way out of the Red Fens with his head on his shoulders. He shook the glass for good measure, sending a splash of Sweetfire in Calhoun's face.

"Horseshit," Calhoun spat as he wiped the stinging liquid from his eyes. "There ain't no way you're going to make it to Dryftwood without getting caught by some bloodhound."

"Think of it this way," Jeremiah responded, hoping to appeal to Calhoun's pragmatic side. "If I can make it out of the Red Fens alive, then I'm going to need to go somewhere that is, let's say, friendly to outlaws. And what place is friendlier to outlaws than Dryftwood? On top of that, I'd much rather have Moss running the place, given our history, than some other killer in his place. I daresay he owes me. It's in both our interests, Calhoun."

Breaker Calhoun glared at his old foe—the evaporating Sweetfire was making Breaker Calhoun dizzy and impairing his otherwise sound judgment.

"Alright, you son of a bitch," Breaker Calhoun, seeing no other choice, shouted up from his glass prison. "I'll throw the hounds off your trail. But, after that, I'm coming with you, wherever you're going, to make damn sure you don't run off on me."

Jeremiah, Ophelia, and Lukas raised curious eyebrows. Where they were going wasn't a place for tourists. Ophelia started to interject, but Jeremiah gave a knowing nod to the Hoodoux Queen.

"You help me, Calhoun, and you can tag along on our little trail ride," Jeremiah answered, his voice cold and calculating. "We are old friends, after all."

CHAPTER 13

A full day after the forging of one of the unlikeliest partnerships in recent memory, Breaker Calhoun, back at normal height, and Lukas Sing-Low, still at normal height, strolled into Kingston's Krossing, an Island Gnome-owned establishment and the largest, rowdiest game hall in the Red Fens. Arcane lights of dark blue and bright tangerine, the national Island Gnome colors, spun above the pair as tropical Gnomish music rang throughout the main hall. The whirl of spinwheels, the tumble of dice, and the flutter of shuffled cards mingled with the groans of lost fortunes. Since the game hall was perched delicately on the docks, a strong, briny waft of sea air filled every corner of the massive establishment. Lukas Sing-Low and Breaker Calhoun made their way through crowds of sailors, merchants, mercenaries, prostitutes, swindlers, and vagabonds all looking for that one lucky strike. All around the pair, glasses clinked and crashed, and shouts both joyous and furious rang out across Kingston's Krossing.

Lukas Sing-Low and Breaker Calhoun, an odd pair but not out of place in the current surroundings, strolled into the raucous game hall armed with only a wild plan concocted by Westhold's most infamous outlaw. They had spent all day arguing and fine-tuning the plan, stretching the bounds of credibility, all in order to throw the hounds off of Jeremiah's trail long enough for them to reach the Priory of Memory. It was a long shot, they all conceded, but every other plan involved Jeremiah taking two steps outside before the Vermillion Guard skewered him with their fancy spears.

"Alright, short-stack," Calhoun, his pale blue eyes alert and wary, whispered conspiratorially. "I know you're famous 'round these parts, but we are following my lead here. I'm the boss of this little outing."

"You can stick them spurs of yours where the Good Light don't shine," Lukas Sing-Low retorted melodically. "Who do you think is going to listen to some roughneck from Dryftwood claiming he caught Jeremiah Blade?

They'd throw you out of here for causing a ruckus before you could look sideways. You need me to make this legitimate. Otherwise, these blades in here are going to cut your lanky ass to ribbons for lying to them."

Breaker Calhoun stopped, defiantly looped his thumbs through his belt, and tapped his boot on the wooden floor planks. His spurs clinked rhythmically with every tap of the boot. Much to his chagrin, Calhoun could already see the patrons of Kingston's Krossing noticing the silver-haired bard. Whispers erupted around them as patrons wondered aloud if it was indeed Lukas Sing-Low. Breaker Calhoun fished a pinch of chewing weed from his belt pouch and jammed the pungent, shredded leaves into his lower jaw.

"What makes you think they are going to listen to you?" Breaker Calhoun spat defiantly. "You know, they say if you ain't famous in Dryftwood, you ain't famous anywhere. And I certainly ain't heard of you."

"Who cares about your shitty backwater?" Lukas retorted, motioning to Calhoun to give him a pinch of chewing weed. "What's the population of Dryftwood? A couple of dusty miners, some drunks and drifters, and a handful of friendly Mesas? The Red Fens is one of the most populous cities in all of Westhold, and you're telling me that I got to get known in Dryftwood to make it big? I've already made it big."

Lukas' words were more matter-of-fact than combative. Calhoun scoured his brain for a witty response. He loudly smacked his chewing weed as he waited for one to come.

"Well, we had the Arkstone," Breaker Calhoun finally exclaimed with a smug grin spreading across his stubble. "That counts for something, I reckon. We could have started a brand new Blight if we had been so inclined. What have yall been doing recently?"

Lukas Sing-Low stared at his companion, arched an incredulous grey eyebrow sharply over his right eye, and ran a hand through his lustrous silver hair.

"Your claim to fame," Lukas started slowly over the riot of Kingston's Krossing. "Is that you shitkickers had the source of the Blight sitting under your asses the whole time?"

Breaker Calhoun nodded sagely.

"Well, at least the marshals ain't running around barging in people's business anymore," Lukas mused once he realized his companion wasn't budging from his position. "If you had a hand in that, Calhoun, I'd sing a song just for you."

"I ain't much of a braggart, short-stack," Breaker Calhoun lied coolly. "But I pretty much found the Arkstone by myself. It wasn't easy, for sure. Especially with that weight around my neck called Jeremiah Blade. To be honest, I'm surprised you hadn't sung my name before today. I had to tell them to hold off on the parade when I rolled into town the other day. It was real nice of the Marchioness to think of me, though."

Lukas Sing-Low rolled his eyes and fended off a drunk, but polite, inquiry as to whether he was the real Lukas Sing-Low. His affirmative answer sent the drunkard and his companions into a tizzy. Lukas shrugged his shoulders with feigned humility.

"If this all goes according to the young Blade's plan," Lukas Sing-Low explained to the begrudgingly impressed Breaker Calhoun. "Then I'll be singing your name a lot more in the days to come. I'll have to write up a song suitable for someone like you."

The two unlikely compatriots volleyed back and forth as the crowd slowly swelled around them. As they maneuvered around a large, loud group of Island Gnome sailors, Breaker Calhoun stopped suddenly and planted his hands on his narrow hips, causing his elbows to jut out at dangerously sharp angles.

"Why are you doing this?" Breaker Calhoun asked unexpectedly. "I mean, he was about to drown me in a glass of Sweetfire. He had me over a barrel. I'll give it to him, he's a lot tougher than he was when he rolled into Dryftwood all them years ago. But, what about you? Yall go way back or something? What do you get out of all this, short-stack?"

Lukas, taken aback by the question, waited a hefty moment as he discerned Calhoun's motives. Word was spreading across the game hall that the legendary bard Lukas Sing-Low had unexpectedly shown up for a rowdy night down at the docks. Drunk patrons whispered to each other, and gamblers took Lukas Sing-Low's presence as a fortuitous alignment of the stars. Kingston's Krossing buzzed in anticipation while Lukas deliberated the character of the man standing in front of him.

"Ophelia helped me search for someone many years ago when no one else would," Lukas replied with unexpected sincerity, surprising both Breaker Calhoun and himself. "It's something that I will never forget. I don't have any connection with this outlaw. He seems alright, though. It's Ophelia that I'm keen on helping. We never found that someone I was looking for, so, maybe, I'm thinking this might be our shot. Me and the witch have been through a lot together, and if she speaks for the outlaw, well, then, I'm with the outlaw, too. You, on the other hand, I ain't too sure about."

"Alright," Calhoun eventually exhaled, satisfied with the answer. "If you're as famous as you claim, now's your chance to make an impression."

Lukas Sing-Low tipped an imaginary hat, ran his hand over his long, silvery hair, scuffed his boots on the floor, and made his way to the bar with astonished glances from revelers following him the whole way. He scrambled up a stool and then onto the bar sticky with spilled alcohol. The bartender started to protest until she realized who was standing on her bar. Lukas Sing-Low stood silently for an extended moment, quietly letting the gawking faces turn towards his person. Breaker Calhoun couldn't help but think of that loud-mouthed Savannah Halfling priest back in Dryftwood, Voros McCracken.

"Ladies and gentlemen," Lukas Sing-Low called out across the bar, his voice powerful enough to raise the dead. The tangerine-colored amulet on his chest glowed softly and blended with the swirling colors of the game hall's Duskstone lights. "If I could have yall's attention, please."

"Lukas Sing-Low!" a voice cried from the faceless horde of onlookers. "Give us a song!"

"I have something much better than a song for you fine folks," Lukas called back, his showmanship swelling to the surface. "I have an announcement that will shake the very foundation of Westhold. I assume everyone heard about the shenanigans at The Stumbling Pelican last night? About the chaos that spilled out into these fine streets and sent the entire Red Fens into a frenzy? About how the most dangerous and dreaded outlaw in all of Westhold ran roughshod through our fair city?"

A tumbling chorus of "ayes" cascaded through the crowd as Lukas Sing-Low paced purposefully along the bar. The bard clapped his hands rhythmically, as if he was timing out the pace of a song.

"It has been done!" Lukas yelled, nearly shaking the rafters from the ceiling. "Jeremiah Blade, the greatest outlaw of our time, has finally been caught!"

The rumble grew louder as more heads turned towards the bar, wondering if the Island Gnome bard was telling the truth. Breaker Calhoun shifted uncomfortably for the first time in his life; he had no idea what Lukas' words were going to do to the rowdy crowd at Kingston's Krossing. He was just as likely to be cut down where he stood as he was thrown atop the shoulders of a drunkard and paraded through the streets.

"That's right, dear denizens of the Red Fens," Lukas purred. He paused a moment, letting the suspense build. Even the spinwheels and dice halted their weary labor to lean in and hear the news. "Jeremiah Blade was right under our noses the entire time. None other than the Shattered Hills outlaw, the slayer of Chief Marshal Godwin Malmont, the most hunted man from here to Alathane and beyond, has been caught!"

Shocked patrons glanced at each other and back at Lukas Sing-Low. Dealers paused their shuffles, chewing weed spit dribbled into beards, and bartenders slowed their pours. Stunned silence shrouded every shoulder in the game hall. After a momentous pause, the bar erupted in wild cheers.

"Where is he?" someone shouted out across Kingston's Krossing. "Where is the murderer? Let's kill him!"

"He is being held in the Marchioness' dungeon," Lukas replied with a dramatic flair, sending a conspiratorial ripple through the horde. "But! That's not the only news I have this evening! We just so happen to have the hero who put him in there here among us!"

Kingston's Krossing exploded. Patrons looked at one another, greedy gleams in their eyes, and the gathered multitude sounded like a chorus of owls demanding to know the identity of the person who caught the outlaw Jeremiah Blade.

"Yes, we have the hero right here with us!" Lukas Sing-Low shouted over the riot, his amulet glowing hot on his throat. "Young man, will you please step up here so your accomplishment may shine as one of the greatest achievements of our time!"

Breaker Calhoun, unhappy with being called a "young man", reluctantly climbed onto the bar and next to Lukas, kicking over a bottle of Sweetfire in the process. He looked around at the gathered crowd, taking in the admiration. Breaker Calhoun always appreciated a good lie, but the stakes were incredibly high. Lukas Sing-Low, standing like a proud father, made a dramatic sweep with his arms towards the rail-thin Calhoun.

"Ladies and gentlemen," Lukas Sing-Low reverberated. "Please welcome a bounty hunter without peer! A name that will be sung by bards for generations to come! Good people of the Red Fens, I give you the relentless, the indefatigable, the Bloodhound of Dryftwood, Breaker Calhoun!"

Breaker Calhoun wasn't sure how much he liked the nickname "Bloodhound of Dryftwood", but the crowd seemed to take to it. Below the pair, patrons raised their glasses and cheered the pretender. Breaker Calhoun could see some members of the crowd whisper malevolently to each other and cast daggers up at the pair, which sent his hand down to check to see if his hatchets were still in place. He wondered if he had sold the Island Gnome short—the bard might actually know what he was doing.

Next to Breaker Calhoun, Lukas Sing-Low clapped and whipped up the patrons of Kingston's Krossing into a frothy frenzy. Among the sea of cheering faces, the pair could see eyes of wonder, envy, and avarice shine back at them. Breaker Calhoun, his irrepressible, smirking grin and brash confidence returning to him, raised his arms in triumph at being crowned the most famous man in all of Westhold.

"Drinks are on me!"

CHAPTER 14

Jeremiah and Ophelia sat on the second-story balcony of Lukas Sing-Low's cottage, watching the stars race towards the morning. An almost empty Sweetfire bottle lounged between them, waiting for the last drop to be drunk. They looked out in silence, wondering if Jeremiah's audacious plan to shake loose the hordes of bounty hunters was working. Jeremiah couldn't help but sigh at the circumstances that led him to rely on Breaker Calhoun to save his hide once more. The smirking, sarcastic Calhoun was like a horse fly that wouldn't stop buzzing around his ear.

Below them, the Red Fens, a city of so much light and fury, stumbled towards an inglorious end to a wild night. Drunks staggered home singing songs of loss and loneliness. Arcane lights flickered in the darkness, casting sharp, otherworldly strangers along the rows of houses and taverns. Off in the distance, some unnecessary, drunken brawl had passed its peak and wound down towards a swollen, bruised morning. The night air was filled with the sounds of a giant slipping off to sleep.

"Do you hear that, cher?" Ophelia piped up unexpectedly, her syrupy drawl dancing on the sweltering heat of the night. "They're on the wind."

Jeremiah, lost in thought, startled at Ophelia's words. He leaned over, spit out a thick glob of bright red chewing weed spit into the spittoon, and shook his head, not knowing where she was going. Jeremiah assumed she was talking about the drunken, mangled rendition of 'Valley So Sweet' that drifted up through the balcony's twisted, wrought-iron railing.

"It's the spirits, cher," Ophelia explained as her long, slender fingers curled around her sharp chin. "They're talking to us."

From his perch, Jeremiah looked out over the Red Fens and strained his ears. Unless the spirits came in the form of cacophonous tree bugs or the quiet hissing of a sleeping Woodroux at Ophelia's feet, Jeremiah didn't hear them. He wiped the sweat from his brow, trying to beat back the unrelenting humidity. As far as Jeremiah Blade could tell, the spirits had nothing to say to a castaway Alathanian hiding from the law.

"What are they saying, Ophelia," Jeremiah asked as he turned the Sweetfire bottle upside down above his lips to wring out the last drops. "I guess I don't have the ear for them."

"The spirits are always with us, cher," Ophelia responded as an intense light sparkled in her emerald eyes. Though they had been drinking for the past few hours, her wits were still as keen as a razor's edge, and her words as crisp as birdsong. "They follow us, guide us, lean on our minds when we least expect them to appear. They hold on because they don't want to be left behind. The spirits are desperate for someone to remember them. Remember who they were."

"Is Lucille there?" Jeremiah asked, though he wasn't sure he wanted to know the answer. "Is she trying to reach you?"

"I'm sorry, cher," Ophelia replied, her voice now barely above a whisper. "I don't hear her. These poor souls that are calling to me, they are grasping for the last shreds of a fading memory. They don't want to be forgotten, but everyone who ever knew them is disappearing from this world."

Jeremiah let the words hang on the humidity. He thought back to that day in the Arkstone cave, cradling Lucille in his arms. From that moment on, he couldn't help but feel that the roles should have been reversed. Despite her protests at the time, he still carried the guilt of her passing on his narrow shoulders. That was why, despite the toll it took on him and the dangers he went through in the intervening years, he hunted down Ophelia, the only person who could lead him back to Lucille Ledoux. He felt he owed it to her.

"Where do they go?" Jeremiah asked the night. "If they are forgotten."

"They just fade away, cher," Ophelia replied as she stuffed more chewing weed in her lower jaw. "They pass from that world just as they passed from this one. We die twice, Jeremiah Blade. We pass once from this mortal coil of flesh and blood and again from the minds and hearts of those we leave behind."

Woodroux, his emerald scales glinting brightly in the arcane Duskstone lights, perked up, raised his head, and slithered towards the wrought-iron railing. The winder's tongue flickered as he peered out into the night.

"How come they talk to you?" Jeremiah questioned as he picked another bottle of Sweetfire off of the shelf behind them. The pop of the bottle's cork echoed towards the stars. "Why do they only talk to the Hoodoux Witches?"

"We are the only ones who listen, cher," Ophelia explained, taking the newly-opened liquor bottle and downing a respectable gulp. "We keep them alive, in a sense. They are desperate for someone to remember them. Thousands of flames still linger because of us. That is our responsibility. The first time you die, it's a part of life. The second, it's a tragedy."

In the street, a pair of Savannah Halflings swayed arm-in-arm, though it wasn't clear which one was holding up the other. Their conversation, loud and obtrusive, wafted towards the heavens, lost words neither they nor anyone else would remember.

Jeremiah was starting to understand why Ophelia was so blasé about death. The dead were still a part of her life—gone but always there, like a brother or sister living on the other side of the world—until, all of a sudden, a misremembered name or a forgotten experience banished them away forever. Jeremiah wondered how many names Ophelia had forgotten.

"Something's been wrong recently," Ophelia said with unexpected earnest. "Ever since that Savannah Halfling woman showed up at my front door. There is a presence on the other side that I have never felt before. Every night since we left, the spirits come and whisper to me. Some sound as if they are scared, cher. Others sound elated, which frightens me even more. But, either way, they won't say what it is. Won't or can't. I don't know if many of the spirits have even experienced something like this. Something terrible has happened on the other side."

Jeremiah didn't know if it was the Sweetfire, the late hour, or a Hoodoux Witch talking to the dead next to him, but his mind swirled and blurred at the edges like a dream. He had a hard time focusing on Ophelia's words—the world started spinning, and it took all of his constitution to focus on a leafy magnolia tree with broad, white flowers directly across from Lukas' cottage.

"I have to admit, cher," Ophelia continued, oblivious to Jeremiah's distorted reality. "This is why I came along with you. I mean, you're alright as far as I can tell, and it would be nice to see ol' Lucille, but I need to know what is happening over there. I had an inkling back on the bayou, but this sense of dread grows stronger every day. You just happen to come at the right time, Jeremiah Blade. No offense, of course, to your quest or my cousin. Your sword arm is certainly welcomed, and you got more control over the arcane than I gave you credit for in the beginning."

Suddenly, somewhere nearby, an explosion of cheers rolled down the street, shaking Jeremiah from his drunken stupor. It sounded like a parade at the annual Fat Spirit Festival—brass cymbals clanging, horns blaring, glass breaking, drinks spilling. Ophelia shot up and leaned over the railing to get a closer look, with Woodroux snaking his way up to the top of the banister to do the same. The cacophony was coming right towards them.

Jeremiah, thinking that the hounds were upon his tail, jumped up, cast about for his blade, and made his way next to Ophelia for a better look once he had his weapon in hand. All that popped into his mind was a mob coming to tear him to pieces. Maybe, he thought sullenly, the plan had failed. Maybe Lukas couldn't convince them, or Breaker Calhoun had betrayed his confidence. Jeremiah should have known not to trust the likes of the former sheriff's deputy.

As the mob materialized through the hazy morning hour, their eyes grew in amazement at the scene below them. Precariously riding atop a horde of revelers, Breaker Calhoun, drunk out of his hat, laughed and sung wildly out of tune. The members of the crowd alternated between chanting Calhoun's name and passing around bottles of Sweetfire. Breaker Calhoun took a bottle and gulped down a long swig before tossing it back to his throng of admirers.

One particularly inebriated Mesa Dwarf woman smashed a pair of shiny brass cymbals together at uneven intervals, and colorful sparks of lights rippled outwards every time the instruments banged together. It was a glorious hero's parade in a city that knew how to throw a good parade. Bloodlust seemed to be the last thing on the minds of the partiers.

Jeremiah relaxed his tense muscles and he heard Ophelia chuckle to herself at the scene. He breathed a sigh of relief as the festive parade passed directly beneath the balcony. Jeremiah felt something poke his forearm and he looked down to see Woodroux weaving drunkenly at him. He thought the winder had bitten him but, when he noticed there were no bite marks on his arm, he realized the familiar was motioning enthusiastically towards someone in the crowd.

On the shoulders of a large and intimidating Plains Human woman, sat Lukas Sing-Low, playing a merry tune on a worn-out, travel-sized squeezebox. The bard led the swaying crowd in a jaunty song as they thundered down the street to the next watering hole. As they passed by Lukas' cottage, Lukas looked up at the inhabitants of his balcony, stopped playing the wheezing instrument for a moment, and gave a victorious thumbs-up to the astonished Jeremiah Blade.

CHAPTER 15

That night, the Sweetfire-drenched nightmare returned. Sky-blue and white flags fluttered aimlessly in the soft breeze that curled around the Plains Human capital of Alathane. The fragrance of hundreds of flowers wafted on the wind, heralding the bright days of spring. People went about their daily business in the warm sunshine, strolling the wide streets and forming neat lines at market stalls.

Jeremiah took in the vivid sights and smells of the magnificent city. Jeremiah was younger, with wisps of hair barely forming on his smooth chin and the haze of innocent youth clouding his worldview. He was running through his grandparents' estate, calling out for his grandma, hoping to hear her lively laughter or see her tending to her flowers in the greenhouse. Her memory made Jeremiah smile. This was the way the dream always started—in absolute peace. Jeremiah wanted to catch a glimpse of his grandma, but then the words of the Exile's Lament sounded out, slow and sonorous.

I left my home in search of another, in the wild world beyond the border. I did not find a home, however. I simply lost the one I left forever.

"Jeremiah," a gravelly voice called from behind the young Blade. "I thought I would see you here."

Jeremiah sighed. It always started with him. He didn't want to answer but he felt the pull backwards in time.

"Hello grandfather," an adolescent Jeremiah called back without looking. "I wanted to ask if you would come see my graduation."

"Jeremiah, you know I am terribly busy," Gerald Blade explained to his grandson. "I have much more important things to do than see you walk across the parade grounds. You didn't graduate at the top of your class like your brother Henric, and you have this stubborn idea of becoming a long-range marshal, something that I will never understand. These are the Alathanian Marshals, Jeremiah. We are not meant to grub around the dirt like some savage Mesa Dwarf. Our family has a reputation to maintain, one that you are ruining. Who do you think you are, that insolent Half-Elf, Sundown?"

Jeremiah felt his face flush hot, even though he knew exactly what his grandfather was going to say. He had heard it countless times before, but each time it still stung as sharply as when his grandfather first said the words.

"The Arbiters say that anyone can be an Alathanian Marshal," Jeremiah pleaded with his grandfather, turning to see the wraith shimmer on the edges of his memory. Gerald Blade, with his intimidating presence and unbent and unforgiving posture, shifted and swirled in the fog of the past. "That means me, too. They said that becoming a long-range marshal is a true honor. Only the bravest of the Alathanian Marshals volunteer to range out."

"Please," the specter of Gerald Blade scoffed, its distorted features shifting in the diffused spring light. "That's just what the Arbiters tell the peasants. They need the lowborns to serve as long-range marshals in the dusty, forgotten corners of the world. We, Jeremiah, are not destined for such pettiness. Your destiny was to become an Arbiter like your brothers. Like your father. Like me. You, Jeremiah, though we share the same blood, might as well serve as our stable boy."

"That's not true, grandfather," young Jeremiah said timidly, though, in the real world, he would have never been brave enough to defy Gerald Blade. "The long-range marshals are the true test of a marshal's ability. Only the most capable enlist for the most dangerous positions. Just like Sundown."

"Ha!" the Gerald Blade wraith laughed, its features grotesque. "The Grey Rider is the one you look up to? That castoff? You would prefer to associate with that commoner instead of the noble line you hail from? You would say that, Jeremiah. You always did love digging through the dirt with the gutter trash, far away from the warmth of the Good Light, sullying the good Blade name. I could never understand you, Jeremiah. I tried telling you this over and over again, but you always hid behind my wife's petticoats."

Jeremiah remembered how the words cut. He had thrown himself into his studies to prove his grandfather wrong, but all he received was scorn and derision. Jeremiah told himself that if he was willing to take the most dangerous outpost available to the Alathanian Marshals, he would make a name for himself and prove his grandfather and family wrong. Little did he or his grandfather know what terrible consequences would come from that decision. All Jeremiah could be thankful for was that Grandfather Blade did not live long enough to see him become the most despised man in all of Westhold and ruin the Blade family name.

Around Jeremiah, the gardens along the banks of the River Alathane bloomed majestically. Cherry blossoms threw pale pink petals into the warm spring air, and the young Jeremiah smelled the sweet fragrance that rolled over the Danathane River. The sky was an impossible blue, the same color as the Alathanian banner. In his memories, it was always spring, and the warmth never faded. Jeremiah hadn't seen a spring blossom in Alathane since he set out with Iron Eyes Ledoux all those years ago. Jeremiah remembered meeting her for the first time on banks of the Danathane, under a cloud of soft cherry blossoms.

I left my home in search of another.

"She's dead because of you," the specter sneered as it transmogrified into a hazy remembrance of Marshal Sundown, complete with a broken arrow hanging from her cheek. "You killed her, Jeremiah, as surely as if you plunged your sword into her heart. You tell yourself that it was Malmont that slew her, but it was you, Jeremiah Blade."

Jeremiah said nothing as the misty apparition swirled around him. Alathane in springtime had transformed too; Jeremiah could now see the red sandstone walls, the glittering, gem-filled pillars, and the ghastly yellow light flashing at staccato intervals. They were all there—Iron Eyes, Moss, Sundown, Shashdurak the Sandscribe, Malmont. Memories of that day, as bright as the noon sun of the Shattered Hills, charged to the forefront of his mind.

In the wild world beyond the border.

"Not only that," Sundown sneered, her road-weary features contorting into a hateful glare. "You destroyed the very order you longed to join and glorify. The marshals have lost their reason for existence, and it is all because of you. Is it not a twisted, cruel fate that you, Jeremiah Blade, brought down the Alathanian Marshals? You wanted to be the best of the best. It is a delicious irony that you are now the worst of the worst. Westhold is a more dangerous and wild place because of you. A place where magic is unregulated and the very seats of governments are threatened by wild brigands wielding previously outlawed Duskstones, despite your best attempts to the contrary."

Jeremiah watched his younger self cradle the dying Iron Eyes Ledoux beneath the Shattered Hills. He always dreaded this part of the dream. Of all the death and destruction that followed that day, her passing still cut the deepest.

"Now, you are an outlaw," Sundown hissed hatefully. "Hunted by the remnants of the order you destroyed, not to mention every glory seeker and opportunist in Westhold. You can never return home, Jeremiah Blade. You know that this is the only way you will ever see Alathane's cobblestone streets again."

"I did what I thought was best," Jeremiah replied as he looked down at a shattered Alathanian Marshal belt buckle in front of him on the red earth of the Shattered Hills. "I didn't expect such tragic consequences."

I did not find a home, however.

"You killed me, Jeremiah Blade!" the wraith exploded as the misty features warped and twisted into Iron Eyes Ledoux, a black bolt protruding from her heart. "You live, and I waste away in the realm of the forgotten!

You breathe, and I wither in the ground! Your life is still yours, while I am shackled in the world of the dead!"

"I'm sorry," Jeremiah struggled. This part of the dream he could never escape—it always came to the same horrible conclusion. "I never wanted you to die. I would give anything for things to be switched. I wish you were still here."

"Well, that's too bad," Iron Eyes spat, fury filling her slate-grey eyes. "I'm not, and I'll never be."

Jeremiah ground his eyes shut, trying to block out the leering visage, but he couldn't close out the rapid flashing of the Arkstone, the ghastly yellow light filling the entirety of his person. Soft weeping filled his ears, try as he might to shut out the noise. There was no escape, just like the time before, and the time before that. The final line echoed throughout the dreamscape.

I simply lost the one I left forever.

The ghastly yellow light exploded, and Jeremiah snapped back to the world of the living.

CHAPTER 16

"Cher, wake up," Ophelia called out softly as she shook Jeremiah's rail-thin frame. "The spirits got you. You're screaming in your sleep."

Jeremiah felt cold sweat cascade off his forehead as the muted light from a morning thunderstorm filtered through the blinds of Lukas Sing-Low's cottage. Ophelia's aged countenance hovered above him, more curious than concerned. The spirits fled Jeremiah's eyes as his bearings returned to him. He sat up groggily, his head swimming in leftover Sweetfire, and took stock of the fallout from last night's festivities.

Across the room, Lukas Sing-Low lay in a Sweetfire-induced slumber underneath the kitchen table, his chest rising and falling softly in step with his snoring. Breaker Calhoun didn't even make it that far. The former sheriff's deputy, his right boot on his left hand for some never-to-be-found reason, lay face down on the bright red carpet mere feet past the entryway. Sweetfire from a broken bottle seeped from underneath the lanky Calhoun like amber blood.

"I don't know if they remember coming home," Ophelia opined. "It seems to ol' Ophelia that your little ruse might have worked. Hopefully, they bought you a little bit of time from the hounds that chase you, cher. Which is good because we need to get to the other side as soon as we can."

"Why is that?" Jeremiah asked, weariness saturating his voice. "I thought the spirits were on their own time."

"I told you last night, cher," Ophelia intoned like an exasperated parent. "You don't pay a dang bit of attention. Something is wrong on the other side. The spirits are restless. Hungry, almost. Something has happened on the other side, and the sooner we go, the better."

This was not the news Jeremiah wanted to hear as he fought the initial wave of his hangover. Spirits were not his specialty, but Ophelia's earnest features, seemingly none the worse for wear from last night's drinking, gave him pause.

"You'll need this, cher," Ophelia continued as she held up a palm-sized, charcoal-grey, burlap bag sown together in the shape of a crooked star. She threw the bag to a barely-cognizant Jeremiah, who caught it after some significant fumbling. "We're going to need all the protection we can get."

Jeremiah eyeballed the surprisingly heavy burlap bag. He shook the crooked charm and held it up in the rain-soaked light, the burlap as grey as the morning. Jeremiah didn't suspect it was made of Duskstones—his Raeller Counter made nary a peep—but it had a certain gravity to it he couldn't quite explain.

"This is a called a zam-zam," Ophelia explained patiently to the uninitiated Jeremiah. "It's a ward against angry, malevolent spirits. And, by the sounds of it, there are plenty stalking the Grey Wastes now. Think of it as a ward against unimaginable forces. A light in the darkness, if you will."

Jeremiah wondered if he was still dreaming, but the dull thudding in his head and creeping nausea wracking his body told him otherwise. He shook the bag and tried to divine its contents—it sounded like it was full of uncooked rice. Jeremiah, deciding to defer to Ophelia's judgment in arcane matters, nodded and tucked the charm away in the pocket of his riding vest directly over his heart.

"I'm going need one of those, too, witch," came a creaking voice from near the door. Breaker Calhoun, still in the land of the living after last night's bender, stood up from his prone position and stumbled forward with unfocused eyes. "Now that I'm the most famous man in Westhold, I'm going need to place to hide."

"Not on my watch, Calhoun," Jeremiah retorted, his patience already thin from his resounding hangover. "You'll just slow us down. Plus, the spirits don't need any smartass comments disrupting their long slumber."

"Are you kidding, son?" Breaker Calhoun responded, his words slurring from the remnants of last night's Sweetfire. There was an unexpected eagerness in his voice; it sounded almost like fear. "As soon as they find out that the outlaw Jeremiah Blade is not thrown under the Marchioness' jail, you think they're going to appreciate having their hats pulled over their eyes? Who do you think they are going to turn their anger on? Oh, that's right, poor ol' Breaker Calhoun from the sticks. I bet the Marchioness is just waiting to throw me a damn parade."

Outside, a persistent rain cloaked the Red Fens, shading the elegant, aging architecture in pale grey. People went about their day, gliding through the sheets of drizzle like lonely wraiths. Despite the early morning hour and the weather, it was hot and muggy outside, and the sticky warmth bled into the room. There was no escape from the relentless humidity in the Red Fens. Lukas Sing-Low's melodious snoring drifted from underneath the kitchen table as the two former adversaries stared each other down in the hazy heat.

"I don't know if you want to go where we are going, cher," Ophelia interjected with a casual wave of her hand. "It ain't a very friendly place."

"The Red Fens ain't a very friendly place," Calhoun shot back. "Especially if you just fooled the whole damn city into thinking you're a hero who caught Westhold's most wanted outlaw. Plus, it ain't like my leg is broke and you got to haul me around on your back. These hatchets are sharp enough to cut anything down to ol' short-stack's size."

Despite the bizarre circumstances and their speckled history, Jeremiah felt an old flower of Alathanian honor and decorum blossom in his heart. Breaker Calhoun had a point and, despite the fact that the former sheriff's deputy had tried to kill him on multiple occasions, Jeremiah felt obliged to see him out of the situation.

"Yep, it don't matter what you throw at me," Breaker Calhoun boasted, hooking his thumbs onto his belt. "I'm going to come out on top. Breaker Calhoun fears no man, beast, nor bug. Wherever we're going, yall will be in good company with me."

"Ol' Ophelia ain't too sure about that, cher," Ophelia retorted. "The Priory is a special place. A gateway of sorts between the living and the dead. Not to brag, but Ophelia was the one who found it all them years ago. I mean, Lukas found the key, but Ophelia did the looking for the hole in the ground."

"How long has it been, Ophelia," a voice from underneath the dining table called out. Lukas Sing-Low crawled on his hands and knees into the soft morning light. "Since that first journey?"

"Not long enough, cher," Ophelia answered softly. The words hung heavy in the void between the four unlikely companions, though they only meant something to two of them. "Something is different now, though. The spirits tell me things are wrong on the other side, and I have to find out what frightens them so."

Lukas Sing-Low said nothing in response, staggered over to the balcony door, and pushed it open, allowing the thick, rain-soaked air to drift into the cottage. He stepped onto the balcony and watched the storm fall to earth. In the course of a few hours, Lukas' section of the Red Fens had turned from a raucous parade of sound and Sweetfire to a drenched, faded painting of old glory. Rusting, wrought-iron facades covered with wet ivy greeted Lukas Sing-Low as he gazed out into the drizzle.

Jeremiah stepped onto the balcony and into the expansive greyness as the droplets pitter-pattered on the awning. He stood next to Lukas and handed him an earthenware cup filled with water. Lukas Sing-Low took it gratefully and chugged it down to start the long process of recovering from his hangover. Jeremiah stepped further out to let the fat drops of rain fall on his tanned face.

"Have you ever been to the Gnomish Island, Jeremiah Blade?" Lukas asked as he stuck his hand outside the awning and watched the droplets pool in his palm. "It's a beautiful sight to behold."

Jeremiah shook his pounding head, wishing he was watching the sunrise on a beach somewhere far away from the hounds that chased him and the past that haunted his every step.

"White beaches, turquoise water, tangerine sunsets," Lukas Sing-Low continued, his voice heavy with wistful nostalgia. "As a child, I would wake up and run through the sugargrass fields on Bastimar Island to the seaside. Me and my sisters would play in the surf, catch fish, baste them with a sugargrass marinade, and grill them right there on the beach over a little bonfire. I would sing songs as the sugar turned the fishes' scales a golden caramel. It was the best-tasting food you could ever imagine. A warm breeze would drift through and carry the smell all across the island. Everyone would say that you could smell the grilled fish all the way to the Red Fens. I don't recall ever smelling sugargrass fish here in the Fens, though."

"You've never been back home?" Jeremiah asked, memories of his own childhood racing back to him. He, too, remembered the smells and sights of his youth—the cherry blossoms blooming in spring, the sweet honey melons from his grandma's greenhouse in the summertime, the cool breeze blowing over the Danathane in the fall. "Not since you were a kid?"

"It's been years since I've been to the Gnomish Islands," Lukas Sing-Low answered. "But, I've found out that home is not a place, Jeremiah Blade. You may become familiar with the lanes and corners of a city or some patch of countryside, but it is the people you surround yourself with and the life you build with them that matters the most. Where you are in Westhold doesn't matter. What we hold onto is the memory of place, and that is somewhere we can never go back to, try as we might. When you are with the people you care for, you are always growing and singing your song together. That's home to me. But, no, to answer your Jeremiah, I haven't been back to the Gnomish Islands, and I haven't been home in longer than I can remember."

Jeremiah looked down to the street below to see a Savannah Halfling bravely fighting the growing storm and selling fried dough sticks covered with sugargrass dust to a family of Swamp Elves sheltering under his cart's large umbrella. The father handed the sweet treat down to his daughter, and she devoured her breakfast with a bright smile speckled with crumbs of dough and powdery sugargrass.

"Who did you lose, Lukas?" Jeremiah ventured cautiously, wondering if time had healed enough of the wound for the old Island Gnome to answer. "Where did they go?"

Lukas Sing-Low turned to face the outlaw Jeremiah Blade, his features outlined against the steady drizzle. He had seen his honest share of winters, and every line on his face told a grander tale than any of his ballads.

"I spent a large portion of my youth searching for a key," Lukas explained finally as he turned his attention back to the Swamp Elf family. "I found the key, and Ophelia helped me find the gate, but once we passed, we never found what I was looking for. This time, I hope we are going to find my home, Jeremiah Blade. It lies somewhere on the other side, and I'll give everything I have to find it this time."

Jeremiah had a feeling his home lay somewhere on the other side as well. Ever since Dryftwood, he had felt lost and adrift, bereft of someone who understands. He thought about his life since that day in the Shattered Hills, alternating between hunting and being hunted. He, too, was searching for his home.

Before Jeremiah could continue the conversation, they were interrupted by Ophelia crashing onto the porch with Woodroux and Breaker Calhoun not far behind. Whatever gravity that possessed Ophelia Delphine earlier had evaporated, and a lightness had returned to her spirit.

"Yall might want to gather your stuff," Ophelia whistled cheerfully. "We're going to visit the Priory."

CHAPTER 17

"Cher, you don't understand," Ophelia explained patiently to the antsy Jeremiah Blade as she handed out fanciful, decorative masks to each of her three companions. The masks, painted in complex patterns and bright colors, only covered half or three-fourths of the wearer's face, leaving just enough to the imagination. "The Priory is the best game hall in all the Delta. We can't just walk in there like we were raised in a barn. These masks mean that we are fancy folks that belong at the Marchioness' court."

"You never told me the Priory of Memory is a gambling den," Jeremiah complained in vain as Lukas Sing-Low and Breaker Calhoun held up their respective masks in the faded light of the rainstorm. "Especially one that hosts a fancy dress party on a regular occasion."

Despite the fact Jeremiah had spent the last few years living in the Red Fens, he had never heard of this supposedly world-famous game hall. Jeremiah could have sworn he knew all the best games in town, but it was as if the Priory of Memory had blossomed through the cracks in the street overnight.

"Why would they put the gate to the other side here of all places?" Jeremiah whined. "Shouldn't it be in, I don't know, a cemetery?"

"Lukas and ol' Ophelia wondered why they would do that, too, in the beginning," Ophelia retorted without expounding on who "they" were. She picked out a rock from in between her toes and flung it down the crowded street. Despite the fact they were going to the fanciest gambling den in the Red Fens, Ophelia refused to wear boots. "If you think about it, it's the last place you would expect to look, cher. I guess they figured the vault at the Priory, which stores a goodly amount of gold, was a pretty safe place to ward off unwanted eyes. Clever, these spirits."

The quartet stood in the constant, annoying drizzle at a busy intersection in the heart of the Red Fens. All around them strode food peddlers, charlatans, and dubious medicine purveyors trying to catch the eye of some obscenely rich Swamp Elf noble. It had been raining all day at varying intensities, giving them some cover, but the four companions figured it would be safest for Jeremiah, Breaker Calhoun, and Lukas Sing-Low if they waited until the sun weighed heavy on the western horizon before venturing into the wilds of the Red Fens. The sky was growing dark, and the Red Fens was starting to stir to life under the glow of its Duskstone streetlamps. Jaunty bayou music dripped out of the taverns and game halls, and the smell of spicy cuisine filled the air.

"You know," Ophelia rambled on. "I had a rather lively cousin who used to own the Priory of Memory, but she lost it on a tumble of the dice. I suppose that's fitting for a gambling hall owner. She had to move out to Dryftwood to hide from the shame. And her creditors. I knew your old backwater sounded familiar when you came clomping into my life, Calhoun."

Breaker Calhoun cocked his head to one side, sending a sheet of rain water cascading off of the wide brim of his black ranching hat as a spark of memory flickered behind his pale blue eyes. Calhoun started to inquire further, but Jeremiah, adjusting the jutting, bird-like nose on his own hooded disguise, interjected.

"Well, whoever owns it now," Jeremiah said, turning the long nose of the mask towards the sky to get his bearings. "If it leads us to Lucille and the answer to whatever is going on over there, then that's where we have to go."

"Yeah, we better get on the road," Ophelia grinned as she tried in vain to straighten her wild hair around her disguise. Woodroux curled around her wrist in a tight coil and, when the winder finally settled, he looked like a piece of ornate jewelry. "Lukas, you ready?"

Lukas Sing-Low nodded his silvered head. His half-moon mask covered the entirety of the right side of his weathered face, and three bright stars circled lazily around the eyehole, obviously powered by some form of minor Duskstone. Silver wisps of hair fell upon the mask like clouds in the night sky. Lukas looked as hesitant as Ophelia looked unperturbed. Maybe he wasn't privy to the spirits' thoughts and presence, not being a Hoodoux practitioner after all, but if he had seen all this before and was still so hesitant, Jeremiah could not begin to fathom what lay at the end of this path.

"Well, cher," Ophelia whistled to no one in particular. "We've put this off long enough. I hope yall are ready. Enjoy the rain while you can."

Ophelia Delphine crossed the soaked street towards the gilded double doors sitting under a looming, Duskstone-lit sign that read "Priory of Memory Game Hall". The flashing green, gold, and purple lights glinted off of the pouring rain, creating an otherworldly, blurry haze that surrounded the entrance like a halo around the moon. Lukas Sing-Low followed shortly after that, his bootsteps heavy on the cobblestone street, leaving Jeremiah and Breaker Calhoun alone in the middle of the intersection.

"Maybe it's a good thing I didn't kill you all them years back, Jeremiah Blade," Calhoun mused as he stuffed his cheeks with a sugargrass biscuit from a peddler's cart. Motes of sweet dust floated into the feathers resting on his bony cheeks. "If I had cut you down like I intended, I would be the Sheriff of Dryftwood, ride roughshod over a townful of innocent folks, and spend my nights drinking my weight in Sweetfire. Now, thanks to my stayed hand and forgiving ways, I'm following some crazy bayou witch into the land of the dead. Mmm, yeah, killing you would have been terrible."

"You don't have to come along, Calhoun," Jeremiah retorted, wiping the persistent rain away from the dark, shaded eyes of his mask. "In fact, we'd probably all be better off if you didn't, but no one expects you to listen. Maybe, I should have killed you all those years ago, and you'd already be on the other side."

"That would have been terrible, too," Breaker Calhoun shot back. "I wouldn't want you stomping through the land of the dead, disturbing my eternal slumber. But, here we are, Jeremiah Blade. Neither of us are dead, and I fully intend to bitch and moan all the way to the other side and beyond."

Jeremiah still couldn't believe he had been talked into letting Breaker Calhoun join their expedition. Given their past, Jeremiah had a sneaking suspicion that this was an elaborate plot devised by Calhoun to get back at Jeremiah for scuffing his boots or some such nonsense. He was regretting his decision to recruit the erstwhile sheriff's deputy into his scheme, but he was a capable—if brutal—warrior, and Jeremiah was banking on Calhoun putting his dual hatchets to good use. Jeremiah wasn't entirely sure those weapons would be effective given where they were going, but Ophelia seemed confident that she could get some use out of him. Plus, despite his grating personality, there was something comforting about having Breaker Calhoun tag along—he was a link to a past long forgotten. He would never tell the insufferable Calhoun that, however. So, Jeremiah Blade kept quiet and stalked towards the haze surrounding the Priory of Memory. Breaker Calhoun finished up the last sugargrass biscuit, clapped his hands in a blinding white cloud, and followed closely behind, his spurs clanking loudly on the cobblestone street.

After coming face-to-face with a pair of burly, tattooed Mesa Dwarves guarding the door, Jeremiah Blade and Breaker Calhoun found themselves on the sumptuous floor of the Priory of Memory Game Hall. Green, gold, and purple arcane lights filtered through magnificent crystal chandeliers and shone down on gilded paintings that depicted the sweeping landscapes of the old Willowgate empire—sprawling oak trees dripping with moss, palatial Savannah Halfling manors, and expansive graveyards with ornate tombs and mausoleums. Well-to-do patrons, many of them decked out in the extravagant clothes of noble Swamp Elf families and wearing mysterious, handsome masks, filled the game hall, playing a plethora of games and watching their gold pouches thin. Aristocratic Swamp Elf tunes, far more refined than the riotous choruses that filled The Stumbling Pelican or Kingston's Krossing, filled the hall, with the music from songbows and tinkling clavichords intertwining around the masked patrons and staff.

These people were the upper crust of society—the countesses, baronesses, and various knights and ladies who ran in circles with the Marchioness, the temporal leader of the Red Fens and the entire Delta. These nobles commanded fortunes unfathomable to the average denizen of the Fens. Forced, empty laughter of the aimless rich filled the Priory of Memory. The fortunes won and lost at these tables would feed entire city blocks for weeks, but such was the life of feckless nobility in the Red Fens.

Jeremiah spotted the barefoot Ophelia Delphine tracking across the gambling floor, her serpentine guise peeking in and out of the crowd, with Lukas' flowing silver hair following closely behind. Occasionally, Ophelia would stop and watch some poor soul lose at the dice, or a blessed spirit reached towards the heavens in victory, giving Jeremiah and Breaker Calhoun enough time to slip their way through the crowd and catch up with the pair.

The quartet watched a young noble in frilly dressage and a slender mask grip a long, spinwheel table with bloodless knuckles. Ophelia circled around him like a vulture eyeing a decaying corpse. When the noble sunk to his knees after an unlucky spin, Ophelia chuckled and moved away to stalk elsewhere in the Priory of Memory.

The four companions wound their way through the stately atmosphere until they came upon a long exchange counter with several barred windows. Ophelia went up to a counter with a golden three hanging above the window and flashed a toothy smile to an old Savannah Halfling accountant handling a large stack of gold coins. The accountant looked up, her features covered by a long-billed cap and shaded green by an arcane lamp off to her side. Ophelia and the accountant stared at each other for a long moment as a whirlwind of gold, music, and perfume swirled around them. Jeremiah, Lukas, and Breaker Calhoun stood off to one side, passing around a chewing weed pouch as Ophelia eyeballed the silent accountant.

"We need to see the Abbess, cher," Ophelia whispered conspiratorially to the old accountant. "I was thinking you may be able to help us."

The accountant looked over her spectacles at the rough-hewn Hoodoux Witch. Another awkward moment passed before she clicked off her green arcane lamp and gave a slight, almost imperceptible nod.

"Thank you, cher," Ophelia smiled as she made her way to the end of the exchange counter, where two hefty Mesa Dwarves stood with their arms locked in front of their burly chests. Ophelia's three companions scurried along after her, scanning around for a spittoon along the way.

One of the Mesa Dwarves, his brown beard swishing softly on his rough chest, craned his head towards counter number three, with the number itself having almost imperceptibly changed to a dull yellow. He eyed up the curious entourage, unfurled his heavily tattooed arms, and opened a single wooden door hidden cleverly between two imposing oil paintings of old Savannah Halfling estates. Behind the narrow portal was a dark, featureless hallway.

Ophelia and Lukas stepped through without a word. Jeremiah and Breaker Calhoun hesitated, looking around the Priory of Memory, with its listless nobles, glittering treasures, and soft, sumptuous atmosphere. The Mesa Dwarf guard grunted impatiently, and Jeremiah and Breaker Calhoun quickly turned and followed their companions, who had already doffed their masks and were disappearing down the dark path. The wooden door closed behind them with a curiously heavy thud, and the pair found themselves in inky blackness. Both Jeremiah and Breaker Calhoun removed their masks and followed the hollow, receding steps of Ophelia Delphine and Lukas Sing-Low.

Going from the dazzling array of the game hall floor to complete darkness was a disorientating affair. Jeremiah ran his hands over bare stone walls to guide his way and followed the sounds of his companions until he came upon the three horizontal Duskstone tattoos under Ophelia's eyes glowing softly against the darkness. The iridescent glow provided enough light to show Ophelia and Lukas standing in front of a dizzying spiral staircase that plunged deep into the earth.

"Watch your step, cher," Ophelia offered as her bare feet pattered against the bare stone. "Don't want you slipping to the other side before we're ready."

The four companions descended the narrow stairs for an eon. The air was hot and muggy, and Jeremiah was surprised that, with the Red Fens being as wet and swampy as it was, the stairs could have been dug so deep without flooding. Before long, stylized skulls filled with somber purple flames lined the walls. The snapping tongues of fire danced from the empty, leering eye sockets of the grisly decorations and threw bizarre shadows on the walls, shading their reality in fantastic hues. Lukas Sing-Low coughed softly, and the sonorous echo rippled deep into the wet earth.

The stairs finally ended in a cavern of intricately carved tombs and mausoleums built into the thick mud of the Delta. A fine mist sloshed around their boots, clinging to the leather like spider webs. Ophelia kicked the mists playfully with her bare feet and called out to the dancing shadows in a language Jeremiah had never heard before. A low, mournful breeze curled around the grim facades of the crypts to answer Ophelia's call.

Despite the sense of dread growing in his heart, Jeremiah stood in awe of the vast, subterranean world. He could see small particles of iridescent light drift on the humid air. Jeremiah fished his Raeller Counter out of his belt pouch and peered at the swirling green and purple lights blooming on the display. He had never seen these profiles before—the shade, the hue, the intensity. The lights seemed to be guiding him away from something, hiding the true face of the reality before him.

Across the cavern, Breaker Calhoun squatted over a moss-covered tombstone, iridescent flecks of light reflecting in his pale blue eyes. Lukas Sing-Low sat quietly on a low rock, the fog almost engulfing him entirely.

Using his Raeller Counter as a guide, Jeremiah looked towards a looming tomb with an emblem of sickle crossing a golden bundle of hay engraved above its marble doors. Tales of grim harvests of the dead told by excitable Arbiters filled his memory. To this day, the people of Westhold would still cry out that 'the harvest is upon us' in times of war, famine, or pestilence. Jeremiah stepped forward to get a better look, but, before he could, the symbol on the door flared to life with a bright golden light, and the mausoleum gates cracked open with the grinding of stone on stone. Beyond the marble gates lay a pool of impenetrable shadows.

Suddenly, an impossibly tall, slender figure clad in swirling grey robes entered the cavern.

CHAPTER 18

"It's nice to see you again, madam," Ophelia called out as the towering figure glided into the flickering purple torchlight. "It's been too long."

The robed figure's hooded, grey clothes gave her a wraith-like appearance, and, as she approached, Jeremiah could see a flash of bone white from underneath her cowl. Delicate, pale hands with slender fingers trailed the top of the mist until she loomed over Ophelia Delphine. The robed figure was taller than all of them, even Breaker Calhoun in his boots, and Jeremiah could see a skeletal grimace etched on the angular lower jaw. A heavy sense of unease settled around Jeremiah's shoulders, as thick and sinister as the mists around them.

"Ophelia," a soft, feminine voice emanated from the walls and echoed through the tombs. The sound coalesced around them despite the figure's mouth failing to move. "Do the spirits not speak to you enough?"

"The spirits have told me of the troubles on the other side, Abbess," Ophelia answered, her voice steady. "Something sinister lies in the Grey Wastes. It is like a gaping wound. You surely must have felt it as well."

The Abbess stood there, her swirling grey robes blending with the haze, as if she were weighing the fate of the four on some invisible, inscrutable scale. Her long shadow wavered in the torchlight.

"I see you bring the key back," the Abbess said, peering down towards Lukas Sing-Low. "Has he not suffered enough?"

Lukas Sing-Low's face contorted into a mask of old pain. The swirling mists lapped at his chin, but he kept his head down, not willing to gaze upon the mysterious Abbess. Lukas suddenly seemed devoid of life, the vigor of his performance at The Stumbling Pelican a faded memory. Shadows highlighted the rivers of wrinkles across his features.

"Who are the other two?" The Abbess asked, not waiting for Ophelia to answer. "Are their spirits hardened enough to stalk the Grey Wastes?"

"Of course my spirit is hard enough, lady," Breaker Calhoun interjected with characteristic bravado. "I got the hardest damn spirit from here to Dryftwood. Ain't nobody better to wander your badlands than Breaker Calhoun."

An intimidating silence loomed over the gathered host as the Abbess' dark cowl turned towards Breaker Calhoun. He spit a bright red glob of chewing weed into the mists, his lanky limbs jutting sharply. Whatever his flaws were, and they were legion, Breaker Calhoun had some fire in him.

"He seeks to hide from the living," Ophelia answered quickly before Breaker Calhoun tried something stupid. "He is hunted and seeks refuge from the hounds."

The towering Abbess turned her cold visage from Breaker Calhoun and glided towards Jeremiah Blade.

"This one looks for a spirit taken forcefully, by violent methods," Ophelia said, motioning with a crooked finger towards Jeremiah Blade. "He feels responsible for her passing and seeks to honor her memory."

A sense of freezing foreboding flooded through Jeremiah Blade. Somewhere deep within the hood, Jeremiah could feel the gaze of the Abbess pour into him like a cold, distant star.

"Who do you look for, young one?" the Abbess asked, her voice echoing among the tombs but her skeletal jaw still. "Who draws you to such a terrible place?"

Jeremiah had seen danger in his young life, but as the void glared down at him from beneath the cowl, he felt an intense fear crawl up his spine like none he ever experienced. Icy sweat cascaded from Jeremiah's temple as he steadied himself and held the gaze of the looming Abbess.

"She died because of me," Jeremiah answered as calmly as he could manage. "Her blood is on my hands."

"Did you kill her?" the Abbess retorted quickly, twisting her head and leaning in as if she were hard of hearing. "Did you deliver her spirit to me?"

"I did not," Jeremiah clarified quickly. "There was another who slew her, the leader of my order, but it was my decision that caused her to be there at that moment. I did not fire the crossbow that sent her to the other side, but her death weighs heavily on my heart."

The mists shifted on the currents of a soft breeze. Jeremiah thought he felt a tendril of fog grasp at his hand, but he dared not look away from the Abbess.

"You come here out of guilt," the Abbess stated flatly. "You wish to say the words you did not get a chance to say while she lived. You do not come here for her. You come here to soothe your troubled conscience."

Jeremiah said nothing in response. He felt the Abbess peer deep through his being, exposing secrets he dared not acknowledge.

"You have the wish of the uncountable multitude," the Abbess continued, the tone of her voice growing sharper. "You are filled with regret and sorrow and have come here to relieve your darkened soul. Such is the burden of the living. The dead have no such concept. You will find no relief on the other side."

The Abbess paused and turned a creaking head towards Lukas Sing-Low, who seemed in danger of being consumed in the rising mists. He did not return the pitiless gaze, instead focusing on the marble gate boasting the sickle-and-hay emblem. The Abbess turned her attention to Breaker Calhoun, who was defiantly clacking on his chewing weed.

"The dead do not care about you," the Abbess continued. "They shed no tears for the living or even for themselves. As time passes, and a spirit's memory is forgotten, they forget what it's like to feel the cool breeze, warm sunshine, or the embrace of a loved one. The dead are not the only ones left behind, Jeremiah Blade."

Jeremiah thought of holding Iron Eyes Ledoux in his arms under the Shattered Hills; he thought of how she told him to move on, live his life, and be content knowing that she made her own choices. But Jeremiah remembered her last words, her desire for him to seek out Ophelia—she must have said that for a reason. It was this litany that had powered him since that day in the Shattered Hills. Jeremiah had searched all over the Delta and beyond to find the Hoodoux Queen Ophelia Delphine, and she had brought him to a portal between worlds. He had to believe there was a reason for it all.

"I understand the risk," Jeremiah Blade replied solemnly. "I am willing to move forward, no matter the cost. I have come this far. I cannot turn back with my goal within reach."

"You do not understand the risk," the Abbess replied, her voice devoid of life and color. "You would not be here if you did. Your goal is not within reach. Your trials are just beginning. Yet, you are allowed to pass, just like others before you. Though your reasoning is ill-guided, it is one that makes you mortal. If you shall remain that way is yet to be seen. You should prepare yourself to never feel the warmth of the sun again."

Jeremiah Blade looked to Lukas Sing-Low, who looked as if he was on a ship watching his home disappear over the horizon. Even Ophelia, one with whom death and spirits were constant companions, stood quiet among the towering tombs. Breaker Calhoun, still wrapping himself in his cloak of false courage, rolled his eyes at the theatrics. All Jeremiah could do was nod in response.

Suddenly, the Abbess' long, slender hand turned upright, and a dull red Duskstone burned in her palm. Jeremiah peered down as the Abbess held the Duskstone out towards him; inside the ore, iridescent specks floated aimlessly.

"Extend your left hand, Jeremiah Blade," the Abbess commanded. "This is your one and only hope of returning."

Jeremiah reached out, and the slender fingers delicately placed the Duskstone on his outstretched palm. Suddenly, he felt a quick, intense heat burn across his flesh. Searing, spiraling red lines etched into the meat of his palm and stretched to his fingertips. The now-bright scarlet ore pulsed like a beating heart before melting into his flesh. The spider web of arcane lines on his skin glistened brightly against the encroaching shadows.

"Breaker Calhoun, step forward," the Abbess ordered, her darkened cowl turning towards the bounty hunter. She produced another scarlet Duskstone as her outline faded into the purple shadows. "Your shield awaits."

Breaker Calhoun hesitated a moment, his bravado dropping for a mere moment. Quickly, though, he strode forth, spurs clinking loudly, and he snatched the Duskstone from the Abbess. The dull red light flared to life again, and arcane lines shattered across his palm like broken glass. Breaker Calhoun hissed in pain and let out a long string of creative curses but held on until the arcane energy burned fully into his flesh. The Duskstone dissipated, leaving behind a glittering blood-red spiral on Breaker Calhoun's palm.

"With this, you will become as the spirits are," the Abbess explained as she turned towards the marbled gates. "Without it, you will be treated as a trespasser on hallowed ground and dealt with accordingly. This Duskstone will defend you against their insatiable hunger."

Jeremiah looked over to Ophelia and Lukas, and they held up their left hands, showing the same red vortex of veins crisscrossing their palms. He had never noticed the markings before, but now they shone brightly with an ephemeral scarlet light.

"Come," the Abbess continued. "Your journey begins. It is time to turn the key."

With that, Lukas Sing-Low's quivering voice began to fill the cavern.

CHAPTER 19

O'er the ocean
My love waits for me,
O'er the ocean
The dark, endless sea.

O'er the ocean
My love lies so low,
O'er the ocean
In its cruel, endless flow.

The words of the old Island Gnome sea ballad filtered through the macabre cavern like dust in torchlight. The crescent moon amulet on Lukas Sing-Low's throat glowed with a warm, tangerine light, and the mists hovering around their boots dissipated, creating a path through the yawning gate.

"You are right, Ophelia," the Abbess stated as her grey cowl flickered in the shadows. "There is a darkness spreading on the other side like a festering wound. I have not felt anything like this since the beginning of my vigil. I fear that it is not just the world of the dead that is in danger. I am bound, but you, Ophelia Delphine, are not. Your companions will need the proper tools if you are to survive."

The Abbess turned her dark vision on the slim frame of Breaker Calhoun. The erstwhile sheriff's deputy met the Abbess' gaze and held it through the purple torchlight.

"Breaker Calhoun," the Abbess called. "You are inadequate and threaten the lives of your companions. Give me your weapons."

"Inadequate?" Breaker Calhoun retorted, appalled. "What? I ain't giving you nothing, lady. I stole these two hatchets myself and I ain't just going to give them away to some creepy beanstalk."

Breaker Calhoun didn't have much say in the matter as his two serrated hatchets formed in the long hands of the Abbess. The blades glinted oddly in the purple light as she turned the weapons over in her palms. Before anyone could react, a bone-white light spread out from the slender fingers of the Abbess and coated the two axes; they turned a dull, matte ivory from tip to tail, the same bone color as the Abbess' hands and lower jaw. Before Breaker Calhoun could protest, the ivory hatchets appeared back in his belt, glowing with a soft, white light.

"Now you have some use, Breaker Calhoun," the Abbess stated emotionlessly. "Your companions will rely on you, as you will rely on them."

"Horseshit," Breaker Calhoun boldly shot back. "I was perfectly useful before these hatchets. Not that I, uh, don't appreciate it. It's just that there ain't nobody better to ride with than Breaker Calhoun, regardless the circumstance."

"Your companions' lives depend on it," the Abbess replied as she drifted above the haze. "You hold more than you realize, Breaker Calhoun."

The Abbess faded further into the twisting, purple darkness. The painted, bone-white chin jutting out from the cowl was the last thing Jeremiah saw before the Abbess disappeared completely.

"The gate is unlocked," the Abbess' voice reverberated through the skulls and gravestones. "The way is open. If you are lucky, you will see the sun rise again."

The purple torch lights snapped off, leaving the companions in almost complete darkness. The only light that pierced the blackness was the sickle-and-hay emblem that hovered over the looming gateway and the orange light from Lukas Sing-Low's Duskstone. The bard hummed softly in the dark, though Jeremiah did not know if it was to keep the gate between worlds open or bolster their sagging courage. Slowly, steadily, Lukas Sing-Low stepped forward, the echo of his boot steps thundering across the cavern. Lukas Sing-Low led the way, followed by Ophelia Delphine, Woodroux coiled tightly around her upper arm, then Breaker Calhoun, his spurs clanking defiantly, and, finally, Jeremiah Blade. As they passed under the golden emblem, some unknown force sapped the heat from their bones. Then, the marble gates closed, and the shadows tightened their embrace.

"Follow Lukas' voice, cher," Ophelia called out, her words sounding faint and distant as they intermingled with Lukas' melodic humming. "One boot in front of the other."

Jeremiah spied a warm, crimson glow coming from his waist; he initially thought it was his marshal belt buckle going haywire until he realized the light was coming from the spider web of arcane lines that crisscrossed his palm. The radiating light from the four companions' hands joined Lukas' amulet as the only bastion against the looming darkness. The lonely beacons of red marched quietly into the gloom, and the further they walked, the brighter the arcane lines grew.

As they moved forward, Jeremiah thought of the mysterious Abbess. She seemed neither alive nor dead, trapped in some kind of limbo, guarding the path to the realm of the dead. Jeremiah had seen terrible power on display, but there was a coldness that radiated from the Abbess. He had never experienced anything like it, and the image of the bone-white jawline jutting out from the grey hood burned itself into his memory.

The four companions walked for an eternity. Dizziness overcame Jeremiah, the claustrophobic shadows playing with his perception of reality. He heard faint voices around him and, as he looked ahead, the lights from his companions' palms distorted and wavered. It was as if the threads of his world were becoming unwound and replaced by a terrifying and alien power.

The sounds around Jeremiah grew louder, drowning out Lukas Sing-Low's continuous humming, and the shadows twisted into leering visages. Some of the faces were curious, others furious, and they swooped and retreated, encircling the companions. Each time a shadow dove, the scarlet light on their palms blazed to life and sent the apparition fleeing back into the darkness. The shadows followed Jeremiah and his companions like a swarm of clinging horseflies, creating a furious chorus of buzzing, clicking, and hissing.

"Don't stop," Ophelia warned. "Or you'll never see your home again."

Eventually, the dark gave way to enough light to show a vast, mephitic swamp cloaked in an ashen film. They were standing on a tiny island of wet grass and black soil, looking out over the endless grey sweep. Though they were standing in a swamp, the humidity and heat had been sapped from the surrounding air, fragmenting their senses and giving them a disjointed perception between what they saw and what they felt. The edges of their vision were blurred and hazy as if smoke from a forest fire coated the land. Ephemeral figures, broken, disjointed, and aimless, moved through the haze, gliding among the indistinct blackwood trees and hanging moss that lazily scraped the surface of the brackish water. It was a mirror of the world they left behind, but a broken one, shattered at the edges.

The red lines on their palms pulsed violently, covering the four companions with a thin, protective shell as forgotten spirits swept towards the intruders. The veil of crimson light held up as their only protection from the oppressive gloom and hungry dead that threatened to swallow them whole. Jeremiah glanced at his Raeller Counter and saw only the bright red Duskstone profiles encircling each traveler; beyond that, the screen was dead and lifeless.

Ophelia Delphine strode to the bank of their little patch of wet land and placed her feet at the very edge of the stagnant water, her dark features furrowed in concentration. Spirits moved in closer, though hesitant of the crimson protection. Jeremiah, Lukas, and Breaker Calhoun gathered around her, awed by their surroundings. Jeremiah and Breaker Calhoun couldn't help but flinch every time a wraith lurched from the fetid bog or drifted past them. It was not an experience that many in Westhold had the honor of beholding.

Ophelia turned to her companions, the Duskstone tattoos under her eyes glowing fiercely, and she brought them in closer as if to hide her words from the damned and forgotten. Woodroux slithered up towards Ophelia's shoulder, his scales glittering the same emerald green as her eyes, and leaned in conspiratorially with the rest of the travelers. They were lost and lonely children in a cold and unforgiving land.

"Welcome to the other side, cher," Ophelia Delphine whispered softly in the gloom.

CHAPTER 20

"I was expecting more theatrics, to tell the truth," Breaker Calhoun exclaimed as he stood boot-high in hazy, other-worldly muck. "You know, the blinding radiance of the Good Light cleansing my spirit. My life of sin finally catching up to me. Being weighed in the balance and all that."

"We are far away from the Good Light here," Lukas Sing-Low replied as he watched the spirits play on the ghostly winds. "We are on the periphery. The place where spirits come to fade away as they are forgotten in the mortal realm. We will find no warmth here."

"The world here is a reflection of the world we left behind," Ophelia explained. "Just as these spirits are a memory of the mortal world, so too is the land a reflection of the realms of Westhold. The world here is pieced together by the collective memory of its inhabitants hoping to find the familiar comfort they left behind. Yet, as their souls fade, these memories of hidden bogs and patches of blackwood trees are consumed by the endless grey tides."

"We all will be forgotten in time," Lukas piped up. The wrinkles etched into his weathered face seemed to deepen with each passing moment. Lukas Sing-Low, once so commanding and full of vitality on stage, now seemed eroded by the unrelenting gloom. "Even the land we tread. All of it will be washed away."

"Well, that's cheerful," Breaker Calhoun stated as he filled his lower lip with chewing weed. "I don't suppose any of these fine folks will know what in the Good Light we are looking for?"

The ghosts around the interlopers howled in response. It was a low, mournful sound, the sound of memories being forgotten and histories lost. The echoes wound their way around the boughs of the blackwood trees, through the hanging moss, and across the flat, dark water. Icy tendrils curled around the living with a growing sense of claustrophobia.

"The spirits, they're telling us we don't belong," Ophelia replied. "I don't think many of the dead will be willing to offer directions."

"I reckoned as much," Breaker Calhoun smacked loudly as he spit out a blob of chewing weed spit. "If they ain't helping, how do we go about finding this 'disturbance'? We just going to wander around until we fall through it? Or will we have to bribe one of your ghost friends to finally start jawing?"

Ophelia Delphine never got the chance to answer. A ripple in the black, brackish water exploded as a hulking shade of a long-dead Swamp Elf burst towards the gathered travelers. The spirit lurched towards Ophelia, causing the scarlet etchings on her hand to flare in defense, and hit her with enough concussive force to send her tumbling across the distorted landscape.

Jeremiah Blade and Breaker Calhoun stood dumbstruck at the sight of the malevolent, sneering spirit; Lukas Sing-Low was not caught so unaware, however. As Ophelia lay numbed and shocked from the attack, Lukas jumped into action with a sudden, unrelenting fury. Lukas' amulet exploded in a hot, orange glow, and a primal roar ripped through the desolate atmosphere. The air surrounding them faltered and wavered as tangerine sickles of energy careened through the gloom and tore through the ethereal wisps of the rampaging spirit. The apparition, surprised by the sudden arcane attack, jerked and whipsawed like a stuck winder.

Lukas' fusillade gave Jeremiah Blade enough time to shake his daze. Jeremiah drew his Alathanian longsword, and the cold steel instantly roiled with the heat of a dying star. With the molten blade held high, Jeremiah thudded across the moist soil and plunged into the fray. As the specter thrashed from the tangerine sickles of energy, Jeremiah brought his boiling edge through the ghost, setting it ablaze and banishing it from living memory in a flash of smoke.

Jeremiah turned, wide-eyed, searching for answers on the weathered features of Lukas Sing-Low. There were no answers from the silver-haired bard, however; three more lurching spirits violently broke from the water's surface and lunged towards Jeremiah Blade just as the smoke cleared. A deep seed of fear blossomed in Jeremiah's heart as he turned to see the mangled, rotting faces of the dead reaching towards him.

A bone-white hatchet glittered in the murk and sliced through the first spirit before it could reach Jeremiah. The weapon crackled with otherworldly energy and engulfed the wraith, dragging the being's ephemeral tendrils beneath the surface of the blade and trapping it underneath the magical coating. As the weapon crashed into the muck, the spirit's enraged features glided towards the edges of the blade, furiously trying to break free from its arcane prison. The enchantment the Abbess bestowed upon the weapon held, however, and all the specter could do was howl in rage.

Breaker Calhoun, chewing weed still firmly planted in his lower lip, charged the two remaining spirits to come to the aid of his old foe with his off-white, offhand hatchet raised high. Before he could reach Jeremiah, Breaker Calhoun suddenly stopped short as one of the dead narrowed and slammed against the magical Duskstone ward coating his bony chest, sending a thundering shudder through the crimson light. The attack was powerful enough to send Calhoun sprawling backwards uncontrollably, and he fell into the ghostly swamp with a loud splash. Paralyzed by the otherworldly force, he drifted on the surface of the water like a ship without a sail. The specter reformed and swooped down to finish the incapacitated Breaker Calhoun.

Before the spirit could feast upon Breaker Calhoun's flame of life, the air froze and the malevolent wraith crystallized, giving it the shape it lost in death. The specter hung in the air, suspended for a heavy moment, before crashing to the ground and shattering into a thousand crystal shards. A few yards back, Ophelia Delphine stood defiant, her heavy, black hair floating on some unseen current and the three lines of Duskstone tattoos under each eye glowing with a fierce, iridescent light. Frosted steam dripped from Ophelia's clawed hands as she exacted her revenge on the raging spirit.

The remaining specter, suddenly unsure of itself, darted through the murk like a fish on the line, encircling the quartet. The ghost faded in and out of existence, cautious of the deadly magic on display from the intruders. Lukas Sing-Low's amulet glowed once more, and a violent thrum filled the air as bright orange lances of arcane power raced to pincushion the darting apparition. The spirit writhed and snapped violently, trying to avoid the arcane onslaught, but, at last, the magical force ripped through its ephemeral frame, and it drifted away like sand in the desert.

The other spirits looked on cautiously, not daring to test the combined magical might of the intruders and risk being evaporated from living memory. Jeremiah, Lukas, and Ophelia scanned the twisted visages of the curious wraiths, waiting for one to risk death a second time. A long vale of silence expanded around them as they took stock of the fallout from the pitched battle. A soft gurgling interrupted their vigil, and they saw Breaker Calhoun slowly sinking beneath the surface of the water and struggling for breath. Jeremiah quickly waded out into the brackish pool and hauled the paralyzed Breaker Calhoun up with his free hand. Calhoun, feeling rushing back through his body, gasped and fought for life-giving air.

"Well, would you look at that," Jeremiah mocked his former antagonist as he pulled him back to semi-solid land. "Jeremiah Blade just saved Breaker Calhoun's life. Never thought I'd see the day. Must be a blue moon or something."

Breaker Calhoun was too busy coughing up other-worldly swamp muck to make a smartass response. He tried to take a step forward, but his knee gave way, and he tumbled forward, slipping from Jeremiah's grasp and crashing into the earth with a heavy thud. Jeremiah let Breaker Calhoun writhe on the ground for a long moment before helping him up from the clinging soil. Eventually, Breaker Calhoun made his way back to his boots, with Jeremiah holding him up by his armpits. Jeremiah's unexpected gallantry drove Calhoun mad, but he had little choice in the matter.

Tense moments passed as the living waited for the dead to renew their assault, but no attack came. Peace had returned to the realm of the dead. The spirits, it seemed, would bide their time.

While Jeremiah helped Breaker Calhoun take an unsteady step forward, Ophelia strode to the edge of the water, stood ankle-deep in the thick mud, and turned her head towards the expansive haze as if she was straining to hear something. Woodroux crawled his way to her narrow shoulders, raised his head, and mimicked Ophelia's movements, his normally bright scales glinting dully in the muted light. Ophelia and her familiar peered out into the world of the dead, searching for answers, as the others recovered from their short, spirited battle.

"Well, I wasn't expecting that," Ophelia whistled through the murk, her emerald eyes twinkling mischievously as she turned to face her companions. "The dead are taking shape, drawing from some unknown wellspring of life. The dead, cher, are rising."

CHAPTER 21

Woodroux stood up straight on Ophelia's shoulder like a flagpole struggling against the wind. None of Ophelia's three companions knew what exactly the winder was doing, and the witch was giving up no clues. Breaker Calhoun's left arm hung loosely at his side; the paralysis brought on by the malevolent spirit was proving difficult to shake. Jeremiah Blade and Lukas Sing-Low passed a pouch of chewing weed back and forth, each silently weighing the circumstances as blood-red spit dribbled down their chins. Jeremiah took in a deep breath. The otherworldly swamp air around them had a peculiar taste—stale and dusty, like an ancient library corridor or a forgotten box of memories.

"I thought yall said these pretty Duskstone lights were going to save us from the dead," Breaker Calhoun, still annoyed that Jeremiah saved his hide, spat as he shook the life back into his arm. "That sure as shit ain't the case."

"That was unexpected, I admit, cher," Ophelia, her normally bright eyes now clouded and hazy, explained as Woodroux gazed into the murk. "But I figure it has something to do with this disturbance the spirits keep harping on about. I didn't quite expect it to be this bad, though. I've never had a spirit attack me before like that. They try to spook you, sure, but the Duskstone wards have always protected mortal travelers from the inhabitants of this world. At least they did the last time we were here. The spirits are riled up about something, and I'm guessing this is a symptom of it."

"Well, that's fantastic," Calhoun drawled, his voice slurring from the unexpected paralysis. "Here I was expecting a cheery jaunt through the land of the dead and now I got to worry about becoming one of them. Ain't that just grand."

"That makes our task all the more urgent," Ophelia insisted, though there was no real urgency in her voice. "It's as if these spirits are taking the shape they lost in life, regaining their lost forms, breathing for the first time in centuries. I'm pondering hard about what could be causing it."

"Great," Breaker Calhoun snorted. "I was hoping we would wander 'round here like chickens with our heads cut off 'til the spirits ate us alive. I should have taken my chances with them frilly red ladies in the Fens."

"You can always turn back," Jeremiah remarked as he gnawed on the chaw of chewing weed in his lower lip. "Or is the mighty Breaker Calhoun getting scared? A little yellow, are we?"

"Son, I ain't never been scared in the entirety of my life," Breaker Calhoun shot back, suddenly on the defensive. "Yall are going to have to try a lot harder than a few ghosts to get Breaker Calhoun riled up."

A low, mournful howl filled the swamp, dancing through the limbs of the blackwood trees. The sound cut their conversation short and sent Lukas, Jeremiah, and Breaker Calhoun on edge, though Ophelia and Woodroux remained unperturbed. The sound died, and a great vat of silence rushed back to fill the void.

"Whatever is going on, Ophelia, it doesn't seem that it affects every spirit," Lukas Sing-Low mused. "There are spirits within eyesight that haven't turned on us. Why wouldn't they join in the fray? Why only four?"

"We are pretty tough," Breaker Calhoun boasted as he examined the furious ghost still trapped underneath the bone-white Duskstone layer on his hatchet. "At least I am. Don't know about hoss over there. Especially with my new toys here, these ghosts need to be afraid of me. They're running scared, I reckon."

Jeremiah regretted his decision to drag Breaker Calhoun along, but he kept his opinions to himself as he scanned the mists for signs of Lucille Ledoux. He had no idea where to begin looking for her, and Ophelia was more concerned with the disturbance in the spirit world. He had spent the last few years of his life trying to find a way to see Lucille again but, if the domain of the dead mirrored the land of the living, he could wander for an eternity and not see her. Though both Lukas and Ophelia had kept mum about their first journey to the other side, Jeremiah had picked up enough bits and pieces to know they had failed in their search. A seed of crippling doubt began to blossom in the back of Jeremiah's mind that he would fall victim to the same fate.

"There are portions of the Grey Wastes," Lukas chimed in as they waited for Ophelia to stop looking for whatever it was she was looking for. "Where the memories are stronger and the world brighter. At these locations lie the recently deceased and the vibrant spirits who sing throughout the ages. Legendary figures still roam here, their spirits undimmed and remembered by the masses. The ghosts here, on the edges, have been gone for ages, and everyone who would have remembered them is gone. Bitterness fills them as they fade away."

"Thanks for that, short-stack," Breaker Calhoun mocked as he finally recovered the use of his left arm. "Jeremiah, maybe you'll see your girlfriend at one of these places and you can stop crying about her all the time."

Jeremiah felt his face flush, and he was about to berate Calhoun for his irreverence, but he knew they were in a dangerous place. As tentative an ally the former sheriff's deputy was, he was still one of the few who stood among the living. Judging by recent developments, they would need as many sword arms as they could find if they had any hope of finding Lucille or the source of the disturbance, so he figured he better find a way to get along with the grating Calhoun.

"Everyone believes the Good Light is the sun," Lukas Sing-Low continued, ignoring Breaker Calhoun. His was low and quiet, as if he was trying to avoid waking the dead. "But the Good Light is the brightness of the spirits that fill the memories of the living."

"Jeremiah, you figure that old windbag McCracken knows that?" Breaker Calhoun asked. "Probably not, I imagine. I ain't never met a bigger sinner in my life. And he was the damn priest!"

"Goes to show the kind of place Dryftwood is, I guess," Jeremiah conceded, rubbing the light stubble on his chin thoughtfully. "How's old Father McCracken doing nowadays, Calhoun?"

"Damned if I know," Calhoun answered as he swatted away a curious spirit. "He stayed around after you wrecked the place, but he fell in love with one of them ranch wives that attended his sermons, pissed off some old boy, and got ran out of town. Last thing he said before he burned out of there on a flop-eared mule was that he was going home. I guess that meant Old Willowgate? I didn't think he had ever actually been there, but where else would he be going? Don't think he had a home, as far as I could tell. I don't think any of them Savannah Halflings have a home, come to think about it."

"That's it," Ophelia piped up suddenly, like a bolt of lightning through the gloom. Woodroux also lashed about as if he had stumbled upon some great scholarly discovery. "Old Willowgate. That's what I couldn't see, cher. That Savannah Halfling back on the bayou, the one that tried to bring you to whatever justice you're running from. There was something about that Duskstone she was using. She kept going on about that Arkstone, but that stone she wielded was powerful and had a very peculiar profile."

Jeremiah thought back to the unique lavender and silver hue Hallincross wielded. He had never seen that particular type of Duskstone before, but he was still a young man, and there was much of the world he had yet to see. Jeremiah couldn't see the connection Ophelia was making, however.

"Old Willowgate has been a ruin for decades," Lukas stated quietly. "The Savannah Halflings are a ruined people. How would they be able to affect the spirit world?"

A high-pitch shriek answered Lukas' question. Weapons quickly flew into thirsting hands and magic curled around eager fingertips as the four cast around for the source of the sound. The normally-still waters of the swamp churned and boiled, sending plumes of twisting smoke into the surrounding haze. After a tense, bloated moment, the water stilled and lay flat again. The living breathed a collective sigh of relief.

On Ophelia's shoulders, Woodroux, after his initial excitement, finally collapsed into a curling puddle around the witch's neck. The light returned to her emerald eyes as she dipped a bootless toe into the water, and the ripple spread out across the brackish pool and into the murk. For another long moment, no one moved as they waited for some vengeful wraith to burst forth to consume the only wisps of life present in the land of the dead.

"In old times," Ophelia started boldly, not waiting for an ancient ghost to devour her before she had said her piece. "When the world was formless and vague, there was no distinction between the living and the dead. There were only ancient gods who vied for power in a vast, endless sea of creation. Among these gods, there were two siblings, a brother and sister, both terrible in their might. You would think that two siblings would be able to get along sometimes, but these two warred constantly, leaving great swaths of creation in ruin. They both strove for power over the other in a constant battle that raged for eons. Eventually, the sister created a prison to entrap her brother. If she could not defeat him, then she would lock him away for all eternity. She created a facsimile of the world they inhabited, a mockery of creation, one that only existed in dull tones and faded edges. She succeeded in locking her brother away in the boundless prison. But, she still harbored a seed of love for her sibling, so she gave him enough of a memory to remember what had passed. That god, locked away for eternity, became the first spirit, a vague shell of his once fearsome might. Yet, he still hungered and, once mortals came into being, reached an agreement with his sister to claim the restless spirits as his own. Thus, he grew his ranks of followers, even if they were hazy remembrances of their former selves. Now, we stand in his domain, the Grey Wastes."

Jeremiah thought back to the Shattered Hills, after the fight with Sheriff High Hedge and the Brightglaive brothers, when he and Lucille, Iron Eyes then, were searching for Sundown in the cramped tunnels of the red rock butte. He remembered the story of The One Who Fell, the goddess who was cast down from the heavens and whose bones created the Shattered Hills and whose blood painted the rocks. He thought it a fairy tale then, but now, standing in the realm of the dead, maybe there was more to the story than he thought at the time.

A soft splash sounded like a thunderous crash as Ophelia took a step into the dead water. The black water crept up her calf, onto her tattered dress, and up to her narrow waist. Her crooked fingers glided across the surface and, as the scarlet lines of power from her palm touched the surface, dark red energy spread across the dank pool. Ophelia hummed as her slim frame left a long, quiet wake behind her. Woodroux curled around her shoulders, his tongue flicking into the mists.

"Where are we going, Ophelia?" Jeremiah Blade called out into the gloom after exchanging bewildered glances with Breaker Calhoun. "I see no path forward."

"The Grey Wastes are a prison, cher," Ophelia called back as she faded into the clawing fog. "Something that should only have one way in or out. But, like any jail, there are those who want to find an alternative path. We go now to find the tear between worlds, Jeremiah Blade."

CHAPTER 22

Their throats did not thirst for water, nor did their stomachs rumble for food. The four companions had no way of telling time as the sun did not streak across the sky heralding the arrival of the stars. They did not tire nor drag their boots, and their eyes did not weigh heavy with the expectation of sleep. Their existence was a strange purgatory, and, as they walked, a sinister sense of dread filled their bones—their only real way of measuring time in the land of the dead. The Grey Wastes mirrored the world of the living, though under an opaque veil, making it seem at once familiar and foreign. They were mortal shells adrift in a dead sea.

The four companions tracked through the mud and muck of the swamp, around copses of blackwood trees and pools of stagnant water. Ophelia led the way, Woodroux perched on her shoulder as a lookout, her laugh ready and easy despite the oppressive circumstances. She was followed by Lukas Sing-Low. The bard's steps were solid and purposeful—he was familiar with this world and knew the toll it would take on mortal travelers. Breaker Calhoun followed Lukas, alternating between bellyaching and spitting bright red globs of chewing weed in the water for Jeremiah to wade through. Jeremiah, bringing up the rear, avoided the pools of crimson spit and kept a wary eye on the spirits that hounded them through the blackwood trees. The ghosts surrounding the companions continued with their chittering chorus, a drone that reminded Jeremiah of long-gone summers and fading twilight.

The scarlet lines of arcane power on their palms both guided and protected the four companions. Ophelia would occasionally remind them to focus on the Duskstone lights in their palms so as not to get lost in the bleakness. It seemed a simple enough task in the beginning, but as they continued their long march, Jeremiah could feel his senses dulling and his mind clouding. The Duskstone lines would then pulse, and he would shake the cobwebs and refocus on the bobbing scarlet hue encircling Breaker

Calhoun's fist. Jeremiah wondered if the other three were experiencing the same thing, but he did not see anyone falter, so Jeremiah concentrated on putting one boot in front of the other.

"Keep up, cher," Ophelia called from the front of the line, her words crisp in the fog. "You might be doomed to wander the Grey Wastes forever without ol' Ophelia guiding the way."

Spirits followed their every step—some were curious, others leering and bitter at the intrusion of the living on their realm. None dared attack them, however. Whether the wraiths could not break the magic etched into the companions' palms or they were just biding their time, Jeremiah couldn't tell. Occasionally, they would hear the weeping of a woman or the wail of a child through the fog.

"Where in the Good Light are we going, witch?" Breaker Calhoun exclaimed, his patience fraying. "These damn ghosts are circling us like a pack of wild dogs. They're just waiting for us to slow before they sink their dead fangs into our flesh."

"The disturbance is faint here, Breaker Calhoun," Ophelia answered. "The tear is still many moons away, if you want to use that reckoning. Plus, you wanted to hide out. I can assure you the Marchioness' jailers ain't going to find you here."

That kept the mouthy Breaker Calhoun quiet, though he still produced a steady stream of obscenities under his breath as he trudged through the swamp. As the four lonely lights of life continued their trek to the tear between worlds, the terrain shifted from swamp to rolling hills, much like the farms and homesteads to the south of Alathane and close to the hamlet of Harrowdale.

"This should look familiar, Jeremiah Blade," Ophelia shouted, though Jeremiah strained to hear through the oppressive surroundings. He could only see the faintest scarlet of Ophelia's Dusktone ward in the distance. "Though it seems to be many years since you've been home."

Jeremiah Blade did, in fact, recognize the contours of the land, despite the otherworldly fog that still clung tightly to the horizon. Jeremiah stopped and focused on the ghosts following him—back in the swamp, many of the spirits had been Swamp Elves, lithe figures gliding through the blackwood trees. Now, he saw faint, bulkier outlines of Plains Humans—farmers with gaunt, hungry eyes. Jeremiah's eyes strained against the crowding murk, searching for anything he might recognize. If the other side was truly a mirror to the mortal realm, he might find a lost memory from his past. Jeremiah took a step into the mists, moving past swirling specters as he did.

Through the blurred, churning miasma, Jeremiah thought he spied alabaster-white crenellations looming above the Grey Wastes. Memories instantly flooded back to him of his childhood home of Alathane. The outlaw was taken back to his childhood days playing with his brothers on his family's estate. In his mind's eye, he saw himself climbing trees with Henric and swimming in the streams and ponds with Alistair and Barnaby. Cherry blossoms bloomed in the warm spring sunlight, their soft, pink petals drifting through the air. Somewhere on the cool wind, playful voices called Jeremiah's name.

Jeremiah felt a warm sensation pulse faintly on his palm, but he continued towards the city of his birth. He saw children chase each other on wide avenues as the sound of laughter filled his ears. Jeremiah hadn't seen Alathane since he set off for Dryftwood; he had never been able to go back due to the events that transpired in the Shattered Hills. It was as Lucille said when she died—Jeremiah was an outlaw through and through. All he had were memories of his home. There would be no parade for Jeremiah Blade down the cobblestones of Alathane.

Faint-but-familiar faces peered from windows and around corners as Jeremiah glided through the streets of Alathane. He saw smiles and returned them in kind; he even tipped a non-existent hat to a flower girl running alongside him. Everything around him seemed so bright and airy, just like he remembered it from his childhood. Jeremiah's hand felt hot, almost burning, but he moved forward anyway, looking for a friendly face or an old haunt.

"Home," Jeremiah whispered under his breath. Though it had only been a handful of years since setting out for Dryftwood, it seemed like a lifetime ago. He felt at peace. "Finally home."

Jeremiah Blade looked around and found himself on the main path of the central gardens in his family's estate. Crisp sunlight filtered through the boughs of oak trees and fell upon the sharp, green spearmint leaves that filled the estate grounds. Around him, smiling Alathanians laughed and danced. Jeremiah looked around and saw a familiar figure glide towards him—it was Agnes, his old governess. Jeremiah hadn't seen her in years. She had died before he even entered the Academy. The heat on Jeremiah's palm was becoming unbearable, flashing in hot, staccato intervals, but he ignored it and moved towards the comforting features of the old woman.

"Nai Nai," Jeremiah called out to the approaching woman, using the term of endearment the old governess preferred. A low howl swirled around Jeremiah, making it hard to focus on Agnes' shifting edges. "It's been too long."

As the figure moved closer, Jeremiah could see the kind, wrinkled countenance of the old woman. A sense of peace filtered through Jeremiah's mind as he extended his arms to embrace his Nai Nai.

The grandmotherly features blossomed into a grim, furious visage as the specter lunged at the mortal interloper. Jeremiah, entranced by the idealized memory of his childhood, didn't realize the noose was tightening around his neck. Only the scarlet etchings in Jeremiah's palm saved him from the hungry, malevolent wraith. A crimson light the color of chewing weed spit rippled across Jeremiah's mortal frame as the specter smashed against the arcane energy like a wave crashing upon the shore. Jeremiah, violently awakened from his radiant nostalgia, was forced several steps back as the glowing, tranquil past degenerated into a dangerous present.

Around Jeremiah, a half-dozen specters appeared and filled the emptiness with their hateful laughter. They came at him from all angles, and only his training and survival instincts honed by years on the lam saved Jeremiah from joining the ranks of the dead. The wraiths circled Jeremiah like a cyclone, dipping and diving to feed on the lonely lifeforce stranded in the Grey Wastes. Jeremiah Blade, now realizing the immense danger he was in, drew his longsword and called upon the power of a raging dust storm.

The heat and fury of Jeremiah's magical blade temporarily stalled the onslaught. Jeremiah could barely make out the spirits long dead against the suddenly murky lanes and gardens of his childhood home. He swept the sword in a wide arc to ward off the seeking shades, leaving a warm, orange wake in the encroaching mist.

The ghosts swarmed like frenzied hornets, whirling around the magic of Jeremiah's longsword. The shrieking, contorted faces smashed against the scarlet light that protected Jeremiah, and, with each attack, the light darkened. In a mad swipe, Jeremiah cut through two specters, their forms consumed by the raging heat. Despite the small victory, panic seized his throat—the spirits were too fast, too dexterous, and too many.

Jeremiah cast around for help from his companions, but somewhere in his nostalgic wanderings, he had lost them. He was all alone, adrift in the Grey Wastes, and hunted by hungry wraiths. Every time the arcane lines dimmed, Jeremiah feared he would be paralyzed like Breaker Calhoun and then be a feast for the dead. Neither Ophelia nor the Abbess told him of the consequences of losing the crimson protection, but he feared he did not have long to find out.

Jeremiah Blade split one more spirit in half as the swarm descended on him and warded off the others as best he could. Suddenly, before him loomed the hulking, incorporeal form of his old Nai Nai. The specter curled, distorted, and flew straight towards Jeremiah's heart. As the impact rippled through the crimson protection, the magical aura shuddered and, finally, failed.

CHAPTER 23

"Jeremiah!" Breaker Calhoun screamed across the desolate expanse of the realm of the dead. "Jeremiah Blade! Where is he, witch?"

"Looks like he's wandered off, cher," Ophelia responded matter-of-factly. "He could be anywhere. I told yall to follow ol' Ophelia."

Ophelia Delphine, Lukas Sing-Low, and Breaker Calhoun stood among the rolling hills, swatting away errant spirits. None of them, not even Ophelia, could reckon how long Jeremiah had been gone, but whether it was one hour or one lifetime, the consequences were equally as dire. They all knew that getting lost in the Grey Wastes was a death sentence—the dead would take their share eventually.

"So, we just plan on leaving him out there?" Breaker Calhoun pressed before catching himself. "Not that, uh, I miss him or anything. It's just that sword of his might come in handy, I reckon. Really, if we could have the blade without the Blade, that'd be mighty fine."

"Look, cher," Ophelia replied after exchanging glances with Lukas Sing-Low. "Jeremiah could be anywhere, and we could spend all eternity looking for his narrow bones. Plus, we are on a bit of a tight schedule here. We need to get to this tear sooner rather than later."

"How long did we wander, Ophelia?" Lukas asked quietly. "How many lifetimes were we gone for?"

"Too many to come up empty-handed like we did, cher," Ophelia replied as she twisted a long strand of her hair into a tight curl. "That's why we have to focus on the task at hand. We have to trust Jeremiah can handle it on his own."

"I think back then we would have appreciated it if someone came and rescued us," Lukas said to the ether. "We barely made it back with our sanity last time."

"Alright, dammit," Breaker Calhoun spat. "Yall best start jawing. Why did yall come here in the first place? How'd yall get back out? If I'm going to wander around this shithole, I want to know that I can get back out if I run off and get lost like Jeremiah. I mean, I probably should have asked these questions before we found ourselves boot-deep in some ghost swamp, but things were tight back there."

Ophelia and Lukas said nothing in response, further infuriating Breaker Calhoun. Eventually, Ophelia turned away as if she was giving Lukas some space for a performance. Lukas Sing-Low peered through the gloom as the spirits played on the spectral winds.

"I don't know if you have children, Calhoun," Lukas started, his melodic voice a jarring sound among the chittering dead. "But, if you do, you know you'd do absolutely anything for them. I was young and wild and free once. Then I met my wife and we had a son. Everything that I thought was important in life faded away the day I held him in my arms for the first time."

Breaker Calhoun stopped relentlessly chomping his chewing weed at Lukas Sing-Low's revelation. Ophelia Delphine remained with her back turned, her glare locked out into the gloom, as if she couldn't bear to watch the coming tale.

"I had given everything up to be a dad," Lukas continued, clambering up a heavy stone as if he was about to perform on stage at a tavern. "I stopped singing, stopped going to bars and festivals. I had made plenty of coin by that point, so money wasn't a concern. It was a chance for me to focus on raising him. My wife and I saw it as a privilege."

Specters crowded in to hear the tale, even dampening their constant chorus to listen to Lukas Sing-Low. The Grey Wastes slowed and stopped as the bard summoned the strength to tell his tale.

"For a few years," Lukas explained, his voice steady and his posture unbent. "We three were happy living in the Fens. I was content with everything we had. Then the pox came to the Red Fens and scoured the city, laying waste to young and old. This was decades ago, but I still remember the churches and cemeteries overflowing with disease-ridden corpses. Everyone thought another Blight was upon us. We laid low, tried to avoid others as best we could, used various Duskstone wards and Hoodoux protections, but it didn't matter. The pox claimed my son and nearly killed my wife."

Lukas Sing-Low paused as memories flashed behind his grey eyes. To Breaker Calhoun, he almost seemed a completely different person than the commanding performer he had seen in The Stumbling Pelican and Kingston's Krossing; this Lukas Sing-Low was heavy with the weight of terrible experience. The old bard took a long breath to steady himself before continuing.

"So, I buried my son," Lukas said almost imperceptibly. "I was shattered. My wife eventually recovered from the pox, but she was scarred for life. Without our son to bind us together, we drifted apart, lonely boats awash in an ocean of grief. It was too painful of a reminder to see each other, so she never came home one day, and I never went looking for her. To this day, I don't know if she is alive or dead. We buried our love alongside our son."

Lukas Sing-Low had aged a lifetime in mere moments; dredging up the past was affecting him physically. The mists of the realm of the dead swirled and snapped, providing cold comfort to the heartbroken bard.

"This is where I come in," Ophelia contributed. "Much like our lost Jeremiah, a broken Lukas Sing-Low searched for any way to contact his lost son. He begged every Hoodoux Witch in the Delta to help him find his son, and they all turned him away. All except ol' Ophelia. His grief was raw and deep, and ol' Ophelia thought she might be able to help. Lukas learned about the spirit world, of how we linger in the hearts and minds of those left behind. He became obsessed with finding his lost son and scoured Westhold for a way back to him. And, with that pretty Duskstone around his neck, we wound up here in the Grey Wastes for the first time."

"We searched for what seemed like lifetimes," Lukas picked up, mechanically rubbing his fingers over the tangerine Duskstone amulet at his throat. "Though it's difficult to reckon time here. Eventually, we were forced to turn back. Our sanity started to slip, and we didn't know if we were alive or dead. I'll always be grateful to Ophelia for sticking by me through the entire ordeal. I didn't want to stop, but Ophelia knew that we risked a fate worse than death if we stayed. So, we retreated, unsuccessful, and I still haven't seen my son since that day I last held his little body in my arms."

Breaker Calhoun had seen brutality and death in his life—living in Dryftwood provided plenty of both—but the way Lukas told the story, his powerful voice trembling even after all the intervening years, softened Calhoun's hide ever so slightly. Calhoun didn't have any kids of his own, his was a rough line of work for a dad, but a pang of sympathy struck his cold, cold heart. Calhoun considered throwing out a smartass comment to lighten the mood but thought better of it for the first time in his life.

"Before all this happened," Lukas declared finally. "I could sing songs about grief and loss, but it wasn't until I lost my son that I had any idea what they meant."

A sharp shriek split the sky. Ophelia, Lukas, and Breaker Calhoun looked up to see a gigantic, snaking shadow slither through the endless murk above them. It was like a shade of a colossal winder with wings floating on some unseen spectral current. The shadow disappeared into the gloom with another ear-piercing scream.

Breaker Calhoun looked towards Lukas, his face a mask of confusion, and then to Ophelia, whose mahogany features had blanched in terror. Ophelia's words tumbled out in a mad, staccato rush.

"Oh, no, cher," Ophelia said to her two companions. "We ain't got no time to look for Jeremiah. He is on his own. It's far, far worse than I feared.

We must follow that shadow, now."

With that, Ophelia bounded over the uneven ground and charged after the fleeting image of the shadow in the sky. Lukas Sing-Low and Breaker Calhoun exchanged worried glances and quickly plowed over the hills after Ophelia Delphine, not wanting to suffer the same fate as Jeremiah Blade.

CHAPTER 24

As the spirit pierced his heart, Jeremiah felt a sharp, cold fire race through his being. His muscles seized, and a bright fear gripped him as he struggled against the creeping paralysis. Around him, he heard the cruel laughter of a thousand hungry souls echo through his home. Jeremiah felt his throat tighten, and he gasped in short, frantic bursts. His longsword slipped from his frozen grip and dropped to the stone pathway next to his boots.

Jeremiah struggled to turn his head, desperately searching for any sign of Ophelia Delphine, Lukas Sing-Low, or Breaker Calhoun, but his companions were nowhere to be found. Jeremiah had gotten lost in the endless murk of the Grey Wastes, lured by the radiant memories of his childhood and separated from salvation. He cursed himself for dropping his guard in so dangerous a realm; now, he was well and truly alone, surrounded by hungry sharks circling their wounded prey.

The specters careened towards the freezing Jeremiah Blade, their hideous shrieks rippling through the opaque surroundings. Jeremiah fell belly-first onto the cobblestones and reached for his still-blazing sword in a mad scramble to save his life. His fingers wrapped around the handle, and, using a well of energy he had not summoned for many years, he twisted onto his back and brought the molten metal in a wide arc above him. The sword cut through several wraiths as they descended upon him and ended their existence in a puff of iridescent smoke. The mighty effort gave him a small reprieve as the spirits regrouped, their shrieking turning into a frenzied, collective whine. Jeremiah tried to rouse himself to his boots, but his legs would not budge no matter what wellspring he drew from.

Beyond the swarm of specters, Jeremiah could see pale-pink cherry blossom petals float aimlessly through the air. He thought back to the warm spring days of his youth, running and laughing with his brothers through the orchards towards his grandma's greenhouse. It seemed so peaceful then, and so long ago. His sword clattered out of his hand once again, the blazing metal searing the cobblestones. Jeremiah thought it a cruel fate to find his way back home in such circumstances; at least, he could see the comforting memories of his childhood, or a facsimile of it, one last time before he joined the ranks of lost souls wandering the Grey Wastes. Above him, the cherry blossoms turned to ash and faded into the gloom.

Jeremiah felt a weight press on his chest from the pocket of his riding vest. He reached into his coat and scraped his fingers against the rough burlap of Ophelia's zam-zam. The Hoodoux Queen's words echoed in his mind—the charm was a guard against the spirits, a light in dark times, a ward against unimaginable forces. Jeremiah thought the burlap sack was just one of the numerous gaudy trinkets one could find by the dozen in the Red Fens, but, if there was a time to find out the truth of the zam-zam, now was the moment. The charm weighed heavily on Jeremiah's chest, as if it had its own special gravity. He tried to summon up the magic of the zam-zam like he would his longsword, but it failed to respond. No blinding arcane radiance erupted from the charm; the zam-zam just sat cold, inert, and unmoving above his still-beating heart. Jeremiah was on his own against the dead.

The constricting cold spread to every corner of Jeremiah's body, and, in short order, all he could feel was his left arm, the last of the arcane lines of energy fighting valiantly against the paralysis. Jeremiah tried to reach upwards to ward off the mocking spirits, who whipped and snapped like banners in the wind, but his left arm gave out, and his hand fell directly onto his Alathanian Marshal belt buckle. The outlaw felt the sword-and-book emblem on the cool metal; he remembered the day he received it and how much it meant to him. At his graduation, he hid tears of joy from his family and classmates when the Lord Arbiter pressed the weighty buckle into his palm. Jeremiah had studied so hard, journeyed through so much doubt—from his family, friends, himself—and the belt buckle was his reward for his dedication. All those hours in the classroom studying over the different uses and combinations of Duskstones and matching them to signals on his Raeller Counter were rewarded the day he held his belt buckle for the first time.

Above Jeremiah, ash rained through the spirits as they fell upon him, hungry for the lifeforce that had so long been denied to them. Their faces were masks of venom and insatiable thirst. Jeremiah thought it a grim irony that he would die in the shadow of his former home—so close, yet so far. With the zam-zam pressing down on his heart and the last fragments of sensation leaving his left hand, Jeremiah's fingers wandered to the cerulean Duskstone implanted on the backside of the belt buckle which powered its protective shield. His fingers plucked the Duskstone from the belt buckle, just as he had seen Sundown do a lifetime ago. The stone was cool to the touch, and he let it roll into his palm, tumbling across the inert lines of scarlet power that once held the dead at bay.

The specters let out a collective shriek as Jeremiah Blade used the last of his strength to crush the cerulean Duskstone into a fine, arcane dust. The energy from the blue stone drifted into the dull lines of power on his palms and rekindled the arcane light in a blaze of magical power. A deep indigo light flared brightly from Jeremiah's palm and bloomed in all directions, shredding the malevolent ghosts as it rippled across the Grey Wastes. Jeremiah's muscles now responded to his call, and he quickly rose to his boots, holding his left hand aloft as an oily indigo fire pulsed into the bleak surroundings.

Arcane energy raced through his body, banishing the remnants of gripping paralysis that wracked his thin frame. Dark flames dripped through Jeremiah's clenched fist as the combined arcane power of the two Dusktones radiated outwards through Grey Wastes. Jeremiah remembered his lessons from a lifetime ago; combining Duskstones led to unique, terrible, and unpredictable powers, and only the highest-ranking Arbiters were allowed to conduct such experiments. Others, like the Gnomish Klinkhammers, created legendary weapons and armor by combining Duskstones. But, Klinkhammer smiths trained for decades to craft such powerful artifacts. Judging by the resulting power that now coursed through his veins, he understood the terrible destruction it could cause.

The frenzied wraiths, furious that their feast was ripped from their pale lips, encircled the lone light of life in a mad attempt to break through the blinding indigo fire. Every time a specter tried to pierce the dark flames, they were incinerated and their memories were wiped from existence. Jeremiah spied the ghost that had paraded under the guise of his old Nai Nai, its wispy frame twisted and grotesque against the falling ash. Jeremiah's features contorted into a hard grimace as the once-crimson lines of energy on his left palm now ran a dark, oily indigo like liquid midnight.

The shrieking specter swelled to gigantic proportions and dove towards Jeremiah. He could see its dead, hateful eyes filled with jealousy of the living. He held back the power long enough for the spirit to come within an arm's length, its spectral claws sharp and reaching. Jeremiah, anger boiling beneath his dark eyes, clenched his fist, and the swirling power expanded outward, consuming the wraith in a violent arcane cyclone. The ghost evaporated, and a gulf of silence fell upon the Grey Wastes.

As the dead vanished from sight, Jeremiah's adrenaline melted from his veins, and the energy in his palm dimmed to a dark purple. For a long, tense moment, he strained his ears against the shadows, waiting for the specters to make another assault. The relentless, buzzing chorus of the spirits had stopped, and all Jeremiah could hear was the thudding of his heart against the heavy gravity of the zam-zam in his chest pocket. When the danger seemed to have passed, he dropped the last of the arcane power and stood abandoned and adrift in a sea of grey. Jeremiah Blade cut a solitary figure against the expansive fog.

Jeremiah peered through the murk and spied a feature of the Alathanian landscape he missed before—a looming, gilded gate featuring a symbol of a sword running down the spine of an open book. Jeremiah blinked to make sure it wasn't another form of otherworldly trickery. He realized what he found once he spied the words "Analyze, Arbitrate, Adjudicate" written above the gate in the old Alathanian script. Here it was, or, at least, a half-remembered mirror image of the real thing—the Alathanian Marshal Academy. A great portion of his young life had been spent in the libraries, training yards, and classrooms behind these walls. Jeremiah thought about all the friends he made and the lessons he learned at the Academy. Those lessons had served him well in his travels and had saved his life on multiple occasions. However, the fervor instilled in him at the Academy had also almost gotten him killed on multiple occasions. Jeremiah remembered the danger he blindly walked into on his first day in Dryftwood—the enemies he made and the lives that would ultimately end by his actions. Everything started here.

On the day he passed under this gilded gate and into the wider world, Jeremiah could never have imagined the circumstances that would lead him back to these letters. After he left Alathane, he would daydream of returning to the city as a celebrated hero—an Alathanian Marshal that had made the world safer for everyone. Jeremiah even thought of the parade they would throw for him as his name was sung alongside legendary Alathanian Marshals like Godwin Malmont or Sundown. Now, after everything that transpired in the Shattered Hills, there would be no parade for Jeremiah Blade now, or ever.

Here, lost in the spirit world, Jeremiah wondered what he would find behind the book-and-blade emblem on the gate. Would the old library still be as dusty? Would the training yard still be filled with wide-eyed trainees? Would Arbiters still stroll along the shaded lanes and cloistered halls while discussing the finer, arcane points of Duskstone use? The marble walls loomed over him, calling him back through time.

Jeremiah could see a seam of golden light peak from underneath the massive gate. The warm light ran the length of the cobblestones towards where his tarnished Alathanian Marshal belt buckle sat next to his cooling longsword. Despite the light seeping from underneath the Academy gate, the once-brilliant sheen of the book-and-blade symbol looked dull, faded, and forgotten. Now that the cerulean Duskstone had been removed, it was just a piece of metal with an abandoned symbol on its face.

Jeremiah thought of all the Alathanian Marshals who had worn the belt buckle—Alban Monroe, Sundown, Chief Marshal Godwin Malmont, his grandfather, father, brothers, teachers, and classmates. The Alathanian Marshals no longer existed thanks to Jeremiah. He thought of what the book-and-blade represented to Alathane and all of Westhold. So many luminaries had passed under the creed of the marshals. Now, none would look up and admire these three words and what they stood for. The Alathanian Marshals were dead and gone. For Jeremiah Blade, there was only one path upon which to walk.

Jeremiah picked up his longsword, sheathed it, and took a long look at the marshal belt buckle. In his chest pocket, the zam-zam sat heavy, quiet, and reassuring. He then tipped his imaginary, long-lost hat to the piece of metal laying on the cobblestones and took off into the mists.

CHAPTER 25

Jeremiah had no idea how long he wandered the streets of Alathane. The back alleys, whitewashed cottages, and leafy parks started to blend together as Jeremiah's hollow boot steps echoed throughout the city. He tried to find his way out, but he kept getting turned around and circling back on his old trail. His guard was up—at a moment's notice, he could summon the oily indigo flames that protected him from the dead—and he was determined not to be seduced by the nostalgic, rose-tinted view of his childhood again. So, Jeremiah Blade marched on, aware that getting lost and wandering the Grey Wastes for all eternity was a clearer possibility with every passing step.

The normal markers of travel and time—weariness, hunger, thirst—had no place in the world of the dead. The only way Jeremiah knew he was getting anywhere was the Alathanian cobblestones passing beneath his boots. He had no idea how he would find Ophelia, Lukas, and Breaker Calhoun, and he began to wonder if he had, in fact, survived the battle with the specters. Perhaps, he was now doomed to roam the realm of the dead like the spirits that followed him like flies in the summer.

Jeremiah visited his old haunts, searching for sparks of ancient memories in hopes they could somehow lead him through the mists. Though he could not reckon how long he wandered, he eventually rediscovered a memory locked deep within his past—the Blade family estate. The land here was brighter and clearer, though Jeremiah made sure to keep his eyes sharp for any more illusions from the dead. He followed the footpaths he created with his brothers as a child, stepping through orchards and gardens that shone despite the oppressive circumstances. The apples above his head were a delicate pink-red and looked appetizing enough to pull off the tree and eat right then and there. Jeremiah remembered climbing up as a child and plucking apples from the branches of these very same trees.

As Jeremiah Blade made his way through the orchards, he came upon his grandma's old greenhouse, a vivid place he spent many summers playing in and hiding from his parents and minders. The structure was long and elegant, and, from the outside, he could see the rows of strange plants his family had imported from far-flung locales around Westhold like the tropical Gnomish Islands and the muggy Swamp Elf Delta. The building had rounded glass angled to maximize the light and heat of the sun, which was useless now in this bleak land. He could still remember the blast of heat and the fragrant tendrils of exotic plants as he entered the humid greenhouse all those years ago. In the world of the living, plants of all shapes and sizes populated the glass enclosure—broad, leafy bastards and narrow, delicate greens destined for a noble's table filled every spare corner in the greenhouse in addition to the hundred varieties of plump fruit that clung desperately to branch and bush. He recalled the awe he felt at the sheer bounty the world had to offer.

This time, however, no such richness greeted him as he opened the glass door and stepped through the yawning portal; the dead had claimed this lonely structure that had been once so full of life. Deep purple plants, snaking vines, and thick fruit were still there, but, now, as he moved deeper into the enclosure, there was only an absence of climate and vitality, a vague, grim mockery of the vibrancy the hall held in the realm of the living. Muted flowers around him reached towards the non-existent sun. It was just as Jeremiah remembered, all except the soulless, haunted visage that had replaced the life and radiance of the greenhouse. Jeremiah steeled himself—if his understanding of the world of the dead was correct, he would find her here.

"Grandma Blade?" Jeremiah called out softly, though his voice sounded oddly detached from his form. "Grandma? Are you there?"

Silence peeked around the fruit, flowers, and plants to glare at the intruder. Jeremiah had kept his newly-created arcane ward up in case the spirits tried to entrap him again, but now he lowered it in the hopes of finding the soul of his grandma. Outside, a low, pitiful howl echoed through the Grey Wastes. Inside, nothing moved or breathed—unlike the world of the living, there were no flies or other insects looking here and there for a nip of nectar. Jeremiah never thought he would see such a fecund realm so devoid of life. A creeping sense of uncertainty made its way up his spine; Jeremiah was starting to regret this as a fool's errand.

"Grandma Blade," Jeremiah called out into the vast stillness again, not entirely sure he wanted anything to answer. "Grandma, are you there? It's me, Jeremiah. I came to see the sugargrass flowers bloom. They're beautiful, just like you said."

There was no answer, so Jeremiah turned to exit the greenhouse when suddenly the apparition appeared inches from his face. His heart stopped and did not resume until he realized whose ancient features he looked upon. Sir Gerald of House Blade, High Count of Alathane, and Jeremiah's grandfather, stood before his very eyes.

Gerald Blade seemed shorter than Jeremiah remembered, or, possibly, Jeremiah had grown since the last time he had seen the old man. Even though the mists distorted his grandfather's form, he could still see the balding head, neatly trimmed beard, and drooping ears as clearly as he did in his memories. The ghost floated there as rigid as a board, his shoulders back and chin up, and the once-rich brown eyes were now dulled by the Grey Wastes. Despite the oppressive setting, not to mention being dead, Gerald Blade still commanded the aura of authority that had sustained him in a fruitful and prestigious life in the court of Alathane. The ghost said nothing, content with hovering in front of his grandson with a grim, dour countenance. There was no joy reflected in the eyes of the spirit at the reunion. Jeremiah hesitated, unsure of whether the specter had malevolent intentions; he squeezed his fist, ready to summon the arcane flames at a moment's notice.

"Jeremiah, fancy meeting you 'round these parts," cackled a hollow, elegant voice. "I thought we left you for the living."

Jeremiah Blade turned and came face-to-face with his grandma, Lady Estelle Blade. Even though her incorporeal form shifted and faded with the hazy surroundings, Lady Blade still looked radiant and vivacious, a testament to her indefatigable optimism. Her neatly-coifed, blinding white hair sat perched on her head like a sleeping owl, and her clothes echoed the latest in Alathanian fashion from the time she passed from life to death. A bright smile snuck across her wrinkled, ethereal features. In death, as in life, Grandma Blade proved to be the antithesis of her taciturn husband.

"I see you finally got some stubble on that chin of yours, Jeremiah," Estelle Blade laughed into the void, the sound distorted but cheerful. "Grandpa said it would never come. But I knew it would. Grandma always knows best. Isn't that right, Gerald?"

The spirit of Jeremiah's grandfather said nothing in response and hovered quietly, observing his grandson. The ghost's eyes seemed to pass right through the lone light of life standing before him. The stern features never wavered; not even death could dim his grandfather's adherence to order and discipline. When his grandfather was alive, Jeremiah was equal parts awed and terrified by Gerald Blade—the old man brooked no dissent and expected all of his family members to fall in line with his demands. When Jeremiah was younger, he never gave much thought to his grandparents' wildly differing personalities and how they stayed together, but he imagined it could not have been easy for his gregarious and free-wheeling grandma to stay married to someone as unyielding as Gerald Blade.

"Don't mind grandpa, darling," Jeremiah's grandma cooed softly. "Being dead hasn't changed that crabby mood of his. You'd think being a ghost would take some of that starch out of his pants. Hehehehe."

Lady Estelle's high-pitched laugh was just as spirited as it had been in life. Jeremiah smiled in spite of the strange and dire circumstances; it was good to hear grandma's laughter again.

"Thanks grandma," Jeremiah responded shyly, reflexively returning to his adolescent self. He thought it absurd how he quickly reverted to his childhood—he had killed and fought in countless battles—but Grandma Blade's presence provided him a comfort he had not felt in many years. "I'm glad to see death hasn't changed you much. That gives my weary mind some comfort. I honestly didn't know if you would be here."

"You were always a clever boy, Jeremiah," Grandma Blade laughed as she glided towards her long-dead husband. "That said, I didn't think anyone would be clever enough to find a way into the realm of the dead without, you know, dying. How did you get here?"

"A Hoodoux Witch," Jeremiah answered quietly. "Ophelia Delphine, Hoodoux Queen, to be exact. Well, I guess she just gave herself that title, but, regardless, she is a traveling companion of mine. I don't suppose you've seen her roaming around here recently? She doesn't have any boots on, if that helps."

"I can't say that I have, darling," Grandma Blade responded, her hazy green eyes sympathetic. "As you might imagine, we don't get many visitors around here and, if we do, they are usually quite dead. But, I can feel their flames burning bright, just like yours, and that's a dangerous thing, my darling."

Jeremiah nodded, the memory of his brush with death still fresh in his mind. The living must be like lighthouses for the dead.

"Things have been strange here, recently," Lady Estelle continued. "There is an unrest here, among the spirits. Maybe that's why you are here, Jeremiah. You were always trying to impress your brothers and old stick-in-the-mud over there."

"Actually, the witch and I came here to find a friend," Jeremiah explained, though his attention turned to the ethereal form of his looming grandfather who was wafting closer to Jeremiah's thin frame. His grandfather bore into Jeremiah with an increasingly hateful glare—something that resembled a base, feral hunger. "Someone I lost when in I was in the Shattered Hills. My actions led to her death as well as the death of many more."

"So, you didn't fight your way through damnation and high water to see your old grandma?" Grandma Blade giggled maniacally, her ephemeral outline shaking against the backdrop of a thousand exotic flowers. "I'm hurt, Jeremiah. Is this 'someone' your girlfriend? Hehehehe."

Jeremiah's face flushed a bright scarlet. He couldn't believe, here in the land of the dead, his sudden prudishness.

"She's not my girlfriend, grandma," Jeremiah stammered, his cheeks warming. "Or she wasn't. I mean, she never was."

"That's a shame, darling," Grandma Blade retorted with a gleeful cackle. "All my friends at court thought you were a very cute young man, hehehehe."

A horrific shriek interrupted their repartee as the dull brown eyes of Gerald Blade flared with a lavender light and a sudden fury. The spirit lunged at Jeremiah, hungry for the flame of life. Jeremiah had just enough time to clench his fist and summon the indigo flames that protected him from the dead. Both Grandma and Grandfather Blade reared back in terror at the protective arcane energy. The ghost of Gerald Blade tried again, searching and snapping at any breach in the magical ward but found the flames too dangerous to tempt.

Grandfather Blade fled skyward, through the glass enclosure, and into the infinite grey haze beyond. Jeremiah quickly turned his attention to his grandma, his battle training taking over any nostalgic, familial feelings. An immense sense of guilt washed through Jeremiah as he kept a wary eye on the specter of Lady Blade. The ghost floated there, her green eyes and long face pained.

"He hasn't been feeling himself lately," Estelle Blade explained to her grandson. "I know he was always a little grim, but he could be quite sweet and thoughtful when it was just the two of us. It's tough being dead. You lose a little bit of yourself every day. If we counted days. He is barely the person I remember him being. Our memories are fading, though his faster than mine. I suppose that's what we are waiting on here, to forget and be forgotten."

"Grandma, my guide spoke of a tear or a rift in the Grey Wastes," Jeremiah said as he surveyed the expansive greenhouse, keeping a wary eye out for his vengeful grandfather. "Something, she says, is wrong here, and all the spirits are suffering for it."

The ghost of Grandma Blade hovered a few feet off the ground, her vivid green eyes searching the face of her grandson. Though her spirit knew no need for rest, Estelle Blade suddenly seemed weary.

"Something is wrong here, I agree," Estelle Blade started slowly, her words edged with a slight metallic grate. "I don't want to worry you, dear, but now there is a foulness in the Grey Wastes. A poison now haunts this land, feeding the mindless hunger of the dead. We are turning into insatiable monsters, Jeremiah. There is a power here that I have never seen before. It is like we wander the desert, delirious from thirst."

The words hung uncomfortably in the void. If Ophelia was to be believed, a tear had grown between the land of the living and the dead, and that must be what his grandma was describing. Jeremiah had no knowledge of anything that could cause such a rift, despite his education and experience. He had seen the terrible power of the Arkstone laid bare and remembered all the lessons he learned at the Academy, but he had never heard of any magic that could tear the seal between the world of the living and the dead.

"The dead don't often feel fear," Estelle Blade continued, though her words were becoming distorted and raw. "But this is unnatural, Jeremiah.

Every spirit hopes to stay bright in living memory, but we are losing ourselves and turning into beasts."

The ghost of Estelle Blade drifted through the glass of the greenhouse and into the wider, greyer world beyond, forcing Jeremiah to chase after the wayward spirit. He stepped out of the greenhouse and onto the soft, rolling fields of the Blade estate. His grandma floated above him, her outline blurring with the surrounding haze.

"What can I do?" Jeremiah called towards the receding spirit. "Do you know where this disturbance is coming from?"

"I don't, darling," Grandma Blade said, fading further into the mists. "But I can show you the way to your little friends. As you might imagine, there aren't many living souls wandering around here. You all stand out like a church's bell tower."

The ghost swept her arm wide, and a bright white line appeared on the soft grass at Jeremiah's boots. It looked like a lightning bolt painted on the ground and ran unbroken as far as Jeremiah could see.

"Follow this to your friends, Jeremiah," Estelle Blade cooed to her beloved grandson. "You might even find your girlfriend, too. I hope you do. I always knew you'd grow up to be a ladykiller, Jeremiah."

Jeremiah looked at the blinding, serrated line speeding off into the gloom. He couldn't tell where it went, but it was his best way back to his companions and the land of the living. He turned his attention back to the ghost of his grandma. Estelle Blade floated there effortlessly and smiled at her grandson.

"I miss you and grandfather," Jeremiah said suddenly as hot tears snuck into his eyes. He felt like he was a child again and leaving his grandparent's estate after a fun weekend. Jeremiah hadn't felt this way in years. Nostalgia overwhelmed him. "I don't want you to disappear, grandma."

"Then don't forget us, darling," Grandma Blade answered softly as she faded into the ether.

CHAPTER 26

Jeremiah followed the bright, jagged line for a lifetime. He dared not stray from the line for fear of losing it and becoming stranded in the mists again. So, whether it was the rolling hills of the Blade estate, the high walls of the city of Alathane, or the rows of tall crops encircling outlying farmhouses, Jeremiah stuck to the light no matter where it led.

Jeremiah kept the ward of oily indigo flames surrounding his lonely frame in case his lifeforce proved too tempting to a hungry specter. The realm of the dead was starting to break down the young outlaw. An insidious weariness, not from want of sleep, but a dulling of the senses, crept through Jeremiah as he waded through the gloom. He had no idea how long he had been in the realm of the dead, but he feared the longer he wandered, the more severe the toll on his mind would be. There were no good choices laid out before him—the only way out was to find Ophelia, and the only way to find Ophelia was to follow the radiant line towards salvation.

The rolling plains and farmlands that surrounded Alathane eventually gave way to scrubby coastal flats. The tough, yellow grass crunched beneath Jeremiah's boots, and he was forced to fight his way through towering phalanxes of sharp pampas bushes. If the Grey Wastes mirrored the realm of the living, Jeremiah figured he was moving south from Alathane past the hamlet of Harrowdale and towards the coast of the Crystal Gulf, the body of water between the mainland of Westhold and the Gnomish Islands. He had never been to this part of the world—he had heard it was full of pirates, rogues, and other questionable company—but he reckoned from his geographical studies that this was the land west of the Swamp Elf Delta.

A light drizzle started to fall through the haze. Jeremiah looked at the grey soup above him in amazement; Ophelia never mentioned anything about weather patterns in the realm of the dead. The Grey Wastes were a shade of Westhold, a shadow that existed alongside the world, but not subject to the whims of the mortal realm. The rain made Jeremiah feel alive, a strange and alien feeling in the land of the dead.

As Jeremiah walked, the rain turned from a drizzle to an intermittent torrent. The coastal marshes that surrounded the Crystal Gulf were legendary in the land of the living for their downpours, and now it seemed to have seeped into the realm of the dead. The tempest drenched Jeremiah, soaking straight through his boots; safe from spirits, he mused, but not from the rain.

Jeremiah sloshed through the growing sheets of water until his ears picked up a curious change in pitch from the constant choir of buzzing ghosts. A rising wind grew alongside the spectral drone; the first time Jeremiah had felt the breeze since entering the other side. The mists swirled around Jeremiah as he fought through the growing gale, and the worsening conditions made it difficult for him to follow the illuminated trail. A peal of thunder ripped across the grey landscape, drawing Jeremiah's attention forward, and he picked up his pace towards the deafening sound. The coastal grass bent under boot, and, as Jeremiah ran towards the source of the thunder, he whipped the indigo flames around his person into a heady froth. The fire and the rain twisted together into thin columns of streaking steam.

As Jeremiah plowed through a salty coastal pond, he heard a strange sound—the cries of the living. Ahead, the mists parted, and he saw a burst of tangerine light spark across the air. A string of foul words dressed in a thick Dryftwood accent skipped across the coastal marshes, and Jeremiah realized that the jagged white line had finally come to an end. In death, as in life, Grandma Blade had led him true—he had found his companions. He was equal parts elated and horrified as he broke through the haze and laid eyes on the violent contest in front of him.

A shade of a gigantic, winged serpent coiled in the sky above Jeremiah's hatless head, and its pitch-black eyes peered down on the three mortal shells known as Lukas Sing-Low, Breaker Calhoun, and Ophelia Delphine. Breaker Calhoun was struggling to his feet as a host of opportunistic wraiths buzzed around him. Lukas Sing-Low's talisman glowed a bright shade of orange as sickles of arcane energy formed around him. Ophelia Delphine launched crackling green bolts of magic towards the colossal, looming shade while Woodroux snapped valiantly at incoming specters.

The monster soared on the gusts of the storm, its dull yellow scales shifting from ephemeral to solid with every beat of its massive, multi-colored, feathery wings. Jeremiah stood momentarily stunned at the sight of the massive beast; there were no creatures like this in Westhold. Legends and myths told of monsters that stalked the primordial lands that would become home to the Five Civilizations, but they had passed from living memory for ages.

Jeremiah remembered back to his days pouring over texts in the Academy library and finding an ancient tome of legendary stories that he assumed at the time were fictional. The soaring serpent resembled the description of the Semby, a giant winged ancestor of modern-day winders that had roamed the coastal plains for food, terrorized early Swamp Elf settlements, and played an important role in early Hoodoux spiritual practice. Everything Jeremiah had read stated that the beast had never existed, that it was a work of early imagination. The creature's presence in the realm of the dead proved otherwise.

The Semby's snapping, serrated teeth soared towards Ophelia as she held the scarlet etchings on her palm aloft in defense. The monster phased in and out of existence, its scales at one moment a faded yellow and a shimmering sunflower the next. The creature reared up, its body arching against the thundering sky and brought its heavy corporeal tail whipsawing into Ophelia. The scarlet Duskstone ward offered no protection against the solid aspect of the beast, and Ophelia was sent flying through the raging storm from the impact, her tattered dress fluttering behind her like a snapping flag. She sailed over Jeremiah's head and into a salty, coastal pond.

Two dozen wraiths streaked across lashing sheets of rain and dove into the pool after the living interloper. Jeremiah drew his blazing longsword, followed after the hungry specters, and plunged into the salty water while summoning up a wall of oily indigo fire. The dead screeched as the dark flames engulfed them and wiped them from existence. Spectral fire danced across the surface of the pool, giving Jeremiah enough time to search for Ophelia. His sword hissed furiously as he swam through the brine.

Jeremiah saw Ophelia near the bottom of the pool, her long, dark hair wafting expansively behind her. She seemed asleep, almost peaceful, as she floated in the salt water. Woodroux curled loosely around Ophelia's thin arm, as numbed from the mighty blow as she was. Above them, the indigo fires flickered, and, beyond that, the shadow of the Semby played along the edges of their watery world. Jeremiah swam towards Ophelia and gently lifted her upwards. Her eyes immediately snapped open and shone with an otherworldly light—the same color and intensity as the iridescent tattoos lining her cheeks.

Jeremiah and Ophelia stared at each other through the distorted angles of the salty pool. Ophelia Delphine flashed a toothy smile to her once-lost companion and rose to the surface, leaving Jeremiah behind as his blade boiled the water around him. He watched her slip through the spectral flames and back into the fray. All she left behind was Woodrow, his curious eyes glittering in the water. Jeremiah held out his hand, and the familiar quickly curled around Jeremiah's right forearm in a tight coil. With the winder securely in place, Jeremiah followed after Ophelia, his boots weighing him down as he broke through the surface.

Jeremiah waded through the pond to dry land as a chaotic scene unfolded in front of him. The Semby corkscrewed on the wind currents, snarling at the diminutive figure of Lukas Sing-Low summoning bright sickles of light in the air around him. Breaker Calhoun defended Lukas from a host of wraiths, attacking and trapping them in the bone-white prisons of his twin hatchets. Though staunch, the pair was quickly becoming overwhelmed by the shade of the ancient beast and a host of opportunistic ghosts. Ophelia Delphine, ensconced in a protective cocoon of iridescent magic, soared towards the Semby, while Jeremiah, earthbound, trudged towards the heart of the battle to aid his long-lost companions as Woodroux urged him forward into the fray.

"Fancy meeting you 'round these parts!" Breaker Calhoun shouted over the ruckus as he cut through two spirits circling Lukas Sing-Low. Dozens of malevolent wraiths writhed in the bounty hunter's bone-white hatchets. "We thought you'd run off to look for your girlfriend!"

Jeremiah ignored the irreverent bounty hunter and focused on blanketing the coastal marsh with oily indigo flames. The swarm of spirits paused momentarily, wary of the magic. The scarlet etchings on the left palms of the three other living companions served as an admirable defense, but the crackling indigo energy that cascaded from Jeremiah's clenched fist was a far more potent source of magic. The combination of the cerulean stone that had powered the Alathanian Marshal belt buckle and the magic provided by the mysterious Abbess proved to be a grave danger to the dead. The seeking flames consumed any spirit that veered too close and soon created enough room for Lukas Sing-Low and Breaker Calhoun to catch their breath from the incessant attacks.

Above the three companions, devastation mingled with the falling sheets of rain. Ophelia Delphine, her full, terrible power on display, sailed towards the Semby writhing among the lightning bolts. The legendary creature still phased in and out of corporeality as if it was torn between worlds. For a brief moment, the witch and the monster hung suspended in the sky, their silhouettes illuminated by every fork of serrated light. The Semby bared a maw of razor-sharp fangs that glistened hatefully in the storm as they stared at each other like duelists underneath an oppressive noon sun. Ophelia hovered there, all might and fury, as wispy green smoke dripped from her clawed hands.

Thunder cracked the sky to signal the start of the duel between the witch and the ancient beast.

CHAPTER 27

Against the backdrop of a raging storm, the Semby snaked towards Ophelia Delphine, with the hurricane gusts of wind from the beast's giant wings nearly sending Jeremiah Blade, Lukas Sing-Low, and Breaker Calhoun flying across the coastal scrub. Ophelia responded by co-opting a bolt of lightning, infusing it with a sickly green light, and hurling it towards the beast. The physical aspects of the Semby shuddered and recoiled from the attack, but it still retained enough etherealness and momentum to bring its snapping jaws down on Ophelia Delphine.

Ophelia Delphine deftly slipped away from the gnashing maw and brought a clawed hand ripping down the side of the beast, leaving behind a trail of dark blue blood against the sunflower-yellow scales. The Semby whipsawed and, this time, caught the dexterous witch between rows of gleaming, corporal teeth. Immediately, defensive magic radiated outwards from the identical lines of arcane tattoos from under Ophelia's emerald eyes. The swirl of scarlet and green protected Ophelia from evisceration, but the Semby still held her firmly in its grasp, and she struggled to break free.

The entire realm of the dead slowed to gawk at the battle raging in the storm-wracked skies. Ophelia's three companions stared up in amazement, both at the terrible power that she wielded and the mythical creature spiraling through the raging tempest.

Ophelia, firmly lodged in the Semby's jaws, couldn't bring her hands around to summon another spell; all she could do was keep her wards up as the monster shook the flame of life out of her. Jeremiah, sensing an opportunity, focused his mental energy towards coiling the oily indigo flames into a tight, twisting column that raced towards the gigantic creature. The hungry flames lanced across the sky and engulfed the Semby, causing it to thrash furiously as the incorporeal parts of its body withered under the magical fire. The creature let go of Ophelia with a violent shake of its serpentine head, and she pinwheeled through the dark sky.

Pressing the advantage, Lukas Sing-Low, his melodic voice filling the air, sent searing sickles of tangerine light cutting through the storm and screaming towards the beast. The arcane light cut through the flesh of the beast, and it screeched violently under the dual threats to both aspects of its being.

The Semby would not be so easily felled, however. The flying serpent twisted suddenly and nosedived towards Jeremiah and Lukas as lightning rippled off its yellow scales. Lukas barely had enough time to scramble out of the way as the colossal beast plowed head-first into the coastal earth, sending a massive shockwave through the ground. Both Jeremiah and Lukas flipped ass-over-teakettle, with Jeremiah sprawling out on the rough grass and Lukas falling into a coastal pool. As the coil of the Semby's body followed its head to earth, it crash-landed directly on top of the pond that held Lukas Sing-Low with a thunderous smack.

Breaker Calhoun, for all of his jeering irreverence, was afraid of no man, beast, nor bug. He leaped onto the downed Semby with his twin hatchets flashing in the wild storm. Dark blue blood sprayed around the bounty hunter as he searched for the fleshiest part of the beast. The Semby writhed and thrashed and, with each gesticulation, destroyed the marshy ground around the pool. The beast regained its balance and sent the pesky Breaker Calhoun soaring through the gloom with a powerful snap of its body. The monster then hauled its massive, rippling girth skyward.

Jeremiah sprinted across the coastal flats and leaped on the back of the Semby before it could leave the earth forever. Grabbing the underside of one of the solid, yellow scales with his offhand wreathed in dark flames, Jeremiah tried to jam his sweltering longsword into the beast's flesh, but the Semby whipped like a bucking bronco as it soared towards the heavens, forcing him and Woodroux, still tightly coiled around his forearm, to hold on for dear life.

A sickly, green lightning bolt split the sky, stunning the Semby, leaving it suspended momentarily above the hazy void. Ophelia Delphine soared towards the floating monster with rippling waves of arcane energy flowing behind her and crashed headfirst into the ancient creature like an emerald comet. The creature shuddered, stalled, and drifted downwards to the coastal marshes below them.

Jeremiah took the advantage and sprinted along the length of the Semby, jumping from one corporeal patch of flesh to another, his boots pounding along the hard yellow scales. Grasping his molten longsword with both hands, Jeremiah sent the oily indigo flames racing along the length of the blade. The sword, already blistering with the heat of a furious dust storm, threw a sharp halo of arcane light across the marshlands. As Jeremiah reached the base of the serpent's head, the Semby popped unexpectedly, sending him into the air. However, the outlaw's momentum kept him moving forward and, as he started to tumble back to earth, he brought the bright edge through the base of the creature's skull. The sword slid through scale and bone, the boiling blade burning through the beast's flesh-and-blood existence, while the oily indigo flames raced along the monster's coiling form, burning away the ethereal light.

Whatever invisible threads that kept the Semby together dissolved, and fleshy chunks of the creature fell to earth like a meteor shower. Jeremiah felt gravity take hold and he flailed wildly for anything to arrest his fall. His sword, which had served him so well for so long, slipped from his grasp and pinwheeled through the lavender-grey sky around them.

Ophelia Delphine, her black hair splayed wildly behind her, swooped to pluck the wingless Jeremiah Blade out of his free fall. Ophelia's bony fingers wrapped tightly around Jeremiah's boot as he watched, upside-down, his Alathanian longsword thunder to earth like a spear of blinding sunlight. The sword cratered into the coastal flats, business-end downwards, mere feet from the awe-struck Breaker Calhoun. The blade stood there among the rough grass like a monument to a fallen hero.

Jeremiah hung there by his boot, facing the grey expanse of scrubland below, as Ophelia lowered him and Woodroux through the storm and next to the panting Breaker Calhoun. Ophelia Delphine, Woodroux, and Breaker Calhoun hurried over to the ruined pond as Jeremiah brought the oily indigo flames up in a wide barrier, keeping the remaining ghosts at bay. Together, they gazed down at the floating form of Lukas Sing-Low nestled in the mud and salt water.

Lukas Sing-Low laid motionless, his body bent and twisted at gruesome angles. Lukas' face was swelling quickly, with purple splotches growing under each eye and a stream of blood running from his significant nose. The tangerine-colored artifact bit deep into his fleshy throat, pooling blood into the divot in his neck.

"He's still breathing," Breaker Calhoun called out as he dropped to his hands and knees. "Don't know for how much longer, though. Lukas, can you hear us?"

Lukas Sing-Low's chest was rising and falling in shallow, irregular intervals. Jeremiah and Breaker Calhoun gingerly lifted Lukas out of the briny coastal earth, and melodic grunts of pain rumbled from the Island Gnome's lungs, providing proof that his spirit still lingered in his mortal frame. The pair placed him as tenderly as they could among the crunchy grass. Outside the ward of oily indigo flames, ghosts peered in at the scene, either curious or hungry.

Ophelia Delphine dropped down to one knee to examine the damage. The scarlet etchings on Lukas' hand protected him from the spirits, but not the weight of a long-dead, half-resurrected, giant sky winder. A tormented grimace crept to the edges of Lukas Sing-Low's mouth.

"Do you think he will make it?" Jeremiah asked Ophelia as he kept a wary eye on the spirits outside his magical ward. "Can you heal him?"

"Don't know, cher," Ophelia responded as she looked over Lukas Sing-Low's shattered body. "I ain't one of those fancy priests yall got in Alathane. Hoodoux focuses on the dead, not the dying. Lukas, you going to make it?"

Lukas Sing-Low looked up, his dazed eyes focusing on Ophelia. He was still in shock from having the equivalent of a castle wall fall on him, but he grasped at the salty grass and focused on forming a coherent sentence.

"I ain't gone yet," Lukas Sing-Low whispered as blood seeped from the corners of his lips. The crescent moon Duskstone on his throat glowed a valiant orange in the falling rain. "I still got some fire in me. Yall can't get rid of me that easy."

"What happens if he dies here, witch?" Breaker Calhoun asked bluntly. "He becomes a ghost, right?"

"Not sure, cher," Ophelia conceded as she dug through one of her pockets and pulled out a sewn burlap bag in the shape of a five-point star. She shook the zam-zam over the prostrate Lukas Sing-Low and hummed deep and low. "The spirits might feast on what's left of his mortal shell, and he would join them in short order. It would be an unnatural death, I presume, one where he does not truly belong to the dead or the living."

"Is that hocus-pocus going to stop him from dying?" Breaker Calhoun asked incredulously, despite the fact that he had just seen the witch fly around and command lightning bolts to do her bidding. "Or is Jeremiah, freshly back from the dead himself it looks like, going to have to haul him around on his back the rest of the way?"

Jeremiah looked at the charcoal-colored burlap charm and once again felt the gravity of his zam-zam against his chest. He thought about his own brush with death and hoped that whatever magic, real or imagined, the charm possessed would keep Lukas Sing-Low from a grisly fate.

"If he lives, it's up to him," Ophelia answered, her words crisp in the rain. "I wasn't expecting we would run into something like the Semby here, and certainly not in the flesh. I can ease his pain, soothe his spirit, but his fire is his own. I'm sorry, Lukas."

Lukas Sing-Low clenched his fists, trying to will movement into his limbs. He tried to move up to one elbow, but his arms gave out in a flash of pain, and he fell back onto the coastal grass.

Jeremiah looked through the rain and haze towards the multitude of grim, hollow faces that watched from outside his enchantment. They were primarily the spirits of Swamp Elves and Island Gnomes who once populated these coastal flats in the world of the living. Their features warped and morphed, occasionally taking on corporeality much like the Semby.

"How was that possible?" Jeremiah asked as the rain cascaded down his tanned features. "How was something like that able to become something of flesh and blood?"

"We are close, cher," Ophelia started as she shook the zam-zam over Lukas. The charm shushed rhythmically over the injured bard. "Close to the rift between worlds. The dead are swarming here to regain the spark of life denied to them for so long. The flame of life gives them form and substance. But it is twisting them, destroying their minds. We have to find the rift and close it all costs, or the two worlds will bleed together and set the dead against the living."

The words hung uneasily in the rain. Jeremiah slid his sword back into its sheath but kept the oily indigo flames up to push back the leering dead. He kicked at a stubborn patch of crunchy, yellow grass next to a chunk of the Semby.

"Do you know how to close it, witch?" Breaker Calhoun asked, his patience fraying, as he helped Lukas into a painful sitting position. "What happens if we run into something like that flying winder again? Are we going to hack our way through the entire damn land of the dead to do this? I get the feeling that we've been duped by this witch to come along on a fool's mission. Do you even know exactly where this tear is? Or are we just turning in circles waiting for a ghost to feast on our flesh?"

"I might be able to help with that, Calhoun," came a hollow voice from outside the dark flames.

The living all looked towards the sound of the voice. Jeremiah froze and he felt his words catch in his throat. The shade stood right outside the arcane fire, her slate-grey eyes bright and vivacious despite the oppressive circumstances.

"I know a thing or two about finding the right way," smiled Iron Eyes Ledoux.

CHAPTER 27

"It's good to see you, cousin!" Ophelia cackled as she popped up and waved to Iron Eyes Ledoux. The witch's aged features suddenly gave way to a girlish beauty that held back the unending dreariness of the Grey Wastes. "I was wondering if we were going to run into you 'round these parts. How long has it been? A lifetime? You've been busy, I see."

"I think the last time I saw you Ophi, I was barely grown," Iron Eyes Ledoux drawled out in her Dryftwood-inflected tones. "Ma and me came out to see you on the bayou before I ran off to the Shattered Hills. You pushed me into a mud pit and left me there for a whole afternoon, if I remember correctly. But, looking at things now, I probably should have stayed on the bayou with you."

"I wouldn't worry 'bout it too much, cher," Ophelia cooed quickly, trying to gloss over the memory of the mud pit incident. "We all end up here eventually."

"You always said that," Iron Eyes responded, though her slate-grey eyes remained locked on Jeremiah Blade. "I never thought it would happen so soon, though."

As the Swamp Elf cousins bantered back and forth, Jeremiah stood rooted to the coastal scrub, unable to speak. After many painful months recovering from his ordeal in the Shattered Hills, years of wandering to find Ophelia Delphine, and literally traveling to the realm of the dead, Jeremiah had finally found his lost trail companion, Lucille 'Iron Eyes' Ledoux. She was still dressed in the clothes she wore the day she died. The ghost came up so suddenly that everything he had thought up to tell her fled his mind. After all the years and countless rehearsals, Jeremiah Blade could think of nothing to say.

"Is that swamp thing?" Breaker Calhoun interjected, walking up to the edge of the spectral flames to get a better look at the shade. Calhoun placed his fists on his narrow waist, sending his sharp elbows akimbo. "Last time I saw you, you were smashing a jar over my head. You know, to tell the truth, I thought you had made it out alive that day, and hoss over here was crying over nothing. You seem to be doing alright, you know, despite being dead and all."

"If I had hit you a bit harder, like I intended," Iron Eyes chuckled. "You'd be here with me."

"You know, swamp thing," Breaker Calhoun retorted as he instinctively rubbed the back of his head. "I never held your violent tendencies against you. You were just doing what you had to do. I can understand that. I always thought you were alright, for what it's worth."

"That's high praise," Iron Eyes smirked, the antagonism they shared in life dissipating on account of one of them being dead. "Coming from the likes of Breaker Calhoun. You always knew how to sweet talk the ladies."

Breaker Calhoun adjusted his wide-brimmed ranching hat and stood almost embarrassed at the ghost's words, as much as it was possible for Breaker Calhoun to be embarrassed. He settled for a tip of his hat to Iron Eyes Ledoux. The shade nodded in response and turned her attention to her old riding companion.

"Jeremiah Blade," Iron Eyes called out with a sly smirk on her hazy features. "I hope you didn't come out all this way just to see me. Ophelia better have put you to work on something."

All eyes, living and dead, turned towards Jeremiah Blade, who stood awkwardly as a lightning bolt shattered the sky above them. Jeremiah still could not believe his eyes. He was afraid this was another trick of the dead to get him to drop the magical flames and doom them all.

Jeremiah suddenly felt years younger, back to the night before he left Alathane for good, unsure and tentative as he cast his gaze out west towards Dryftwood. He and Iron Eyes had met at a tavern that evening, finalizing the logistical details of their upcoming trip. Even at that point, their personality differences had begun to shine through—he had probably grated on Iron Eyes' nerves before they even left the gates of the city. But, through fire and tribulations, they had grown close, until she passed and left him behind for good.

Jeremiah knew he had a special opportunity—many do not get the chance to speak after the final goodbye has been said. Yet, he couldn't think of anything to say. The words were trapped in his throat, threatening to choke him. He took a step closer to the edge of the magical fire, summoning up the courage to speak.

"I..." Jeremiah Blade started, his head still swimming in the face of the surreal reality before him. The sound of his voice tumbled out, raw and heavy. "I...just wanted to say that I am sorry...for everything."

"What did I tell you, Jeremiah Blade," Iron Eyes scolded, exasperation shading her words despite the intervening years and events. "There ain't nothing to feel sorry for. I made my own decisions. I ended up here of my own accord. Don't you remember what I told you back there?"

"I know, but," Jeremiah stuttered, the words blocky and awkward in his mouth. "I insisted on investigating, on informing Alathane, on trying to find a peaceful resolution to everything, and it all backfired. You paid the iron price for it. I'm still on this side of the flames. It wasn't fair."

"You're telling a ghost it wasn't fair?" Iron Eyes asked, incredulous. "There ain't nothing but to move forward, Jeremiah. I'm gone from the world of the living and I had to move on when I got here. You don't forget, but you always move forward."

"How can you move forward?" Jeremiah retorted, suddenly feeling nervous and frantic. The pair couldn't help but fall into familiar patterns despite death itself. "You're stuck here in the land of the forgotten."

"She might not be trapped here for too much longer, cher," Ophelia interrupted before her cousin could berate the clueless outlaw. She shook her zam-zam and walked over to the pair. "If we don't find this tear between worlds, then the line between the living and dead will blur. We've already seen it with the Semby and the storm raging around us. The spirits will seep into the realm of the living and become whole again, with all the terrible ramifications that entails. There is a reason the dead and the living are kept separate."

"Ophelia is right, cher," Iron Eyes conceded as she floated softly outside the indigo fire. "The souls of the dead are flocking to the rift. The memories of everything that has ever lived now have a way back to the mortal world. Something has blown apart the seam that holds the worlds together, and now the dead are rushing towards the opening like water from a broken dam."

"Well, shitfire," Breaker Calhoun exclaimed. "I was afraid of that. You know what Moss told me before I left Dryftwood? He said, 'Calhoun, don't go get mixed up in some scheme where the dead are flooding into the land of the living through a magical tear between worlds. It's going to be nothing but trouble.' But did I listen? Sure as fire, I didn't."

"You know, cousin," Ophelia mused, ignoring the incessant complaining and running her bony fingers through her thick black hair. "I always thought you'd make a good Hoodoux Witch. You were so hard-headed, though. You were always talking about going to the Shattered Hills. Me and your ma could never understand what was so interesting about that place."

"I always thought talking to the dead was too spooky," Iron Eyes admitted as she lifted her ephemeral head towards the falling rain. "I guess the joke is on me now."

The grim irony brought the conversation to a halt. Only the pitter-patter of rain filled the void between the living and the dead. No one said anything for an agonizing moment until Iron Eyes broke the silence like a peal of thunder on the horizon.

"I can lead you there, cousin," Iron Eyes said as she moved as close to the indigo flames as she thought prudent. "But it will be more dangerous the closer we draw. As much as I enjoyed being alive, the unimaginable chance of reclaiming the flame of life is driving the spirits mad with hunger. Jeremiah Blade, I led you around in life, and I guess I'm doing it again in death. You're like stubborn old trail dust. There just ain't any way to get rid of you."

Jeremiah looked past the words frozen in the falling rain and towards the spirit of his long-gone riding companion. He wanted to run and hold her, as he had when she lay dying in the Arkstone cave, but he knew that would be impossible. They were careening towards something opaque and dangerous—Jeremiah doubted even Ophelia knew exactly what lay ahead of them—just as he and Iron Eyes had all those years ago. He could only guess at the terrible ramifications that lay beyond.

"Well, that's awfully sweet of you, cousin," Ophelia opined as she shook the zam-zam over Jeremiah Blade and Breaker Calhoun. "Your ma always told me you were a helpful child. In death, as in life."

"The closer to the rift, the more frenzied we become," Iron Eyes explained, her drawl just as pronounced as when she was alive. "I feel it myself. It's an insatiable hunger for the flame of life, something I never felt in life or in my time here in the Grey Wastes. The worlds are coming apart at the seams, Ophi."

Ophelia stood in the pouring rain, scratching an itch among her tangled curls. Lukas Sing-Low laid on the crunchy coastal plains, his breathing shallow as the rain pelted his aged features; occasionally, he would turn his greying head and spit out a splash of crimson red, whether blood or chewing weed spit, his companions did not venture to guess. Breaker Calhoun dug the heel of his boot into the salty mud, his sharp features illuminated against the occasional crack of lightning. Jeremiah's deep brown eyes watched the wavy outline of Iron Eyes Ledoux, of Lucille, blend into the grey haze around them. He thought about the intervening years and events since the two last saw each other.

"It's good to ride with you again, Lucille," Jeremiah said eventually, moving closer to the flames that separated them. "I never thought we would get another chance."

"I don't think you are going to like where we are going, Jeremiah Blade," Iron Eyes responded, her voice growing more distant and hollow as she hovered away from Jeremiah's magical protection. "It's not a place for the living or the dead."

"And just how long we got, swamp thing?" Breaker Calhoun interrupted, his boots wet and his patience thinning. "Where is this place exactly? I'm itching to get eaten alive by angry ghosts."

The spirit of Iron Eyes Ledoux turned to the opposite direction and stared off through the haze that shrouded the coastal marshes. A dull light glowed through the haze; Jeremiah first thought it to be the shadow of the indigo flames or the radiance of a dying lightning bolt, but the light persisted, muted and lavender on the horizon.

"It's out there," Iron Eyes responded, sweeping her ghostly arm through the sheets of rain. "On the shores of the Crystal Gulf."

CHAPTER 29

After some lively back-and-forth about who was going to carry the bruised and battered Lukas Sing-Low, Breaker Calhoun begrudgingly hefted the broken bard across his shoulders, causing Lukas to howl in pain.

"Don't expect me to carry you the whole way, short-stack," Breaker Calhoun complained as the four living companions set off after the shade of Iron Eyes Ledoux. "I can't be cracking ghostly skulls with you hanging on like a babe at the teat."

"Maybe I should strangle you now and be done with it," Lukas Sing-Low shot back defiantly, though his face grimaced with every step Breaker Calhoun took. He tightened his grip around Calhoun's neck for emphasis. "At least that way, I'll save everyone your bitching and moaning."

"You're as pleasant as always, Calhoun," Iron Eyes called back as she hovered outside the oily indigo flames. She melded with the swirling spirits that kept a wary distance from the powerful magic. "I sure did miss that when I left Dryftwood."

"Just 'cause you're dead, swamp thing, doesn't mean I can't make your life miserable," Breaker Calhoun retorted, shifting his weight and causing Lukas to squirm in agony. "The only reason I came along on this little jaunt is because your boyfriend cried and begged me to find you. He obviously needs my help after he moseyed off by his lonesome. We thought he was going to wander the Grey Wastes for all eternity looking for you. Jeremiah, these other two had given you up for dead. But not ol' Breaker Calhoun! I said, 'I got to find this young man so I can keep making his life miserable.' Where did you end up going anyway, son?"

"I...thought I saw something that ultimately wasn't there," Jeremiah explained through gritted teeth. He regretted not drowning the cocksure Calhoun in the glass of Sweetfire. Even if he had, Breaker Calhoun would have found a way to float across the Grey Wastes and harass him. "I was not prepared for that level of manipulation."

"The spirits will do that to you, cher," Ophelia piped up cheerfully as she walked behind her dead cousin and occasionally stopped to examine the crunchy grass in between her toes. "They will play on your memories. That's all they have, if you think about it. That's the only way they exist, in the minds of the living. So, if they can manipulate that, it helps keep them 'alive', so to speak. Ain't that right, cousin?"

Iron Eyes Ledoux nodded her spectral head without looking back. The ground beneath their boots turned from coastal plains to dunes of thick, gritty sand covered in brown seaweed. The rain had subsided, but for the first time since they entered the Grey Wastes, they could smell. There was a salty tinge to the air, mixed with the aroma of tilled earth, and the combination left a gritty sheen on the skin of the living. Off in the distance, Jeremiah thought he could hear the cries of gulls mixed in with the constant, mournful drone of the dead. Each step they took, the haze receded, and the world around them sharpened into focus.

The four living companions had not felt hunger, thirst, or weariness for as long as they could remember, but, as they moved forward, the burdens of the living returned and weighed heavy upon their beings. A great wave of lethargy crashed over Jeremiah—it was as if the sand and weeds were clinging desperately to his boots to slow his stride. Ophelia, however, seemed unperturbed, shaking her zam-zam hypnotically and cheerily mumbling to herself as she walked barefoot through the sand. If hunger, thirst, or fatigue burdened her narrow shoulders, Ophelia made no mention of it.

Once they made their way to the top of the dunes, the living could see the Crystal Gulf laid out in true splendor at their boots. The water was a light brown color, complete with foam the color of old buttercream frothing on top of each wave. The swells were small but sustained, rhythmically eating away at the shoreline. Coarse, brown seaweed covered the beach, enough to where they could hardly see a patch of dirty, yellow sand. It was not the most majestic sight in the world—in the realm of the living, all the silt from the Danathane River flowed westward, muddying up the waters to the west of the Swamp Elf Delta—but it was rich with life and a unique biome not found anywhere else in Westhold. Jeremiah looked down and saw a tiny brown crab skitter across his boot.

At the top of the dunes, Ophelia and Iron Eyes stood on opposite sides of the oily indigo flames conversing in their native Swamp Elf language. Ophelia shook her zam-zam, the contents of the bag swishing in sync with the crash of the waves, and whispered conspiratorially to Woodroux, who was loosely wrapped around her slender neck. Woodroux swayed in agreement, or perhaps disagreement, and the two Swamp Elves nodded sagely.

"You know, the Gnomish Islands are well-known for the beauty of their beaches," Lukas Sing-Low stated from his perch on Breaker Calhoun's shoulders, his eyes wistful despite his obvious pain. "Beautiful turquoise water, white sand, leafy green fronds lining the shore."

"I'm sure it's majestic, short-stack," Breaker Calhoun snorted as he swatted away a host of opportunistic beach bugs. "I'll have to visit it one day. That is if I don't get eaten alive by these stupid bugs first."

"Better than getting eaten alive by the dead," Jeremiah remarked casually as the sea wind blew his black hair back. He turned his attention to Ophelia Delphine. "Are we close?"

"The marks of the living are upon us, cher," Ophelia declared as she drew her hands in circles in the salty air, her fingers sparking with an iridescent light. "I do not know how long these flames will protect us, Jeremiah Blade. It is not just the dead we have to fear now."

Suddenly, far down the coastline, a flash of bright lavender light blazed through the lingering gloom. For a moment, all was quiet until a deep, protracted roar rippled outwards, racing in every direction. It was the sound of stones shattering, trees uprooting, sand melting, and worlds being torn asunder. Even the specters and sandflies swirling around them paused their restless flights as the shockwave rolled over them like a cresting wave. The sand roiled with energy, forcing them to catch their balance so they didn't roll down the dune and into the brambles of dirty seaweed. All gathered peered anxiously through the haze, but, once the lavender light died, the murk returned, and visibility evaporated.

Another coil of lethargy grasped at Jeremiah's consciousness. He looked towards Lukas Sing-Low and Breaker Calhoun and saw uncertainty and awe reflected in their eyes. Jeremiah then draped his gaze on Iron Eyes, his old riding companion, and saw her phase in and out of corporeality. Life was returning to Iron Eyes Ledoux. Ophelia remained unconcerned, running her old, bony fingers through her tangle of hair and quietly mumbling to herself while Woodroux stood ramrod straight on her shoulder, staring at the flashpoint. Ophelia let out a low whistle that trilled like birdsong.

"Does anyone have a damn idea what we are going to do when we get to this tear?" Breaker Calhoun spat loudly. "What do you got, witch? You going to shake that little bag, crumple some leaves on the beach, and we call it a day?"

"The portal where we entered the Grey Wastes is similar to this, I suspect," Ophelia said as she squatted down to examine a batch of white flowers in the sand. "It, too, is a tear between worlds, though a small one. A tiny nick in the fabric between the realms of the living and the dead. The Abbess maintains the tear so that travel between the two is possible. She also guards against intrusions and ensures the denizens of the two have minimal contact. But now, something has found that terrible power for themselves and intends to destroy the barrier between the living and dead."

"So, we just find whoever is doing this," Breaker Calhoun surmised, running his hand over the stubble on his sharp chin. "Do a little hacking, a little slashing, close the door, and be back home in time for supper. Maybe except for you, swamp thing. I guess you're already home."

"To seal it," Lukas piped up, his eyes peering out over the coastline. "There must be one on each side of the divide. It is a door that locks on both sides. One hand must hold the wound together while the other hand stitches."

The words froze on the sea wind. Jeremiah thought about what kind of terrible magic it would take to create a rift between worlds. He thought of the Arkstone, the ghastly yellow ore that once laid beneath the Shattered Hills, and the terrible power it held. Had someone found it and turned it towards this unimaginable purpose? The color profile didn't match the ghastly yellow ore, but the dark indigo etchings on his hand told him that Duskstones were malleable. Either way, why would someone utilize such dangerous magic to destroy both the world of the living and the dead?

Jeremiah's thoughts were interrupted by the loud smacking sound of a red globule of chewing weed spit hitting the sand. Breaker Calhoun had set down Lukas Sing-Low and passed his chewing weed pouch to the Island Gnome, who took a solid pinch as he maneuvered into a sitting position.

"Well," Breaker Calhoun said finally, his words slurring through shredded chewing weed. "I sure as shit ain't staying here. Can't ol' swamp thing close it? She lives here anyway."

"Everyone here knows damn well, I can't," Iron Eyes explained. "If you had paid any attention when I was alive, you'd know that I don't know anything about these damn Duskstones. Plus, the closer I get to the rift, the greater the stress on my spirit. Even now, I have to control the urge to eat you alive, Calhoun. Not that I need an excuse to get rid of you, mind."

"I was too busy to go through your whole life story, swamp thing," Calhoun retorted. "I figured you might have learned a thing or two on this side of things, but I guess I was wrong."

Another flash of lavender light cut through the remaining gloom. Like before, a terrible howl radiated from the flashpoint and crashed around the companions like summer rain. The ground quaked and the sand shook, causing Breaker Calhoun to lose his footing and tumble down the dune to the seaweed-strewn beach in a cloud of foul words. Taken by surprise, Lukas Sing-Low started to roll painfully down the sand and scrub as well, but Jeremiah grabbed Lukas by the collar of his tunic and hauled the bard back up to the top of the dune. Lukas writhed in agony as the aftershocks subsided, and the beach fell quiet once more.

"We must hurry," Ophelia called out as she quickly made her way down the dunes and towards the receding lavender light. "There is no more time, cher. We must stop this before it is too late."

Lukas wheezed heavily as he tried to shift into a more comfortable position on the trembling dunes, while Jeremiah caught eyes with the ghost of Iron Eyes Ledoux.

"You're causing more trouble, Jeremiah Blade," Iron Eyes said quietly so Lukas wouldn't hear. "I never expected to be haunted by the living. I'm impressed, though, coming all the way through the Grey Wastes for little old me. But don't you feel no guilt for what happened, Jeremiah. I made my own choices, and I lived and died by them. That's all anyone can ask for out of life."

"You wouldn't have been in that cave if it hadn't been for me," Jeremiah insisted earnestly. "I just figured if I could come here and explain that I never wanted that to happen. You said don't feel guilty, but I do. Things could have been so different if I had just left well enough alone. Your light should still be lit, and I should be in here, adrift in the Grey Wastes."

The shade of Iron Eyes Ledoux turned on Jeremiah, her slate-grey eyes glowing furiously.

"It wasn't your decision to make, cher," Iron Eyes whispered coldly. "That's what I'm trying to get through your damn thick skull. It was always my decision. I wanted to be there with you. That's what you can't see. I was happy riding with you, Jeremiah. Despite what happened, I wouldn't trade that time for anything. Don't you come here telling me it wasn't my decision."

Jeremiah stood on the shifting sands in stunned silence. It was the most honest and earnest thing he had ever heard. He grasped for the words, but their jagged edges caught in his throat. Jeremiah came through the worlds of the living and the dead to apologize, but the recipient of that apology was having none of it.

"I just wanted to say thank you for everything," Jeremiah Blade choked out eventually. "I just miss you."

The ghost of Lucille Ledoux stared back at Jeremiah, her lean features an ethereal patchwork of skin and spirit.

"I miss you too, Jeremiah Blade," the ghost said quietly. "More than you realize."

A third lavender light flared down the coastline, followed by a third terrible rending sound. This succeeded in sending Lukas Sing-Low down the dune; at the bottom, he lay among the seaweed, wheezing like an old squeezebox, running his fingers through the rough sand and trying to summon the strength to get to his feet. Ophelia Delphine and Breaker Calhoun, twin hatchets at the ready, were already moving down the coast towards the source of the explosions.

"I hope that sword of yours is still hot, cher," Iron Eyes whispered to Jeremiah as she floated towards the rift between worlds. "We're going to need it."

CHAPTER 30

Jeremiah's boots clomped through the seaweed as Lukas Sing-Low grunted in agony on his shoulders. Ahead of the pair, Ophelia Delphine, Breaker Calhoun, and the shade of Iron Eyes Ledoux raced through the gritty gusts of sea wind rolling onto the beach. Jeremiah kept up the oily indigo flames, but they could all see the wraiths taking physical shape the closer they moved to the flashpoint. The air around them distorted, much like it did when they entered through the Priory of Memory. The haze faded away—only a grey film that shaded the edges of their reality remained—leaving them to run under an endless sea of stars. Dirty seaweed crunched beneath the companions' boots and bare feet, with the occasional seashell shattering underneath their weight.

The explosions grew in frequency and strength, threatening to evaporate the very beach they ran upon. Their entire world started to warp and distort, and the sands boiled and rolled like crashing waves. Terrible screeches filled the air as the dead also raced towards the growing rift, seeing it as their one chance to reclaim the flame of life. Jeremiah gazed upon Iron Eyes Ledoux as she phased in and out of existence, dancing along the line between life and death. For Jeremiah, it was almost as if the intervening years had never happened. There was a comfort he had not felt in as long as he could remember as he followed Iron Eyes' blurred outline soaring above the beach. Despite the immense danger they were charging into, Jeremiah felt more at home than any time since he left Alathane all those years ago.

As they neared the source and cut through the final curtain of haze, a giant outline of an eye in shades of lavender and silver hung in the salt air. A wild congress of spirits and forms made flesh scrambled and clawed for a gigantic, jagged rift suspended just below the eye. A terrible chorus, one of ruin and damnation, echoed around them, joining the endless drone of the dead. As Jeremiah dragged his gaze towards the source of the haunting, calamitous refrain, shock rippled through his being.

Seven people the height of Island Gnomes or Savannah Halflings stood in a wide semi-circle under the eye, their arms spread towards the sky as their black robes fluttered wildly in the face of the raw arcane power. The ritualists wore ornate silver masks crafted to look like dragons wreathed in thorns, and silver tendrils of lightning sparked off the sneering visages. Coils of lavender arcane energy cascading off the seven fed the growing eye and expanded rift above them. Before their very eyes, the worlds of the living and the dead were being torn asunder.

Ophelia Delphine's journey had come to an end. In a language none of the other companions had ever heard, Ophelia's voice boomed outwards and joined the cacophony of worlds ripping apart. Arcane power surged through Ophelia, and she launched a streaking orb of raw magic towards them, but the swirling green miasma crashed upon an invisible barrier and dissipated into the electric atmosphere.

"Be gone, witch!" a female voice boomed over the riot. "Your powers do not register here. The dead no longer whisper to you, Ophelia Delphine. They are now the domain of our people, from this day until the end of days! We can offer the dead something that you have hoarded to yourself for too long—the flame of life! They shall be held down no longer!"

In unison, a half-dozen voices cackled across the coastline like thunder.

"Under the thorn, the rose shall grow!"

The words rolled over dune and wave, stretching into both the world of the living and the dead. Before the echo faded into the distance, Breaker Calhoun, his hackles raised, dove into the breach with his twin hatchets glinting bone-white in the lavender-tinted atmosphere. He jumped as high as his skinny legs would allow him and brought both blades down at the point where Ophelia's magic had dissipated, but the invisible barrier bloomed once more, and the resulting concussive feedback flung Breaker Calhoun deep into a dune. A plume of salt, sand, and curses exploded around him.

"It is no use," the female voice thundered again. "Your tools are useless here, witch. We are the avenging blade of our people. Our ancestors will reward us for granting them their freedom. No longer will we be doomed to wander the earth, like the living dead, away from our ruined homeland. We will reclaim what is rightfully ours. We have been scorned by the other nations of Westhold, but no longer!"

"Under the thorn, the rose shall grow!"

The sea wind swelled to tempestuous proportions, and the waves bore down upon the shoreline with a primal fury. Spirits, hungry for life, swirled and danced around the rift, eager to capitalize on the opportunity to find their way back to mortality. It wasn't just the dead of the Five Civilizations clawing for the exit—ancient beasts, virtually erased from the collective memory of Westhold, scoured the skies and the earth, rampaging towards the rift.

To Jeremiah, it was like a child's fairy tale book split wide open. Great galloping monsters rampaged over the dunes. Flying creatures that resembled giant scaled bats winged overhead, screeching at competing specters reaching for life. Ghostly warriors clad in ancient armor fought spectral battles with one another around the great rift, desperately trying to reclaim their former glory. Myth and legend were taking shape before their eyes, all desperately trying to make their way back into the land of the living.

"Unbelievable," Lukas Sing-Low cursed under his breath. "What devilry is this?"

Before Jeremiah could answer, he noticed Iron Eyes Ledoux shuddering under the great surge of power, her face contorted in unimaginable pain. Her flesh formed and hardened and then faded back into etherealness. She wheeled away, resisting the dreaded pull of the arcane nexus, but it was as if she was being dragged towards a horrid, gnashing whirlpool—swimming against the tide only prolonged the inevitable. The magic the ritualists commanded was raw and brutal, and the spirits heeded its unrelenting call.

"We are the Ash Knights," the female voice roared a third time. "And the time is upon us to reclaim what was so cruelly taken from our people! We were sacrificed for Westhold, and how were we rewarded? Scorn! Destitution! Death! But no longer. We will reclaim our past glory!"

"Under the thorn, the rose shall grow!"

As Iron Eyes and Breaker Calhoun recovered, one of the Ash Knights stepped forward from directly underneath the looming, lidless eye and jagged rift between worlds. The silver dragon mask turned towards Jeremiah, and a hateful darkness peered out from the eye holes nestled among the glittering scales.

"It's nice to see you again, Jeremiah Blade," the ritualist purred, her voice commanding over the chaos. "I must thank you for your tender mercy. Your weakness kept me alive, and we continued to flourish. You did not unburden yourself of your knowledge of the Arkstone, but it is no matter. Our plans continued, with or without your help. You were useless then, as you are now."

"Under the thorn, the rose shall grow!"

Suddenly, a stark memory of a muggy swamp and insect-filled bayou flashed in Jeremiah's mind—a Savannah Halfling left to die among the hanging moss. He now recognized that the right sleeve of the Ash Knight's robe whipped wildly in the arcane wind; no hand peeked out from the darkened folds. Slowly, a blade of pure, lavender energy laced with snapping bolts of silver magic replaced the missing limb. Jeremiah had seen that weapon before, long ago in the humid bogs of the Delta, its remnants seared into his memory. Slowly, the ritualist's one good arm removed the silver dragon mask and let it drop to the boiling beach.

Jeremiah now gazed upon the malevolent features of the Halfling

Hallincross.

CHAPTER 31

"How?" Jeremiah mouthed wordlessly, though in the stunned silence he might as well have screamed. "How could this be?"

"You naively believed I wanted the reward on your head, Jeremiah Blade," Hallincross hissed as the worlds around them exploded back into ruin. "But, what I truly wanted was your knowledge of the Arkstone. I did underestimate you, though. I did not realize the power you wielded since your time in the Shattered Hills. I paid for my arrogance, but I shall not make the same mistake twice."

Hallincross raised her good arm and the magical blade skyward and started to chant in a language long-forgotten. The other ritualists removed their silver dragon masks, each one a Savannah Halfling, and joined in, continuing the ancient and malevolent chorus. Silver and lavender arcane energy swirled around them and grew to a furious froth as their song reached its haunting crescendo.

"No!" Ophelia Delphine roared over the wailing. There was a desperation in her voice that Jeremiah had never heard before. "Stop them! Stop them now!"

Jeremiah unseated Lukas Sing-Low and unburdened his longsword from its casing. He called forth the power of a raging dust storm—one he had ridden through long ago—and the weapon answered the call, its shining steel boiling to life. Waves of heat radiated off of the hissing blade, and Jeremiah charged towards Hallincross to put a violent end to their chorus.

Jeremiah, remembering roughly where the invisible protection around the Ash Knights lay, brought his sword to bear, and the steel bit deep into the magical ward. Ripples of power glided over the invisible surface, but the ward held firm, and the Savannah Halflings continued to sing unabated. Jeremiah brought down his longsword once more with a mighty overhead chop, but the magic held again, resisting the full fury of the storm trapped inside the blade. Coming to his companion's aid, Lukas called forth the magic from the crescent moon Duskstone upon his throat, and sickles of power cut through the gritty air and smashed into the invisible field. But still, the ward held.

The muddy water of the Crystal Gulf churned and boiled. A gigantic whirlpool began to circle and exhale sprays of foam and brine. Jeremiah had no idea how deep the water along the coastline ran, but from the conflagration raging along the shore, it seemed like the ancient god imprisoned in the Grey Wastes was coming to the surface. All gathered, even the specters drawn to the maw between worlds, paused to watch the ocean tear itself apart.

Jeremiah barely had time to register the full calamity unfolding before them when a colossal claw covered in salt and seaweed shot out of the water and crashed into the surf, sending a massive shockwave along the coast. Jeremiah, Lukas, Ophelia, and the returning Breaker Calhoun struggled to hold their balance as the sand trembled beneath their feet.

Out from the whirlpool emerged a beast of unimaginable terror. Its gnarled arm and shoulder, covered in a tangle of writhing tentacles, emerged, followed shortly by the beast's malformed, horned head. Its elongated snout narrowed into a terrible maw of jagged, broken teeth which split open into a cruel and leering grin. Tufts of coarse, black hair sprouted at irregular intervals on the monster's face, and pale yellow eyes cast a horrifying gaze upon the land. The tangle of tentacles writhed around the creature's muscular shoulders like a shroud, occasionally snapping like whips and creating thunderous cracks that threatened to shake the world off its hinges.

The dusty library at the Academy flashed to the forefront of Jeremiah's memory. The monstrosity matched the description of an ancient creature called the Typhos. The castle-sized monster was like a god to the ancient world—legend had it that the Typhos was a being designed to serve as punishment to the progenitor tribes of the Five Civilizations, at a time before the Good Light arrived and banished the beast to the dark corners of Westhold. The Typhos' memory had apparently been kept alight by ancient myths and tales, a haunted shell just like all the rest of the spirits in the Grey Wastes. Now, the Typhos had answered the call of mortality.

Even the Savannah Halflings, arms raised in ecstatic glory, were awed by the horrendous monstrosity they had summoned. Despite the fact that the creature was only waist-deep in the waves, it towered over the coastline, taller than the tallest keeps in Alathane. Out of the massive maw burst a guttural shriek that had not fallen on mortal ears in eons. The accursed sound rent the coastal air and sent the living to their knees in agony as blood streamed from their ears. One clawed hand reached towards the widening rift between the lands of the living and the dead, casting a dark shadow over the coastline.

"It cannot be released upon the mortal realm!" Ophelia screamed over the chaos, her normally carefree features now desperate and frantic. "If the

Typhos makes its way through the rift, it will rampage across Westhold and bring untold destruction upon the world!"

"Exactly!" Hallincross' voice boomed in undulating waves. "The civilizations of Westhold shall pay for the tragedy inflicted upon the Savannah Halflings! Our people were cast out and turned away like so much trash. No longer! With these legendary creatures back and hordes of our ancestors scouring Westhold, we will extract justice and revive our great empire!"

Jeremiah realized this was what the mad Savannah Halfling wanted him for—he was one of the few people in Westhold with first-hand knowledge of the Arkstone. To concoct such a devastating plan, the Savannah Halflings needed a Duskstone of unparalleled power, strong enough to tear the veil between worlds. Jeremiah believed the Arkstone had the capability of doing so, but did the Ash Knights find it after only a few years following the events in the Shattered Hills? Or had they found something equally as terrible? Jeremiah thought about the Alathanian Marshals and their role in policing errant Duskstone use; maybe the marshals were misguided on the cause of the Blight, but they had kept magic from being used for malicious and destructive purposes. Without the marshals, dangerous magic was allowed to flourish, and criminals and the mad could wield power that would bring entire nations to ruin. The shadow of his actions in the Shattered Hills had grown long indeed.

Before Jeremiah could rue his errant youth any further, another colossal claw plowed into the seaweed-covered beach, sending another shockwave shrieking along the coast. Like the Semby and the surrounding army of specters, the Typhos phased in and out of corporeality. Whole swaths of skin and meat dissolved into grey shadows, while the ethereal tentacles on the monster's shoulders looked like smoke ringing a mountaintop. The Typhos roared again, decimating the coast of the Crystal Gulf.

Like a streaking, emerald star, Ophelia shot skyward. Wrapped around her arm was Woodroux, his scales glinting wildly in the cacophony. She hovered high over the lavender eye, staring down the gargantuan Typhos, a tiny speck next to the ever-growing, otherworldly monster. Ophelia unwrapped Woodroux from around her forearm, held the writhing animal above her head, and cast him down towards the Typhos.

Against the starry backdrop of the cosmos, Woodroux spiraled towards a grim fate. As he neared the Typhos's head, the winder straightened into a living, breathing arrow plummeting from the sky. Floating above the pandemonium, Ophelia Delphine weaved an intricate spell as sparks of iridescent light cascaded off her thin frame. Suddenly, the microscopic familiar exploded in size, his dimensions multiplying exponentially. The once-tiny, heroic winder now took up virtually the entire sky, his emerald coat glittering like dragon scale.

The gigantic winder careened into the Typhos with a world-shaking crash. The Typhos, not expecting a similar-sized creature to fall out of the sky and onto its head, staggered backwards as the colossal familiar snapped and bit, taking chunks of writhing tentacles out of the legendary monster's shoulder. Woodroux, drawing from a wellspring of fury that matched his new size, hissed and wrapped himself around the stinking, fuming head of the monster. The Typhos, having recovered from its initial shock, now fought back with a rage unknown to the world since ancient times.

As the two giant creatures battled it out in the surf, the Ash Knights scrambled to restart the ritual to tear the veil between worlds. Another pulse of lavender light flared from the unblinking eye, and the earth shook and the sky bled once more. Jeremiah looked towards Ophelia, who still floated above the maelstrom, concentrating on keeping Woodroux in his giant form. Breaker Calhoun plunged forward through the chaos, his hatchets undimmed and undeterred. Lukas Sing-Low stood tentatively among the seaweed, his amulet burning hot as great sickles of arcane, tangerine energy formed around his mane of silver hair, bright blades in sharp contrast to the grim surroundings. Even Iron Eyes Ledoux, still reeling from the terrible cost of being so close to the rift, gathered the strength and conviction she was so well known for in life and dove towards the Savannah Halflings, her body phasing in and out of substance.

Jeremiah joined his rallying companions and, at the risk of exposing himself to the swarming ranks of the dead, drew the oily indigo flames in close and along the length of his searing longsword. The fire swirled and danced on the weapon's edge, throwing off powerful waves of arcane energy. Jeremiah strode through the crunchy, crusty seaweed to bring his marshal longsword to bear once more on the invisible barrier protecting the Ash Knights.

From across the beach, Breaker Calhoun launched one of his bone-white hatchets through the briny air and it connected with the invisible force protecting the chanting ritualists. The hatchet immediately ricocheted off at a sharp angle, but the weapon sent a flood of energy rippling through the barrier. Not wasting a second, Lukas Sing-Low whipsawed his spinning scythes of magic into the barrier near the same spot. The invisible field shuddered once again and, this time, they could see sideways glances from the Savannah Halflings. Locking onto the spot where the force field wavered, Jeremiah strode the last lengths and leaped skyward. The oily indigo flames fluttered off the boiling steel as Jeremiah struck the arcane ward with the fury of a raging dust storm.

CHAPTER 32

The resulting explosion sent Jeremiah flying high over the dunes and into the rough, scrubby coastal plains. The rift shuddered as the Savannah Halflings' ritual came to an abrupt halt with Hallincross and her followers pinwheeling in every direction. A cloud of shredded seaweed, sand, and arcane dust floated through the salt air above the cratered earth as living and dead alike gathered their bearings. Despite the disruption, the lavender eye still hovered in the sea spray, lidless and severe.

Dazed, but knowing time was critical, Jeremiah dug himself out of the sandy cave he had created in the coastal vegetation and stumbled for his longsword. He picked up his weapon just as the heated blade set the brittle grass on fire and staggered back to the dunes, fighting his way through the pain filtering through his head and claiming his limbs. As Jeremiah reached the top of the shifting dunes, he saw the bone-white handle of Breaker Calhoun's lost hatchet sticking up from the sand. Jeremiah snatched up the mystic weapon in his offhand, watching the oily indigo flames from his palm coat the hatchet and the spirits trapped inside. A guttural roar caught Jeremiah's attention, and he surveyed the catastrophe strewn before him.

The Ash Knights were scattered, dazed, and shocked that their magical shield had failed. Lukas Sing-Low, on the opposite side of the beach, writhed in pain in a patch of brown seaweed. Breaker Calhoun had burrowed out of a Breaker Calhoun-sized hole in a dune and cast about for his lost hatchet. He quickly found a recovering foe nearby and pounced with one bone-white hatchet flashing. The Ash Knight, seeing the threat of violence incoming, fired narrow lances of silver and lavender energy from an outstretched, splayed hand; the bolts of energy hit true, one going through the meat of Breaker Calhoun's shoulder and another searing across his skinny leg. But, Breaker Calhoun's momentum propelled him forward and he fell upon his enemy hatchet-first. The bone-white blade came down on the Savannah

Halfling's sternum, and a loud metallic clank and the sound of shattering Duskstones echoed over the beach. The Ash Knight struggled to free himself, but Breaker Calhoun, undeterred, brought the hatchet down into the meat of the Savannah Halfling's neck. A blood-filled scream echoed over the din of battle and press of chittering specters.

Out in the gulf, Woodroux and the Typhos continued to battle, unperturbed by the magical destruction and wanton violence wrought upon the shore. The Typhos had pulled itself fully from the surf to its full, terrible height, shrinking the giant emerald winder by comparison. The mythic beast's malformed head scraped the bottom of the stars and loomed over the flying outline of Ophelia Delphine. The Typhos' legs, both scaled and hairy, and its feet, cloven like a bull and webbed like a duck, emerged from the muddy water. The beast took a step forward, and its hoof smashed into the surf with the force of a meteor. The salt air itself twisted and wavered under the strain of the destructive powers at work.

The tentacles and clawed hands of the Typhos tore into Woodroux as the winder wrapped his coils around the beast's neck, sending sheets of blood cascading into the frothy surf. Woodroux reared up and sank his fangs deep into the nest of tentacles and tightened his body like a noose. The two creatures bit and tore at each other with blood, hair, scales, and tentacles drifting through the salt spray. The Typhos clenched its colossal claw around Woodroux's body and squeezed, cracking ribs and forcing rivers of crimson between its claws.

Ophelia gathered sickly green energy around her as the two titans fought in the crashing waves. A cloud of virulent energy pulsed and surged around the Hoodoux Queen, completely obscuring her from the host gathered on the beach. Ophelia then launched the orb of arcane energy through the salt air, and the sphere smashed deep into the Typhos' hairy, chitinous chest. The resulting shockwave jolted the gigantic creature backwards and, as the Typhos tried to catch itself, Woodroux renewed his attacks, throwing the legendary creature off balance. Like an ancient tree felled by a small axe, the Typhos tipped backwards and sped towards earth.

The Typhos took an eternity to fall, grasping at empty air as it drifted downwards. Time slowed to a crawl, and, when the monster finally hit the waves, it felt like an earthquake had ruptured the very seams of reality. The realms of the living and dead shuddered and threatened to implode at the impact. A massive groundswell ripped outward, throwing the awed onlookers on the beach high into the briny air. Jeremiah saw the swell race towards him, leaving broken bodies in its wake, and, as it reached the towering dunes, Jeremiah leaped over the titanic wave of earth, water, stone, and sand. The swell roared underneath the floating outlaw, who then crashed through the blizzard of sand, seaweed, and ocean water into the hard earth. Jeremiah found himself next to Breaker Calhoun, and they quickly hauled themselves up to their boots.

"Never a dull moment with you, son," Breaker Calhoun whistled as he took his offhand weapon from his former enemy. Calhoun tipped his wide-brimmed hat and wiped dirty sand off of his bone-white hatchet as the trapped spirits howled in madness underneath the surface. "That's a pretty fancy trick the witch cooked up, but I'm not sure how long that winder is going to last. I don't think anyone wants that big bastard running 'round their backyard, but I ain't sure how we are going to stop it from doing that. I don't mind chopping up a few cultists, but I'm a man who knows his limits, and my limits are at that monster splashing around in the surf."

Breaker Calhoun knew the truth of it. If the Typhos broke through the rift and into the world of the living, there would be no way to stop it from rampaging through all of Westhold. At least, as the monster shifted between spirit and mortal shell, it was still effectively in prison, unable to bring ruin upon the living world. As the two old foes watched the titanic beast thrash around in the Crystal Gulf, they wracked their brains for answers. Their only hope lie in closing the rift—they had no idea what Ophelia had in store, but they needed a way forward in case she fell. Jeremiah Blade and Breaker Calhoun spied Hallincross struggle to her feet and wordlessly sprinted across the seaweed and sand towards the master summoner.

Four Ash Knights had recovered and rushed to meet the oncoming Plains Humans, their hungry hands filled with wavy short swords that glowed with a silver-and-lavender energy. Jeremiah took the two on the left and Calhoun the two on the right as weapons clanged and clashed, adding to the riotous symphony on the beach. The Ash Knights were no squires—their speed and deftness took both Jeremiah Blade and Breaker Calhoun by surprise and immediately sent them on the defensive.

Jeremiah brought his molten blade down on one of his foes, but the wavy blade proved powerful enough to stop the magic sword dead in its flaming arc. It had been a long while since anything had been strong enough to halt the raging dust storm that boiled beneath the blade, and it caught Jeremiah off-guard, sending him backwards to rethink his attack.

It proved fortuitous for Breaker Calhoun that Jeremiah had returned his lost hatchet as it commanded all of his experience and dexterity to fend off the deadly Ash Knights. It took every hatchet stroke Breaker Calhoun could muster to deflect the incoming, Duskstone-infused blades. Iridescent sparks flew off kissing blades as Breaker Calhoun struggled to hold off the two onrushing Savannah Halflings. One curved blade snuck past Calhoun's defenses and drew a bright red gash across his thigh, sending Calhoun down to one lanky knee. Breaker Calhoun cursed loudly and fought his two foes from one knee, his injuries mounting.

Seeing his companion in dire straits, Jeremiah drew his sword in a wide sweep to get some space and rushed over to boot one of Calhoun's attackers in the temple. Blindsided, the Ash Knight sprawled out into a scratchy carpet of seaweed, his sword diving point-first into the sand. Jeremiah then thundered down onto the other Savannah Halfling, who barely had enough time to deflect the incoming longsword. Jeremiah pressed his advantage, raining down molten steel on the backpedaling ritualist.

Breaker Calhoun proved tougher than old boot leather. With adrenaline roaring through his lanky frame, he jumped to his boots, caught the two foes chasing after Jeremiah, and tore into them with a renewed fury despite his mounting wounds.

As Jeremiah Blade and Breaker Calhoun fought for their lives in the land of the dead, Jeremiah caught a vision of a specter in the swirling miasma of memories that threw him off-guard and nearly sent him tumbling to the dirty sand under his boots. The shade glared at Jeremiah as he fought—a cold, dead, calculating stare that observed Jeremiah's every sword-stroke and defensive maneuver. It stuck out to Jeremiah as this ghost was all sharp lines and hard angles, compared to the soft, fuzzy edges and twisting forms of the gathered host of the dead.

Jeremiah pushed off his darting foe and risked a quick glance over to the ghost. The specter's balding head, neatly trimmed beard, and drooping ears were all dead giveaways. There was no mistake—the ghost of his grandfather, Sir Gerald Blade, looked on as his grandson fought for his life.

Suddenly, Jeremiah was transported back to the Academy training yard. He was barely old enough to swing a wooden sword, and the older trainees took advantage of that and beat him mercilessly. He was awkward, clumsy, and not able to protect his head from the beating. The entire time his grandfather looked on with an impassive grimace painted on his craggy face. Even as Jeremiah lay bloodied and beaten in the sand, Gerald Blade didn't raise a finger to help.

Jeremiah was brought violently back to the present as a slender, curved blade nicked his chin, sending a spray of blood across the otherworldly battlefield. The Savannah Halfling stunned from a boot to the head had recovered and rejoined the fray. Jeremiah ducked and dodged, but the skilled Ash Knight was pressing him sorely, and he couldn't shake the waxen stare of his long-dead grandfather.

As he dueled with the Ash Knight, Jeremiah noticed a reddish hue radiating from his foe's left hand. Between sword slashes, Jeremiah could see a scarlet Duskstone embedded in his foe's palm, the very same that protected the four companions as they made their way through the world of the dead. Though the chorus of ghosts sung all around them, Jeremiah realized that the surrounding spirits could do nothing while the scarlet Duskstones protected the Ash Knights.

Jeremiah danced away from the swirling blade only to come face-to-face with his grandfather. Sir Gerald Blade stared at Jeremiah, his dead eyes hungry for the flame of life. Looking in the milky orbs of the specter, Jeremiah saw everything his grandfather represented—honor, arrogance, and rigidity in his worldview. Jeremiah had tried to live up to his grandfather's ideal but always fell short. He had tried to impress his grandfather by following his example; he had tried being stern and unrelenting, and it almost killed him in the Shattered Hills. At this moment, Jeremiah realized the truth of things—no amount of battlefield glory or proper decorum could satisfy his grandfather. Ingenuity would have to do. This would be the last chance Jeremiah would have to impress Sir Gerald Blade.

As Jeremiah watched the ghost of his grandfather, he could see the scarlet hue of his foe's Duskstone reflected in the dead man's eyes. Without turning back to face the onrushing Ash Knight, Jeremiah dropped to one side and, as soon as the ritualist overextended himself, instead of going for a wide, killing blow, he flicked his sword upwards and sent the sizzling steel through his foe's left hand, cutting it neatly in half and shattering the scarlet Duskstone.

Immediately, the cacophonous specters ceased their endless tide and turned their attention to the now defenseless Ash Knight clutching half a left hand. Gerald Blade, his thirst for the flame of life overwhelming him, snapped his attention towards the reeling Savannah Halfling. In one fluid motion, the ghost of Gerald Blade led the host of spirits spiraling towards the only unprotected flame of life in the entire Grey Wastes. The feast had begun, and the sound of riotous specters drowned out the Ash Knight's screams.

As the cloud of ghosts dispersed, their hunger satiated, the outline of Gerald Blade, his features now a patchwork of skin, spirit, and bone, hovered over the newly-passed Ash Knight. The two Blades stared at each other like duelists, waiting for the other to blink. All Jeremiah wanted to do as a child was impress his grandfather by joining the Alathanian Marshals and bringing glory to the Blade name. But, instead, the Blade name was now spoken with derision and scorn across Westhold because of Jeremiah. His grandfather didn't know that, a small mercy given to Jeremiah. However, fate had provided Jeremiah a chance; maybe, here in the realm of the dead, trying to save Westhold from a grim fate, Jeremiah's grandfather would realize that his progeny was made of the same fortitude that brought the Blade name to prominence in the first place. Even if Gerald Blade had lived long enough to see Jeremiah fully grown, they never would have been close, but Jeremiah still hoped he could earn a modicum of respect from the old man, even in death.

Despite the tumult around them, all Jeremiah could focus on was his grandfather. Suddenly, the long-dead Blade gave an almost imperceptible nod to Jeremiah, giving him the answer he needed and the validation he had yearned for his entire life. The corporeal aspects of Gerald Blade faded and the old man blended into the swirling cauldron of wraiths surrounding them. The ghost was finally laid to rest.

CHAPTER 33

"Calhoun!" Jeremiah hollered across the beach. "Their hands!"

Breaker Calhoun tipped his hat up with the point of his hatchet and set upon his two adversaries who were temporarily stunned into inaction as their companion shuddered and twitched. With a swift, thunderous strike, Calhoun brought down the bone-white hatchet blade through the wrist of one of the ritualists, lopping the left hand off neatly. The skittering swarm of specters immediately turned their attention to the reeling Savannah Halfling and raced towards the unprotected flame of life. It was a grim sight, and it sent a chill down Jeremiah Blade's spine at how close he came to a similar fate on the streets of Alathane.

Jeremiah and Breaker Calhoun wasted no time gawking at the new feeding frenzy. They set upon their remaining foes, who were immediately put on the defensive. Despite the chilling sight of their comrades being eaten alive by the host of the dead, the remaining Ash Knights refocused and dove back into the melee. Wherever these Ash Knights came from, they had incredible skills and magical resources at their command.

The Ash Knight dueling with Breaker Calhoun held his ground admirably, deflecting the incoming hatchet blades with deft, well-placed parries. Breaker Calhoun's mounting wounds and proximity to the world of the living were starting to weigh on his lanky frame. Lethargy grabbed at his limbs and gave his foe a fighting chance. Breaker Calhoun, hoping to replicate the same ghostly success as he had with the other Ash Knight, overextended with a vicious downward chop aimed at the Savannah Halfling's left wrist, leaving his midsection exposed for a killing blow. Calhoun could do nothing save grit his teeth and wait for the cold steel to slide into his insides.

Yet, the stroke never fell, and Calhoun's insides remained inside his torso. The Ash Knight stopped suddenly, hesitation clouding his features, and looked up to see tangerine sickles of energy swirling in the air above him, an orange glow reflecting in his dark eyes. Then, like an avalanche on a snow-capped peak, the magic rained down upon the Ash Knight, shredding his robes and eviscerating his body. The wavy blade dropped onto the ruined beach below with a soft clank.

Lukas Sing-Low crawled on his hands and knees through the broken seashells and ruined earth towards the pitched battle. Despite the pain evident on Lukas' face, he sent more sickles of energy towards Breaker Calhoun's foe to rip through his mortal form. The ruined threads of the Ash Knight's black robe fluttered to join the sword among the seaweed.

Now outnumbered three-to-one, the remaining Ash Knight broke off from the melee, turned, and sprinted down the beach, strategically regrouping with Hallincross and the other ritualist closer to the lidless eye. Rage was evident on Hallincross' face as her plans crumbled before her. She screeched at the incoming Ash Knight, though with all the sound and fury roaring around them, the words were lost forever. Desperation shaded her pale features—whatever planning went into her scheme was now becoming undone at this most unexpected of arrivals. The tide was turning against Hallincross and her Ash Knights.

Jeremiah Blade and Breaker Calhoun sprinted over to check on Lukas Sing-Low. Lukas managed a small chuckle when Breaker Calhoun took off his wide-brimmed ranching hat to fan him.

"Mighty obliged for the help, short-stack," Breaker Calhoun stated. "Jeremiah over here had left you for dead, but I knew you still had some fire in you."

"This is it, there is no other option left for us," Lukas said as he motioned for the last of the chewing weed from Breaker Calhoun. "If we do not kill them, the portal will grow, and that monster will tear through the veil and be reborn in Westhold. The only reason we stand a chance now is that its full, living strength has not returned to it. As soon as it goes through and reclaims the flame of life, there will be nothing that can stop it from bringing ruin to our entire world."

"Well, no pressure, Jeremiah Blade," Breaker Calhoun stated flatly as he handed over his last pinch of chewing weed to Lukas Sing-Low. "Who would have guessed that an up-jumped former marshal and some shitkicker from Dryftwood would be on hand to save all of Westhold? Everyone is thrilled, I'm sure."

Across the beach, Hallincross and the remaining two ritualists desperately restarted the spell to rip the rift open wide enough for the Typhos to storm through and be reborn. Jeremiah caught the gaze of Hallincross, her eyes swirling with liquid lavender, just as they did in the Delta so long ago. Jeremiah could have ended her then and there, but he chose life instead of death. Now, watching the cackles of silver lightning cascade off of her lavender energy blade and ancient incarnations tumble from her mouth,

Jeremiah couldn't stomach the situation. He had done the right thing in his mind, just as he had in the Shattered Hills all those years ago, but was once again grappling with the dramatic, unforeseen consequences of his actions. Hallincross sneered across the divide, and silver lightning swirled around her like the tentacles on the Typhos' shoulders.

Out in the tide, the Typhos and Woodroux fought tooth and coil, and blood mixed with the muddy sea water and buttercream-colored foam. Their movements seemed slow and onerous due to their titanic size, but each hit landed with the force of a battering ram. It was difficult for the observers on the beach to stay focused on their own battles—forces of nature of this magnitude had not been seen on the face of Westhold in millennia.

Above the brawl, Ophelia still hung suspended over the coastline, gathering foul, arcane magic around her for another apocalyptic blast of energy. Ophelia was desperately trying to buy time for Woodroux, who had lost a significant amount of blood and was quickly fading against the overwhelming might of the Typhos. Time was running out for the heroic familiar.

The Typhos struggled its way to a sitting position with Woodroux still tightly coiled around its neck. The legendary monster tore madly at the giant winder, finally got a good grip, and ripped the winder away from its throat, losing a large clutch of tentacles from its right shoulder in the process. Jeremiah, Lukas, and Breaker Calhoun looked on in horror as the Typhos held the glittering familiar aloft in both hands like a sacrificial offering to some forgotten deity. Ophelia, still concentrating on summoning the sickly green energy around her, could only look on helplessly as her long-time companion writhed in the crushing, cutting grasp.

In one fluid movement, the Typhos grasped Woodroux by his thrashing neck—who latched onto the scaled claw in retaliation—and ripped the triangular head from the winder's snapping body. Woodroux's head held on tight with his fangs, firmly lodged between the Typhos' fingers, unwilling to leave the battle and his mortal coil behind. Likewise, the winder's body whipped and lashed, not realizing it no longer lived. Emerald scales fluttered to earth like leaves in an autumn breeze.

CHAPTER 34

The sickly green energy swirling around Ophelia Delphine evaporated as the link between her and her familiar snapped like a tree branch. She faltered and wavered, her mind and body wracked by the arcane feedback from Woodroux's death. Her companions on the beach, both living and dead, looked up in horror as she slowly started to drop to earth. The witch picked up speed, hurtling towards the beach in complete free fall. Unable to take to the skies themselves, all Jeremiah Blade, Breaker Calhoun, and Lukas Sing-Low could do was watch helplessly as Ophelia plummeted towards the beach.

Iron Eyes Ledoux, still phasing in and out of corporeality, took off and surged across the sky as fast her ethereal body could take her. The ghost met the falling witch and, using whatever solid piece of flesh she possessed, lifted upwards on her cousin to arrest her fall. It was a curious state of being for Iron Eyes Ledoux, but she used her half-existence to slow her cousin's descent until Ophelia crashed in a pillow of rough seaweed and shells near the rift between worlds. The cloud of sand settled, and Ophelia lay still. Iron Eyes Ledoux was nowhere to be seen.

Seeing Hallincross and the remaining two Ash Knights race towards the fallen witch, Breaker Calhoun—running on pure adrenaline—broke out in a full sprint while Jeremiah hauled Lukas onto his shoulders and quickly gave chase. The Ash Knights launched rays of piercing silver-and-lavender light towards the onrushing companions, one errant strand ripping through Breaker Calhoun's wide-brimmed hat and another lancing through Jeremiah's shin and sending him and Lukas Sing-Low crashing face-first into the ravaged earth. Jeremiah rolled around in agony to see the perfectly symmetrical, gaping hole that went straight through the meat of his lower left leg. The pain was an unrelenting, searing fire that burned through his leg. Lukas Sing-Low lay beside Jeremiah Blade in a bruised heap, his breath slow and movements deliberate.

Breaker Calhoun slowed for no man and reached Ophelia just in time, deflecting rays of piercing light intended for the unconscious Hoodoux Queen with his hatchet blades. The two leading ritualists leaped into the fray and began a fearsome hand-to-hand melee with Calhoun, hatchets and short swords flashing under the lidless lavender eye. Hallincross took to the skies, her silver-and-lavender blade in place of her right arm leaving behind a wake of iridescent sparks, and brought her full, terrifying power down on Breaker Calhoun. The bounty hunter held up both bone-white hatchets, crossed into an X, and caught the energy blade in midair. Hallincross hung suspended over Breaker Calhoun, the power radiating from the magic weapons holding her aloft. For a few unlikely moments, all that prevented utter destruction of Westhold was Breaker Calhoun.

As magic coursed through the air around them, one of the ritualists slashed her blade across Breaker Calhoun's unprotected side. The former sheriff's deputy roared through gritted teeth as his foe painted the sand with his blood. Before Breaker Calhoun could react, the other ritualist rolled past his left side and drew his blade across the back of his skinny thigh. Breaker Calhoun buckled to one side and barely managed to deflect Hallincross and her terrible energy blade from slicing him in half.

Hungry blades immediately turned on the prostrate Calhoun, looking to end the threat so the ritual could be completed. Before they found their targets, however, an enlivening melody overcame the battlefield. Lukas Sing-Low, his body bolstered by the power flowing from the amulet hanging around his neck, rose to his feet and filled the air with his sonorous refrain. It was the same aria that the bard sung as they entered the Grey Wastes a lifetime ago. Power returned to Lukas Sing-Low and he stood despite his grievous injuries, his voice rising above the devastation around them.

Jeremiah, struggling to stand on his one good leg, expected the slim sickles of tangerine light to shred Hallincross and the remaining Ash Knights, but instead, the lavender eye faded slightly, and the rift between worlds began to heal. The air twisted and melted at the edges of the rift, like broken glass mending itself.

"No!" Hallincross screeched, seeing her plans becoming undone right at her moment of victory. "Stop him!"

Hallincross left Calhoun and Ophelia behind, leaving behind a shallow, silver mirage as she leaped into the sky and thundered down with her energy blade snapping with silver electricity. Lukas Sing-Low stood, unbent and unbroken, his song swelling as Hallincross descended. Lukas' eyes never wavered from her malevolent lavender orbs.

Jeremiah's sweltering sword stopped the lavender and silver energy blade mere inches from Lukas Sing-Low and knocked Hallincross off her trajectory and to the beach. Hallincross looked towards the starry sky, temporarily dazed from the unexpected impact.

Seeing their leader knocked sideways and in mortal danger, the two remaining Ash Knights left Breaker Calhoun and Ophelia Delphine and launched a flurry of attacks at the defiant Jeremiah Blade. Jeremiah held them off valiantly, sweeping the molten metal in wide arcs to push them away from Lukas Sing-Low. The bard's song continued to rise over the din of battle, stitching the veil between worlds back together.

Soon, though, Hallincross rejoined the fray, pitting three against one, forcing Jeremiah to use every fiber in his body to defend Lukas Sing-Low. A wavy short sword snuck past Jeremiah's defense, cutting deep into the flesh of his thigh and, shortly after, Hallincross' energy blade found a brief opening and sliced through his riding jacket and tunic, splitting the skin covering his ribcage wide open. Still, Jeremiah held firm, protecting Lukas from the onslaught. Above them, the tear in the sky healed slowly and painfully.

Out in the Crystal Gulf, the Typhos finally made its way back to its cloven hooves, and, as the creature rose to its full height once again, its jagged maw split wide and out tumbled the sound of ruin. The Typhos raised its leg high and took a step towards the beach where the eye hung. As its colossal hoof crashed into the surf, a shockwave rippled outwards and sent the living sprawling. A cloud of disturbed sand drifted through the surrounding chaos like snow, and those conscious and living struggled to their boots. Another roar burst from the Typhos—it, too, sensed its window of opportunity to grasp the flame of life closing.

Jeremiah found himself rolling through the sand until he crashed into one of the Ash Knights. Both combatants had the presence of mind to reach for their weapons, but Jeremiah's molten steel lay closer, and he quickly plunged the sword into the gnashing Savannah Halfling's chest until his spirit joined the chittering chorus around them. It was an act of pure, distilled desperation, one that, given normal circumstances, Jeremiah would have done everything to avoid, but now too much was at stake. Jeremiah was struggling to his boots when he felt a warm hand touch his shoulder; he quickly twisted around to see Iron Eyes Ledoux staring back at him.

"You must go," Iron Eyes said mournfully as she conjured enough corporeality to help Jeremiah to his feet. "You're still brave and young and stupid, Jeremiah, but you must go now. The only way to close the portal is from both sides. You must take Ophelia and Calhoun back to the world of the living and seal it for good."

Jeremiah looked at his former riding companion in shock. Her rough features in life had been smoothed in death. There were no tears in her slate-grey eyes, only the sadness of a reunion cut short. She phased in and out of etherealness, her former spark of life an ember trying to catch and flicker back to its former glory.

"What about Lukas?" Jeremiah asked as the grim reality settled upon his narrow shoulders. He looked at Hallincross and the final Ash Knight recovering from the titanic shock. Breaker Calhoun was also getting to his boots and trying to shake an unconscious Ophelia Delphine back from her slumber. "Is there no other way?"

Iron Eyes Ledoux gazed upon the still-young countenance of Jeremiah Blade. For one terrible moment, even with worlds tearing apart around them, all was quiet. The ghost took Jeremiah's hand and shook her head. Jeremiah felt a flash of warmth from the ghost's touch, a reminder that Lucille would always be with him.

"This was always their plan," Iron Eyes responded. "That's why Lukas needed to come with you. Ophelia couldn't do it on her own. Any hope of closing this rift lies with both him and my cousin."

The pair were interrupted by two searing lances of silver-and-lavender magic piercing Jeremiah's extended forearm and another racing across his shoulder blades. He reeled in agony as Hallincross and the remaining Ash Knight bore down upon Jeremiah and Lukas Sing-Low. The two Savannah Halflings launched a furious barrage of sword strokes that Jeremiah barely had the consciousness to parry. Iron Eyes jumped to her former riding companion's defense, though her shifting etherealness and the scarlet Duskstones protecting the ritualists prevented her from interrupting the melee. Jeremiah, blood weeping from several wounds, now replaced Breaker Calhoun as the solitary shield against the ruination of worlds.

The Typhos took another thunderous step towards the beach and the rift, sending another shockwave along the coast. The legendary monster now only needed to reach down towards the eye and claim the fire of life so long denied to it. The towering creature extended its long, scaly arm across the sky; its shadow crept along the shoreline, menacing and inevitable.

As the shockwave rippled across the beach, Jeremiah and his foes were tossed to the gritty coastline once more. Lukas Sing-Low held firm, his melodious voice still patching the torn veil. As Jeremiah scrambled to reach for his sword, the last ritualist shifted her momentum against the quaking ground and lunged at Jeremiah, the wavy short sword pointed towards his throat. Jeremiah stretched for his blade but was too late as the cruel steel cut through the salt air.

Yet, the blade never fell. Jeremiah looked back and saw the Ash Knight suspended in mid-air, her body contorting and her face a mask of surprise. Jeremiah looked past the breaking ritualist and saw Ophelia Delphine, all might and fury, her body cascading iridescent sparks and her dark hair flowing wildly behind her, raise her hands towards the sky as the Savannah Halfling writhed against her powerful, magical grasp. As Ophelia clenched her fists, the Ash Knight broke and snapped in a thousand places. She crumbled to the ground, her dark robes fluttering then laying still.

"Jeremiah!" Ophelia roared over the cacophony as the Typhos' outstretched arm moved towards the lidless eye. "Through the rift, cher! We got no time!"

Behind Ophelia, Breaker Calhoun, surrounded by swirling, snapping spirits, slipped through the opening and back into the land of the living. Jeremiah intended to follow, but Hallincross, her energy blade burning brightly, had other ideas. She jumped through the air once more, her face contorted in a desperate fury, towards Lukas Sing-Low, in one last attempt to keep the portal open.

Jeremiah was there to meet her. He swung his sweltering blade in a wide arc, like he was chopping down a tree, and summoned the primal fury of the storm. The oily indigo flames roiled along the molten edge, melding with the bright orange heat. The two weapons met in a flash of arcane radiance, surging with enough raw Duskstone energy to ignite Hallincross' swirling robes.

"We will return, Jeremiah Blade," Hallincross hissed over the crossed blades. "If not today, then tomorrow. If not tomorrow, then the next. We will not be denied. We have been forgotten and cast off for too long. We have been treated as detritus for decades, but no longer. Thornshadow will lead us to reclaim our glory..."

She did not get to finish. The silver-and-lavender energy blade sputtered and died as the magic of Jeremiah's sword overwhelmed and shattered the Duskstones embedded in Hallincross' arm. The superheated tip dove through her breastplate, destroying the Duskstone wards and plunging into her heart. The lavender light disappeared from her eyes as the life fled from her mortal coil. Hallincross slid down the molten blade, coughed, shuddered, and faded into lifelessness, her head resting softly on Jeremiah's shoulder.

CHAPTER 35

"Jeremiah!" Ophelia screamed as the Typhos' arm soared through the sky towards the rift. "Now!"

Ophelia's body swirled with a blinding blizzard of iridescence and she focused her entire being towards the Typhos, arresting the arm's descent. Her body quaked as she held back the titanic mass of the ancient monster from breaking into the land of the living.

Jeremiah gently laid Hallincross' body down on the dirty sand and took one last look at Lukas Sing-Low. The Island Gnome continued to sing, his powerful voice rising to a thunderous crescendo. It was a harmonious sound, one of rejuvenation, and it raged against the chaos boiling around them. Jeremiah's dark eyes found Lukas' stoic visage, his weathered face crisscrossed by many years, and he tipped his imaginary hat towards the noble Island Gnome. A small smirk crept onto Lukas Sing-Low's haggard features and he gave a quick wink to the departing Jeremiah Blade; no fear shone in his aged eyes. Jeremiah turned and hobbled towards the suspended lavender eye until a voice arrested his momentum.

"Goodbye, Jeremiah," Lucille Ledoux called out through the bedlam. "This time, it's you leaving. I won't lie, it's hard being the one left behind. I had forgotten how nice it was to ride with your young, hopelessly naive self. You still possess the bravery I admired so much in life. I'll miss you one more time, Jeremiah Blade."

Jeremiah had traveled so far and so long and traversed so many dangers just for these precious moments to be with Lucille. He thought about all the steps that led him here as he took the spirit's solid hand. Lucille's palm was still rough, her days on the trail more than a forgotten memory. He had given up everything to be back with her, and, now, it was to be taken away all over again.

"Come with us," Jeremiah pleaded. "It's our second chance. We can turn back time, start all over again. Be together again."

"You and I both know I can't join you, Jeremiah," Lucille whispered mournfully. "As tempting as it is, we can't go backwards. We can only go forwards. Plus, I'm pretty sure my cousin would send me back here real quick and in a hurry if I tried to sneak into the land of the living."

Jeremiah felt the warm hand fade into nothingness. As he looked down, all he could see was the ghostly outline of Lucille's hand covering his. Jeremiah felt his heart ache—the same pain he experienced under the Shattered Hills all those years ago.

"We will be together again, one day," Jeremiah said softly. "I promise."

"I'll be waiting for you," Lucille answered as she drifted away. "Until then, don't forget me, Jeremiah."

"Never," Jeremiah promised. "Goodbye, Lucille."

"Jeremiah!" Ophelia roared as she struggled to hold back the Typhos. "The portal, now!"

Jeremiah gave one last smile to Lucille, whose ghostly features gave a sly grin back, and, using the last bit of adrenaline available to him, sprinted across the sand, his long, loping strides reaching the rift in short order. He dove through the tear and landed in the surf of the Crystal Gulf. The chittering of the spirits stopped, and the haze faded, leaving him under a crystal clear blanket of stars. The beach around him was destroyed from the riotous energy pouring out from the land of the dead; sand and seaweed lay in ruined ripples radiating outwards from the rift between worlds. Waiting for him was Breaker Calhoun—his face streaked with blood and sand—who quickly hauled Jeremiah to his boots. The pair turned at the same time to see Ophelia soaring through the tear between worlds, the last strands of ghostly essence evaporating from her dark skin.

Ophelia Delphine landed in a cloud of buttercream-colored foam and wasted no time in conjuring the spell to mend the wound. With Lukas Sing-Low on one side and Ophelia on the other, the air quickly stitched itself back together. Light bent, broke, and reformed to shut the door between the land of the living and the dead forever.

Before they could finish repairing the tear, a gigantic, jagged, chitinous finger reached through the portal and into the realm of the living. Like a nightmarish siege engine crashing through a castle gate, the Typhos pushed its way through, re-tearing the portal as Ophelia and Lukas desperately tried to seal it. The hardened claw—just the tip of its finger but still the size of a wagon—reached and grasped, the rift growing with each movement. The Typhos now had a hold on the world of the living, the flame of life within its grasp.

Ophelia's body shook violently as she tried to close the rift, and Jeremiah could only imagine the torment Lukas was going through on the other side of the veil. The ancient Hoodoux Queen summoned every ounce of her power, the three matching lines of Duskstones under her eyes blazing with the intensity of the sun. Her skin blistered, and her flowing black locks started to smolder and smoke. Ophelia was quickly becoming overwhelmed, however. After an eternity in the Grey Wastes, the Typhos had returned to Westhold.

Jeremiah, feeling true sand between his fingers and surf swell around his legs, not some sort of hazy facsimile, gazed up at the horror unfolding in front of them. Out of the corner of his eye, he saw his blazing sword steaming the lapping waves and turning the grit on the beach into glass. Jeremiah, sensing their last opportunity, grabbed his sword and trudged through the crashing waves, pain flowing through his body in white-hot flashes as the salt water entered his gaping wounds. Jeremiah then sprinted towards the tear between worlds, lining himself up perpendicular to the Typhos' hungry claw. The sword exploded with the heat of a dying star, and Jeremiah brought the blinding silhouette down on the spirit-made-flesh.

Shards of hardened shell splintered underneath the molten edge, pincushioning Jeremiah's unprotected face, neck, and forearms with serrated scale. From the other side, an unearthly shriek filled the air, echoing among both the living and the dead. Jeremiah did not falter; he dragged his sword through shell, meat, blood, and bone, carving a neat line through the appendage. After what seemed like an eternity and a fraction of a second all in one, the claw crashed into the dirty sand, and the Typhos jerked back into the Grey Wastes, giving Ophelia and Lukas just enough time to release their full, combined power. The air distorted and twisted under the powerful magic until, finally, the rift was sealed, once and for all.

Suddenly, all was quiet. Where the rift once hung suspended was nothing but salt air. Jeremiah glanced around the shattered coastline, at Ophelia, who had collapsed from the immense effort and lay face-first in the seaweed, and then at Breaker Calhoun, whose face was a wide-eyed visage of fear and confusion. The two looked down at what remained of the legendary Typhos—a smoking, wagon-sized claw-tip of a creature long forgotten from the world of Westhold. Jeremiah expected the Typhos to break through once more, but whatever magic that separated the worlds of the living and the dead held, and only the rustling sea breeze filled the void.

CHAPTER 36

Jeremiah Blade passed his pouch of chewing weed to Breaker Calhoun just as the sun was rising over the Crystal Gulf. Calhoun took it gratefully, fished out a pinch, and placed it in his bottom lip as the sky blossomed into a majestic rose-and-gold color. Breaker Calhoun then passed the pouch of chewing weed to Ophelia Delphine, her ancient body recovering from the tremendous trauma of closing the rift. Ophelia dumped out the last bit of the pungent leaf in her palm and placed it in her cheek. The three of them sat in the surf, their wounds field-dressed as best they could, Ophelia had made a poultice from some coastal flowers to help staunch the bleeding, and watched the rose-and-gold dawn spread across the world of the living.

Jeremiah was exhausted, mentally and physically; all of the processes of the living that had been denied to them in the Grey Wastes now came washing over him like the rolling sea at his boots. All he wanted to do was lay down as the warm sun spread across the land, but he knew it was too beautiful a sight to miss. All that remained of their battle on the other side of the veil was a claw tip from a legendary beast and a blasted shoreline where the arcane energy had spilled over into the land of the living. But, they were alive, and a disaster of cataclysmic proportions had been averted. It was a good day.

"You know," Breaker Calhoun said quietly, as if not trying to disturb the sunrise. "You're alright, Jeremiah Blade. I might have had you pegged wrong when you were in Dryftwood. Maybe that was short-sighted of me."

"Thanks," Jeremiah snorted in response, not sure if he was being serious. "That's high praise coming from you, Calhoun."

"I don't want you to start expecting this on a regular basis, son," Breaker Calhoun grinned, his teeth stained a bright blood-red. "But I figured we did just save Westhold. I mean, I did most of the heavy lifting, but I guess yall helped some. That ought to count for something."

"No one will know," Ophelia interrupted as she splashed her bare feet in the surf. "I doubt anyone other than us will even lose any sleep over this."

"What will happen to Lukas?" Jeremiah asked, thinking of the old bard now locked away in the Grey Wastes. "He is the only living creature in the entirety of the world of the dead."

"Lukas lost someone a long ago, cher," Ophelia explained as she dug her toes into the wet sand. "And he means to find him. Now that the rift is closed, and as long as he has the Duskstone in his palm, he is protected from the spirits, even from the Typhos. His journey is not over. Plus, my cousin is on the other side to help him find the way. But, we will see many dawns like this one before Lucas Sing-Low returns to this world, if he returns at all."

It was a steep price for the privilege of watching the sunrise. Jeremiah could see far out across the muddy water and leagues down the coastline. It was immensely peaceful—this area of the coast was sparsely populated, with only a smattering of Island Gnomes and Swamp Elves making their life on the scratchy, salty marshes and scrubland. That was perhaps the reason Hallincross and her ritualists chose this area; they knew they would be left in peace to bring so much ruin upon the land.

"Do either one of you know the name Thornshadow?" Jeremiah asked suddenly as he replayed the events in the Grey Wastes in his mind. "Hallincross said that 'Thornshadow will lead us to reclaim our glory'. I've never heard of them, though, which is surprising if whoever it is controls magic powerful enough to tear worlds apart. I know the Alathanian Marshals don't exist anymore, but it would be exactly the type of enemy they stood guard against."

Both Ophelia and Breaker Calhoun shook their heads, possessing no answers for Jeremiah. The fact Hallincross could have been working with or for someone with the capability of controlling such terrible magic weighed heavily on their shoulders.

"We will have to be mindful, cher," Ophelia answered as she crossed her legs and rested her elbows on her knees like someone a lifetime younger. "You're right. The marshals ain't around to watch for something like this. We are the ones who will have to be vigilant."

"I never thought I'd see the day that I'd be doing the job of the Alathanian Marshals," Breaker Calhoun whistled, a cheeky grin creeping across his stubble. "I kind of like the ring of 'Marshal Calhoun', though. I could get used to that. You got an extra belt buckle you ain't using, son?"

"I don't even have one for myself anymore," Jeremiah answered, his words carried away by the cool morning breeze. He wondered if the standard-issued marshal belt buckle still sat outside the Academy gates in the land of the dead. For a reason he couldn't quite elucidate, Jeremiah smiled. "Looks like you are on your own, Calhoun. With you on watch, I fear for the world."

"Me too," Breaker Calhoun replied coolly, the grin never leaving his face.

"Me too, Jeremiah Blade."

The three unlikely heroes of Westhold chuckled and fell silent. They watched as the rose-and-gold dawn faded and the sun brightened the sky. Daylight was upon them, and a majestic sight it was.

"What will yall do now?" Jeremiah asked, though he wasn't sure if he had ever used that pronoun before. "It seems that we still got a lot of life left in us."

"Dryftwood for me," Breaker Calhoun answered, taking off his wide-brimmed hat and laying it down on the wet sand. His angular features cut through the morning sunlight, throwing sharp shadows on the beach. "I don't know how long we've been gone, but by now them Swamp Elves in the Fens have probably realized that the outlaw Jeremiah Blade ain't sitting in the Marchioness' dungeon. Looks like I ain't getting that reward. Moss is probably going to be a little pissed about that. Still, the old Mesa probably needs my help. Yall couldn't do this without me, and I doubt he can make it on his own either."

"Maybe I'll come with you, cher," Ophelia said as she threw a seashell into the waves. "The spirits are resting now, and, if you found this Arkstone out there in those red hills, maybe that's a good place to start investigating how these 'Ash Knights' pulled this off. Who knows, I might even help you out with your little bandit problem, cher. Plus, I always wanted to see Dryftwood. Lucille was awfully keen on the place."

Both Jeremiah and Breaker Calhoun looked over at Ophelia Delphine, their surprise barely concealed on their stubbled features.

"You know, I told myself," Ophelia continued, unaware or unconcerned with her companions' shock. "'Ol' Ophelia, you ain't getting any younger, cher. You can't just spend all your days on that bayou, stomping around and swatting swamp bugs.' I think Woodroux would have appreciated it a bit more if we had seen more of Westhold."

Jeremiah thought about Ophelia's familiar, Lukas Sing-Low, and the sacrifices made this day—sacrifices that few living souls would ever know. There would be no glory for them—in fact, Jeremiah was still an outlaw, someone to be hunted, reviled, and feared—but deep in his heart, the outlaw was okay with that. He thought about the remarkable events that led him to this particular beach. A promise made long ago flashed in his mind.

"See, Calhoun," Jeremiah smirked in the radiant morning sunshine. "I told you I'd help get Dryftwood back. You don't have any need for an old outlaw like me when you got Ophelia Delphine, Hoodoux Queen, on your side."

A ripple of laughter danced across the lapping surf.

"Alright, Blade," Breaker Calhoun stated as scarlet spit ran down his chin. "You did well enough back there to earn a free pass. Where do you plan on going, though? Last I checked, you're still a wanted man."

Jeremiah had thought about that on his long slog to find his companions—if he survived, where would he go, what he would do. He didn't have a good answer then; maybe, somewhere deep down, Jeremiah didn't think he would make it back. Now that he sat looking out over the restless tides of the Crystal Gulf, all he could think of was how soothing the lapping of the waves sounded. It was tremendously peaceful on the quiet stretch of coastline, and the rising sun chased away the chill from his bones.

"I might go to the Gnomish Islands," Jeremiah said finally as he grabbed a handful of wet sand and let it fall between his fingers. The indigo Duskstone was still firmly planted in his left palm. He examined how the gritty brown sand covered the gleaming gem. "I've never been before and, maybe, it is far enough away that I can lie low, start over, and leave this outlaw life behind me."

"If there was a great place to retire, the Gnomish Island would be it, cher," Ophelia offered as the sea breeze wrapped around them. "They are a long way from the mainland, and, if you're careful, you could live there for many years without anyone knowing who you really are. Plus, ol' Ophelia heard that it has the best Sweetfire in all of Westhold."

Jeremiah Blade, Ophelia Delphine, and Breaker Calhoun fell silent and watched as the last of the rose-and-gold sunrise turned into a powder blue sky. It was a beautiful sight, one made all the sweeter by their return to the world of the living. Jeremiah thought of Lucille and all the years he spent trying to find her. He smiled knowing that she would be there as long as he held tight to her memory. Jeremiah had spent all that time looking for Lucille Ledoux, and he had no intention of leaving her again. She would always be with him, and he with her. He looked out over the endless ocean as the sunlight glittered on the rolling tides. A fish jumped out of the water, happy to be alive.

With the water splashing on his boots and the gulls singing lullabies overhead, Jeremiah laid down in the sand, closed his eyes, and fell into a deep, well-deserved slumber.

ABOUT THE AUTHOR

Originally from Sour Lake, Texas, James "Bo" Brennan lives in Shanghai, China, with his wife Vicky and daughter Olive. He has lived in China for over ten years and traveled extensively throughout Asia, Europe, and the Americas. Since graduating from the University of Texas at Dallas in 2009, he has been a teacher, translator, editor, writer, researcher, and commercial real estate peddler.

BOOKS BY THIS AUTHOR

DRYFTWOOD DUST ON THE TRAIL

In the fantasy western world of Westhold, First-year Alathanian Marshal Jeremiah Blade sets out across the badlands of the Shattered Hills to the dusty frontier town of Dryftwood. Marshal Blade is coming to this lonely outpost of civilization to round up arcane criminals flouting Alathane's magical Duskstone regulations. The marshal has his work cut out for him—Dryftwood is a rough place filled with dangerous outlaws, ornery mayors, and raging dust storms. Jeremiah will soon realize that it is going to take a lot more than words to bring to heel a land that has no intention of being tamed.

DRYFTWOOD OUTLAWS ON THE BAYOU

Down in the Swamp Elf Delta, on the bayous and backwaters, the spirits are restless. An infamous outlaw stalks the swamps for the Hoodoux Queen, a legendary witch of unimaginable power, to help him find someone he lost a lifetime ago. But he is not alone—bounty hunters of every shape and size haunt his boot-steps, looking to bring Westhold's most wanted criminal to heel, and it will take everything he possesses to shake loose his deadly pursuers. If the outlaw is to reach his goal, he must find allies new and old, for where he is going is filled with dangers far beyond anything he has ever encountered. There are some dark days ahead on the bayou, cher.

DRYFTWOOD RUINS ON THE SAVANNAH

Dryftwood Ruins on the Savannah will be released at the end of 2022 and conclude The Tall Tales of Jeremiah Blade Trilogy.